GRIM HORIZONS

Tales of Dark Fiction

ANDREW VAN WEY

Tentacle Press
Andrew Van Wey
Visit the author online: www.andrewvanwey.com

ISBN: 0-9840157-5-2
ISBN-13: 978-0-9840157-5-7

DEDICATION

For Phillip, Casey, Marissa, Matt, Hannah, and Eumee.
We built stories together, we built worlds.
We made memories, we made each other laugh.
Most of all, we built friendships to last a lifetime.

Thank you.

TABLE OF CONTENTS

INTRODUCTION
SOME THOUGHTS ON BEING A GRIM
FELLOW

"BUT YOU SEEM LIKE A PLEASANT FELLOW..."

It's a line I hear regularly, usually in response to the discovery that my literary interests gravitate toward the macabre, specifically horror and grim fantasy. The question that prompts it is often the same: "What do you write?"

It's a fair question, a great question actually, but I've never quite known how to answer it. I write what I like to read, stories that go down the dark alleys and into the whispering crypts of the imagination. Stories that dive into worlds just a bit beyond those I've walked. Stories of real people in unreal settings that rarely merit happy endings.

"What do I write? Horror, fantasy, and a spot of sci-fi. What I like to read, I suppose. Stories that go to grim places."

My response ultimately feels like a let down, to me most of all.

Which brings us back to the proclamation of me seeming to be a pleasant fellow. Aren't most people? Isn't the world built by and populated with mostly pleasant folk? Sure, there's a serial killer here and a terrorist there and sometimes an asshole in a Tesla cuts you off on the freeway, but most people—the overwhelming majority of people, in my four decades of experience—seem to be quite pleasant indeed. And besides, maybe that asshole in the Tesla was racing to get to the bedside of her dying mother.

———

In fifth grade my teacher asked us to bring a book to class and give a report. I chose Stephen King's *The Gunslinger*. My teacher was horrified. This was a book about wizards and cowboys and mutants, and it even had naughty words and violence, and here I was gleefully describing it all to thirty wide-eyed kids.

This teacher also disliked Shel Silverstein because he wrote for Playboy at the beginning of his career, but that's beside the point. Back to the book report. While I wasn't officially reprimanded, I was thoroughly informed that my choice for my next class presentation should be more tasteful. We don't read that kind of stuff here.

That curriculum "lesson" stuck around far longer than it had any right to.

———

For years, such conflicting thoughts have circled in my mind.

I've wondered why there's this knee-jerk reaction to writers of macabre? Or why do the literati and card carrying members of Good Society™ sneer over their latest New Yorker at the genre writers of the world? Perhaps it's the same reason some teachers of literature dismiss students interested in books beyond the very curriculum they grew up with. Perhaps it's a way for some readers to feel good about their own decisions. Perhaps it's an ancestral reflex, an evolutionary instinct to stay close to the safety of the fire. Perhaps it's a fear of the *other*, that strangeness that lays at the edges of the light and beyond.

"But you seem like a pleasant fellow," might be really translated to: "I've got my eye on you, and soon the neighborhood playgrounds will too."

If only they knew the *real* me.

Playgrounds, after all, are such a poor place to find fresh meat...

I had the good fortune of marrying a woman who also likes to read a fair bit of twisted fiction. If my first drafts are for my own dark heart, the near-final drafts are always for her. She's my first and final reader, and I can usually tell if I've cooked up a good literary dish based on how much responsibility she'll set aside to taste-test my creation. If she pauses Netflix, that's a good start. If she turns it off altogether, that's even better. And, on rare occasions, I've seen her forgo sleep to turn page after page, finishing a story in one sitting when she had declared it would have to be split in two.

I live for those moments. I wish other writers such joy. And if my literary career is nothing more than that, I'll consider it a success. Every writer is after someone's heart, metaphorically speaking.

Without her, I'm not sure if I would have the confidence to embrace my inner darkness. Without her, I'm not sure if these stories would exist. Yes, I may still *seem* like a pleasant fellow, but my wife knows otherwise. And still, she's fine with that. I'm learning to be, as well.

"Embrace your freak," I want to tell my younger self. When someone dismisses horror literature as unworthy of their time, size up their skull and tell them it would look good on your mantle. When Professor Killjoy sneers at your book report on a Joe Hill's latest, sneer right back. Read what makes you happy. And, if there's frightening stuff at the edge of the shadows, it's only because others are still scared of the dark.

We live in the shadows, don't we?

And we know the truth. It's quite nice out here. It just *seems* the other way.

Grim Horizons represents some of the short(er) fiction I'm most proud of writing over the past half decade. Works of different lengths and different settings. Looking back now, the title seemed so obvious, but at the time I had no idea how these pieces would be unified. Don't expect puppies and rainbows between these pages. But I do hope you come to be entertained.

I have included the original afterwords for each short story together at the very back of this collection. From a craft perspective, writers are always improving and building new skills, and I find it interesting to chart my own growth. I hope you agree. I took a few risks writing some of these stories, but nothing good ever comes about staying close to the campfire.

Most of all, I hope you enjoy reading them as much as I enjoyed writing them.

Cheers!

—Andrew Van Wey—

April 2018

BOOK ONE
DECEMBER 20TH, 1986

"A people free to choose will always choose peace."

— RONALD REAGAN

His hair was still wet when the first guests arrived. The BMW pulled up to the curb of 515 Magnolia Drive, shark-sleek grey metal belching cotton exhaust into the crisp wind. The sky was silver, the clouds fat with the hint of snow. From the living room window, he could see Dr. Levin's argyle flat cap as the old man shuffled around the car and stopped at the trunk. Rose, his wife, wiped cigarette ash from her fur coat. The Levins were two steps onto the property when Scout began barking.

"Quiet!" Floyd hissed, and snapped his fingers. The dog begrudgingly complied, a low growl lingering behind his teeth. He scampered past the Christmas tree and settled onto the window seat. Floyd released the curtain and checked his watch. It was a Seiko, digital, a gift last Christmas from the very clients he was now cursing. 5:44 pm. They were early.

The Levins were halfway up the walkway, nicotine grins over an armful of gifts. Red and green wrapping paper glistened, spotted and striped.

"Pwesents!" his daughter Melody squeaked, peeking out the window. "Can I open one?"

"After dinner," Floyd said, tying his tie. "Now go brush your hair sweetie, and ask your mom to start some coffee."

Melody ran off, Scout trailing. Floyd took a deep breath. He couldn't control when his guests arrived, he reminded himself, but he could control everything else. He counted down from five. Then he opened the door.

"Folks, folks!" he said. "Happy holidays! I hope those presents aren't for us."

"You're darn right," Dr. Levin said, handing Floyd the largest one. It was heavy, wooden. "Wouldn't you know it? We got our directions mixed up. Rose wanted to take Stillwater Canyon, and I thought the highway. We—"

"The highway is always bad this time of day," Rose said, and gave Floyd a kiss on the cheek. "Always."

The Levins were old and slow; they spoke as though the world would always wait for them. For the most part, it always had. They were wealthy, and this last fact Floyd knew well.

"I'm glad you both could make it," Floyd said. "But really, I thought we agreed: no gifts."

"Presents schmesents," Dr. Levin said. "What kind of Jews would we be if we showed up empty handed. It's a Christmas party."

"Well, a *holiday* party," Floyd said, "but still, it's more than we deserve." He led them to the porch. "Now, let's get you folks inside, find you something warm to drink."

Dr. Levin nodded but his fingers said otherwise. They pressed a trembling cigarette to his lips. Floyd could feel the warm air escaping through the front door, could smell the Cornish game hens his wife was starting to cook. Scout's snout jutted out through the crack. Melody was back at the window, peeking out through the curtain.

"Floyd, a word," the old doctor said, lingering by the porch swing. "If you don't mind. Rose, dear, head on inside, put the boys' present under the tree, will you?"

"Don't stay out too long," was her parting advice.

Floyd closed the front door. His sweater and slacks did little to keep the winter at bay. For a moment his mind drifted to the den, and the boys. Had they finished cleaning up? It was almost ten to six, and they needed to be presentable by 6:30.

"Dr. Levin, really, you shouldn't have gotten us anything—"

The old man waved the sentiment away. "Floyd, please, it was the least we could do. You know, we were in Belgium when we heard the news. Honestly, who starts the holiday season with lay offs? Bad people, that's who. It should've been your name on those partner papers."

Floyd shrugged. "I suppose Mitch and Murphy want to take the company in a different direction."

"Mitch and Murphy," Dr. Levin groaned. "Tweedledum and Tweedle-dumber. You've made them a fortune."

"Technically, you did, Dr Levin," Floyd said, and buried his hands in his pockets. "I just move it all around."

"You're too humble, Floyd. I just don't understand their thinking, their logic. They had a good thing going."

Floyd nodded. "It's like the saying goes: there's two types of people in this world, those who need closure, and."

Dr. Levin squinted, waiting for Floyd to continue. But he didn't. A grin spread across Dr. Levin's face. "That's clever Floyd, that's clever."

"Well, that's kind of you to say." Floyd suppressed a smile. The old doctor had arrived early, but he was exactly where Floyd wanted him. If the rest of the holiday party went half as well, Floyd would be ringing in the New Year with Mitch and Murphy's top clients. "Anyway, I haven't really planned out the next move. Let's just enjoy the holidays, shall we?"

"Fair enough," Dr. Levin said, and tapped the green present. "It's a doll house, by the way. This one's for your daughter. Melanie, is it?"

"Melody, actually."

"Melody, right, what a beautiful name," Dr. Levin said. "We

picked it up in Brussels, from a little antique shop. Supposedly, it's one of a kind. Girls are sure hard to shop for, aren't they?"

"She's got quite the imagination," Floyd said. He could faintly perceive the outline of the structure beneath the ribbons and wrapping. "I'm sure she'll love it."

"And the boys," Dr. Levin continued, "we got them one of those TV gadgets, you know, the games the Japs make?"

Floyd winced. "A Nintendo? Wow, doc, they'll be thrilled. But really, you didn't have—"

"Nonsense." Dr. Levin stubbed his cigarette out and gave Floyd a pat on the shoulder. "You're a good man, a good father too. I'm sure you'll land on your feet."

One step ahead of you, Floyd thought. Instead, he said: "C'mon, doc, let's get you inside."

"BUT THAT'S WHAT HE GOT US LAST YEAR," DANIEL WHINED, PULLING the collar of his red sweater, stretching it out.

"Well, now you have two." Floyd tucked in the boy's sweater. "Besides, you weren't supposed to hear that. And don't either of you dare say a word, okay? He's an old man, sometimes he forgets things."

"Like grandpa?" Elliot asked, burying his finger knuckle-deep in his left nostril.

"Like grandpa," Floyd agreed. "Only with a checkbook that doesn't bounce. Now wipe your nose." Floyd handed him a tissue. His watch beeped. 6:25.

"Okayyyyy," Daniel sighed, "but I get to use the new one."

"Nuh-uh!" Elliot instantly whined. "Not fair!"

"Is too!"

For a moment Floyd considered returning the Nintendo. Without a receipt, it might be problematic. Besides, were they really that desperate? Not yet...

"Listen," he said. "Neither of you will ever touch a Nintendo again if you don't act civilized and surprised. Good manners, good behavior. That's what we need from you tonight, got it?"

"Got it," Melody said, swinging her feet from the edge of the couch.

"Course you do sweetie," Floyd said, clipping the buckle on her pink sparkling shoes.

"And did I get a pwesent?"

"Of course you did."

Her eyes sparkled and widened. "What is it?"

"A surprise!" he said, fastening the other buckle. "But only if you're good. No peeking."

Melody nodded. The doorbell rang. A half second later, Scout was barking from the back yard. Barbara poked her head in the den, her apron no longer spotless. "Floyd, doorbell."

"Heard it the first time," he said, rising. "Okay kids, best behavior now, got it?"

"Aye aye," Daniel said, and hurried off. Elliot trailed behind his big brother, and Melody *clomp-clomped* to catch up.

"Close the door honey!" Floyd shouted, but she was already gone.

For one blessed moment, there was silence. Floyd could hear only his thoughts, echoing inward. You have one shot tonight, Floyd. Don't you screw this up. Don't you dare.

With a beep, his digital watch signaled 6:30. A distant car door slammed shut. Scout howled from the living room, and the doorbell echoed out. The dinner party was starting right on time.

———

SEVEN OF THE TOP FIFTEEN ACCOUNTS AT MITCH, MURPHY, & Benton, LLP, now sat around Floyd and Barbara's candlelit dining table. Old money. New money. And a few moving between. Seven clients and their families. One hundred and fifty million dollars, all stuffed into holiday sweaters and corduroy blazers. The Beauforts, with their silk suits and cocktail gowns from Saville Row. Art dealers with offices on six continents. The Sannicandros, yacht builders for people who summered in Mediterranean comfort, Larry with his nautical blazer, Elise in her wide-shouldered power suit, a pearl necklace dangling around an Ibizia-tanned neck, like ice upon leather. There were the Del Roys, the Donovans, both patent attorneys. Madame Helsinki, who made the good decision of being born into Scandinavian royalty. Gerald, an architect, and his latest boy toy, a Brazilian model named Felipe who smelled of coconut oil. The Sutter clan took up the far end, Brigham and Julia, proud Mormons presiding beside four golden haired boys, and affable smiles and empty blue eyes, always eager to clear the plates between courses. Floyd would have have welcomed the help on any other day. But the plates were fine China from Neiman Marcus; the receipts were still in the boxes. Tomorrow, the set would need to be returned. But if the guests took to his pitch tonight, Floyd could buy the whole set next month. Hell, he could buy out the store.

"Barbara, Floyd, that was an impressive feast, truly," Mr. Del Roy said, and wiped his lips. Nods and murmurs all around. Indeed, Floyd agreed; his wife had cooked each course to perfection, and he'd paired each dish with the right wine. Scout slept by the presents and the Christmas tree, locked behind a baby gate in the living room. In the lazy contentment that followed, Sting and Bono and Boy George's voices drifted in from the stereo, singing in synth pop glory. *"Feeeeeeed the woooooorld. Let them know it's Christmas time again."*

"No presents until later," Barbara said, giving Daniel a stern glance. The boy's brown eyes snapped back, from the shiny boxes and the sparkling Christmas tree, to the plate before him and the half-eaten feast. "Now go on," Barbara continued. "Finish your vegetables."

"Broccoli salad," Daniel grumbled, poking the glazed greenery with a fork. "More like *barf*-li salad."

Eliot's laughter was instant. To a kindergartner, the words of an eight year-old were comedy gold. Eliot clapped his hands, banged a knee beneath the table. "Barf-li!" he cackled.

Melody hadn't heard the comment, but that didn't stop her from joining in.

"*Barf*-li," Elliot repeated, then added: "Baked *poop*-tatoes."

For a moment the meal teetered on the edge of a chaotic abyss. The children's side of the table was in full revolt. Even the Mormon boys had begun snickering.

Order was restored with three thumps of Floyd's knuckles on wood. "Kids? That's enough," Floyd said, straightening the silverware. "What did we discuss about manners, hmm?"

"Sorry dad," Daniel said. "I... I should't have said that."

"Sorry," Elliot added, grinning with a missing tooth.

"So-wee," Melody squeaked.

"Apology accepted," Barbara said, patting her lips with a napkin. "Now go on, finish your, *ahem*, broccoli. And the potatoes too."

Silverware scraped as the boys took up the task at hand. Melody squirmed in her booster chair. "Well, Floyd, I would tell you it gets easier," Dr. Levin said, swirling his glass of wine, "but I'm afraid I'm not a very good liar."

A few chuckles from both sides of the table. The abyss widened. Floyd could feel the wine bringing a blush to his cheeks. It was 8:15 and all was not well. If he couldn't present a unified home front, how could he manage their money at work? Time to deflect with humor. "Well then," Floyd said, and raised his glass. "A toast! To, uh, the imagination of youth. To the wisdom that comes with age. And, to all the humbling chaos found in between."

"Here here," Mr. Donovan said. Stems were raised, glasses clinked. The Mormons toasted with sparkling apple juice. The abyss was beginning to recede.

"And that's it for the cabernet," Mrs. Beaufort said, placing the empty bottle on the coaster. "T'was quite splendid, I must say. Lovely choice, Floyd."

"An inspired pairing," Gerald added, and Felipe nodded.

"Honey, we're out of the pinot noir as well," Barbara added, checking the bottle. Floyd took inventory. Three bottles were empty, and two more were at less than a quarter.

"Fear not, friends," Floyd said, the world tilting leftward as he stood. "Like our celebrated messiah, I shall provide more wine. Transubstantiation! The holy of... holies." Silence. The joke went over like a fart in church. Floyd cleared his throat. "Donna, you liked the cab?"

"Oh, if it's not a bother," Mrs. Beaufort said, and adjusted her diamond bracelet.

"No, no bother."

"And honey," Barbara asked, unbuckling Melody's booster seat. "Would you take her?" Potty break, said their daughter's sparkling eyes.

———

"What's a twans-sub-sub-fistication?" Melody asked, as Floyd put the potty seat atop the toilet, and his daughter atop the seat.

"Nothing sweetie," he answered. "A bad joke, that's all." While she did her business, he thought of his. A bad joke, indeed. A bad idea. The wine had relaxed his tongue, he'd need to go light for the rest of the night. Loose lips, sunken ships, or so the saying went. He'd planned the pitch for 8:45, and he'd need to turn this vessel soon.

"All done," Melody said, then flushed the toilet.

"Can you be a big girl and go join the party?" Floyd asked, putting Melody down in the hall by the cellar. "Tell mom I'll be right there."

Melody nodded; got it. He rubbed her chestnut hair, then tickled her. With a squeal she was off, down the hall, pink shoes clomp-clomping on the hardwood floor. Transubstantiation, Floyd thought, and opened the basement door. God what an idiot you are.

Like half the house, the cellar was a work in progress. When viewed from the top of the stairs, it almost looked regal. Dusty portraits hung over peeling wallpaper, forlorn relatives looking on in black and white judgement. Oak bannisters descended past pine cabinets. The stairs took a hard left at the landing. To Floyd, the cellar had once held the possibility of secret deals and whiskey promises. Of cigar smoke and ventilation. Of leather couches and Sunday football on a big screen Hitachi TV, perhaps even thirty inches. And, most of all, a wine collection. A mahogany rack, from floor to ceiling, two hundred and fifty six slots, each filled with a bottle that told its own story, from seed and soil to vine and vintage.

When viewed from the bottom of the stairs, the cellar revealed its true form. It was a halfway house for abandoned dreams. Legos lay in bins where leather couches should have proudly resided. Daniel's asthma had banished all cigars to the back yard. Even the nook where a big screen TV might have stood was now home to a stack of old blankets earmarked for the Goodwill and a set of brass curtain rods Floyd had forgotten to install. Only the wine rack stood, a cobwebbed mahogany, eighteen lonely bottles protruding from a vast lattice of empty shadows fastened to old brick.

Floyd let his fingers dance over a few bottles. There was a Richbourg from '78 that would pair well with the dark chocolates. A Chambertin from '74 that went with anything. A Rossinni from '71 and a Arabatto-Frenz from '67. There was even a Chilean cabernet sauvignon. Would Felipe like it? Or was that like serving fortune cookies after sushi?

Then Floyd saw it. The Lafleur from 1948, the year of his birth. The bottle had been presented in a gilded box by his father-in-law the night before he married Barbara. "You're family now, son. Family takes care of its own. Whenever you uncork this bottle, keep family in your heart. Drink to them, and you'll never drink alone."

His father-in-law had died two years later, with a liver full of rum and his secretary's lips around his dick. Had the old man had family in his heart then? Floyd wondered. Cocaine as well, according to the toxicology. But Floyd had thought of the family. He had paid the legal fees to seal the autopsy.

"Here's to you, pop," Floyd said, and withdrew the Lafluer '48. "You're welcome."

He took the Rossinni and the Richbourg as well, then yanked the light bulb string. A moment later, and he was at the top of the stairs. The hallway glow was like a lighthouse, the distant conversation a welcome shore. His watch beeped: 8:20. Almost time for dessert.

Then, Floyd felt it. It was odd, a penetrating shiver, as if he was being watched.

There was a creak, a groan from the shadows beyond the base of the stairs. Something moved by the wine rack. Something caught the light at an odd angle. Was a bottle loose?

Floyd descended again, glass clinking. With each step, that sensation grew, as if he were, somehow, no longer alone. Even the air seemed to have changed. The muskiness of the wine rack had given way to a damp, saline odor. Floyd reached up, tugged the light bulb string.

Then a gasp left his lips. "JesusFuckingCHRIST!"

An eyeball, a single, enormous, ocular orb, wet and glistening, protruded from the wine rack. Or rather, where the wine rack had been. The mahogany lattice had been torn apart. From the hole a massive, blinking, green eye peered into the cellar.

That Floyd didn't drop his wine bottles was one holiday miracle. That he made it up twenty steps in three seconds was another. He hadn't covered such a distance since high school track. Then he came to a crashing stop just short of the doorway.

There's no way, he told himself, as he caught his breath. No way you just saw that. It was your imagination. There wasn't a giant eyeball in his basement wall, it was absurd.

Floyd took two steps back down the stairs, and crouched to look beneath the shelving and into the cellar. No, he hadn't imagined it. The eyeball was there, watching him, a black pupil the size of a car tire, an emerald iris even larger.

"What... the fuck?" Floyd whispered. He stood up, face to face with the photos of his grandparents from half a century ago. Eyes that were smudges beneath dust and glass. Eyes that were still. Eyes that were a normal size. Floyd placed the wine bottles on shelving at the top of the stairs. Then he crouched again.

The eyeball was still down there. A circular protrusion from floor to ceiling and wider still. Veins as thick as fingers traced their way beneath ivory sclera. The pupil swallowed light, panning around the room, then spotting him, focusing in. Every few seconds enormous lids closed, lashes like rustling palm fronds. Skin glazed the eye with moisture. A faint breeze followed each blink.

"Hey..." Floyd said, finding his voice. "Hey! What... what are you doing? Hey! I'm talking to you!"

The words returned to his ears as a childish echo. What it was doing was obvious: it was looking at him. It was an eye, after all. A giant fucking eyeball, right in his cellar wall. Right where the wine rack was. Should be. Had always been.

Floyd took a tenuous step down, then two more. His full form emerged erect at the landing, hesitant, lingering halfway between the basement floor and hallway. If there was an eye, then there might be a mouth. Perhaps it was like those Angler fish, deep undersea. Perhaps this was some Lovecraftian entity, some aberration out of time. There might even be teeth. Floyd checked the bannister, the steps. Old wood, old screws. Everything as it should be. Everything except the giant eyeball looking in through a hole in the wine rack.

"You..." Floyd hissed. "You... you go away now. Shoo!" He waved his hands as if fending off a troublesome cat. The eyeball blinked, its pupil dilating. It didn't shoo. It didn't go away. It tracked Floyd, from the landing down the stairs, until he teetered on the final step.

"No. No, no *nononono*," Floyd muttered, and closed his own

eyes. A flashback at an inopportune time, that's what this was. Soon, the walls would begin breathing, the bannister would become a snake. The Grateful Dead would echo out from inside his mind. He never should've dropped acid back in college. A deep breath, a rub of the eyes, and it'll all be gone. Just count down from five.

Floyd opened his eyes. It wasn't gone; the vision persisted. The eyeball was squinting, studying him from the hole in the wine rack. "What are you?" he hissed. "What are you doing? Dammit, what... do you want, huh?!"

The eye didn't answer. Of course not. Floyd was beginning to understand that, despite its size and bizarre intrusion, it was, after all, just an eyeball. A big, blinking, eyeball.

"Eyes don't talk," Floyd mumbled. "You're an eye, of course you don't talk."

That statement settled his mind as a comfortable fact, a lifeline he could clutch on to. There was a logic to this world. Rules that kept order. Kept the seas from boiling. Kept everyone glued to this spinning earth, and not sailing off into the sky. It followed, then, that this singular eye peering in to his cellar might follow similar rules.

"Okay... you, you can see me at least, can't you?" Floyd asked, hesitating on that final step. "You can hear me?"

The eyeball blinked. Curtains of skin folded a faint *whoosh*. Communication. A good enough foundation for any relationship. If it could hear him, it could respond.

"Okay, uh, I... *ahem*, I want you to blink," Floyd said. "If you can understand me, blink once for yes, twice for no. Understand?"

The eyeball blinked once.

Holy shit. It understands. Floyd felt his heart flutter up into his throat. Neil Armstrong had his moonwalk. Jane Goodall had her chimps. Floyd had just made first contact with, well... an eight foot tall eyeball in his cellar wall.

"That's... that's amazing." He stepped down onto the basement, scooting beside an old cooler, past a pile of children's soccer

balls. The eye tracked him, each and every step. "Okay, now I uh...
I want to know, why are you here? Wait wait wait..." Too compli-
cated, he realized. The eyeball hesitated, lids narrowing. The
pupil shrank as he drew closer. Ten feet away. Nine. Eight. He
could smell a salty odor, a vague dampness.

"So, are you friendly? Blink once for yes, twice for no."

The eyeball blinked twice. Two quick flutters of motion that
stirred the basement air with a damp breeze. It was Floyd's turn
to hesitate.

"You... you're *not* friendly?"

Two more blinks. Twice was no, wasn't it? Or was it confused?
No, I'm not friendly? Or: no, I'm not unfriendly?

"Wait... okay, let's reset." Floyd took a deep breath. "If you're
friendly, blink once. If you're not friendly, blink twice."

The eye blinked once. So it was friendly. Good news. Then it
blinked again. And a third time. It narrowed as he drew closer.
There was no consistency. It was just an eyeball, after all.

Floyd stretched out a nervous hand. The pupil shrank, the lids
squinted. Five feet. If he could just touch it he could confirm its
tactile reality. Three feet. The eye drew back, receding a foot
deeper into the wall. Somehow, the fissure in the wine rack
seemed to shrink.

"Floyd, honey?" called his wife from the hallway upstairs.
8:25. Shit, they were waiting on the wine. But he'd found something far more interesting than the perfect Merlot. He'd found an
eyeball in his basement wall.

"Down here," he shouted, studying the eyeball as it studied
him. "Babe, you have *got* to come take a look at this." That statement spawned a sudden thought. This ocular intrusion, as fascinating as it was, would bring about a swift end to the holiday
party. Barbara would scream, the guests would converge, and
Floyd would miss his only chance. After all, no pitch could
compare to an eight foot tall eyeball protruding from a basement
wall.

"Come see what?" Barbara asked, her shadow now at the top

of the stairs. In three bounding steps, Floyd was back at the landing, just in time to intercept his wife.

"I uh, I need your opinion," he said. "About the Lafluer." He passed the bottle from the shelf to her hands, making sure to block the view beyond the turn of the stairs. "Do you think it will go with the truffles or the fruit?"

"I thought you wanted me to see something." She studied the bottle's label. "I don't know, wine's really your thing. What do you think?"

"Is the fruit already cut?"

"Of course it is, you helped me. Goodness, what's that smell—"

"Mochi."

"What?"

"I've got it now. Honey, why don't you bring out the mochi? Add some of the fruit slices to it. Dress it up wit the chocolate shavings. Perfect."

Barbara hesitated. "But, it's not time for the mochi. The fruit should be served first—"

"Says who? The Sannicandro's just got back from Japan, they'd love a surprise. I'll be up in just a minute. Oh, and start a pot of coffee, will you?" He placed his hand on the small of her back, gently guiding her up the last few steps, away from the basement. Away from the eye.

"Well, I suppose."

He planted a kiss on her cheek. "Love you."

And then she was gone, a bewildered shadow in the light of the hallway above, shuffling off. Floyd sighed. Not a perfect solution, but a temporary one.

The eyeball awaited him at the bottom of the stairs. He could feel its gaze, a cold sheet upon his skin, ever present. His reflection grew in its massive, plate-like pupil. Around its rim the wine rack had been torn away. Peeled back, like something had ripped a hole in reality.

This is it Floyd, he thought, you're going crazy. No, wrong tense. More like gone. Next step: Bellevue. Population: you.

And yet, a more comforting thought emerged: crazy people don't know they're going crazy, do they? Every day, Floyd passed dozens of shattered souls in the city. The drug addicts, the broken veterans of the Vietnam war, the mentally destitute. Human husks, once confined to hospitals now closed by Reagan, their maddening chatter now filled the city sidewalks. Had Floyd brought their delirium back to the safety of the suburbs? Had some of it stuck to him?

No. The mere fact that he was asking such a question eliminated such an answer. It was like the card said: *Jesus is the Reason for the Season!* There had to be goddamn reason for this. There had to be something behind this eye.

"I'm going to take a look, okay?" Floyd said and stepped within an arms length of the eyeball. Like a convex mirror at a convenience store, Floyd could see his distorted reflection upon the surface. Each blink refreshed a wet glaze. He pushed aside the stack of old blankets. Pushed past the curtains still in their box, past the forgotten brass curtain rod. Past the sputtering gas furnace.

And then he was at an angle to the wine rack and the wall. The eyeball looked at him sidelong, but couldn't turn. The cold blanket of its gaze began to fade.

"I'm still here," Floyd said. "I just... I want to see something."

The house was a colonial revival, like most others in the neighborhood. With it came the usual problems: the mortgage was a stretch, the furnace was failing, and each minor remodel revealed a major failing. Lately, the maze of crawlspaces between the floors and foundation had become home to rats. Brittle droppings sat atop cement, blanketed in dust. The living room was above. Bing Crosby and Doris Day drifted down through the floorboards.

"Baby it's cold outside..."

But it wasn't cold down here. It was warm and musty and most of all, it was empty. Behind the wall the wine rack stood against, the crawlspace stretched on into shadows. And yet, there was nothing else there. When viewed from the base of the stairs, the eye protruded into the cellar. When viewed from this opposite side, there was only a filthy plane of darkness nestled between the cement foundation and the living room above. Like a tree without roots, or a ship with no hull beneath the waterline. It made no sense, and yet, Floyd wasn't sure what he had expected to find behind the wall and the eyeball. Some giant head, some enormous optic nerve, or worse, a portal to a world of giants. It was just an empty crawlspace.

"So really I'd better scurry..."

Floyd slid back into the basement. The eye was looking side-long at him, squinting, blinking. That sensation returned, the damp blanket of an unwanted gaze. Floyd shivered.

"Your eyes are like starlight now..."

If there was a logical explanation, it was fast escaping him. By his own deductions, he wasn't insane. And yet, this meddlesome eyeball seemed unbound by the laws of physics. It wasn't coming from within the crawlspace. And there was nothing on the other side of the mahogany wine rack, just the backside of the brick wall, lathe and plaster and old wires. The eyeball only protruded when viewed from one side, a lump on a flat plane, yet otherwise vanishing. An illusion, optical or otherwise.

"Doesn't make sense," he mumbled, three little words becoming the theme of the evening. Then he reached out and smacked the back of the wall. Lathe and plaster shook. A webwork of old wires jostled.

He smacked it again. Again. Feeling, fumbling, struggling to find a seam or a fissure, some crack in reality. Instead, he accidentally struck the old junction box. With a pop and a shower of sparks, shadows consumed the crawlspace. The circuit was blown.

"Baby, it's cooooold oooooout—"

Then Bing Crosby crooned down through the floor no more. Fingers twitching, Floyd yanked himself back, smacking his head on a crossbeam. Curse words filled the dark basement. The amber glow of the gas furnace struggled to dispel the shadows. But it was just enough.

The eyeball was gone.

"Whoa whoa whoa," Floyd said. The wine rack loomed before him, same as it had for years now. Two hundred fifty six holes, most empty, a mahogany mockery of his failed collection. There was no colossal eyeball, nor its gaze, nor its salty odor and faint breeze. There was no hole in the wine rack and the wall beyond.

A voice called out from the hallway. "Floyd? Honey?"

He could hear Barbara's heels upon the floor. He was halfway up the stairs when her shadow filled the door way.

"Floyd, what on Earth is going on down here?"

"Nothing," he said, in near total darkness. "Actually, I was just trying to fix something."

He didn't need a flashlight to see the bewilderment on her face. "Fix what? You've been down there for ten minutes and now the whole house just lost power and—"

"Yeah, no, that was intentional," he said, and gave the light-switch at the top of the stairs a useless flick. "The Christmas lights were messing with the, uh, transformer. Overload. Safety first, right?" He stepped into the hall and closed the basement door behind him. "Unless, of course, you want a fire."

It was bullshit. He knew it, Barbara sensed it, but didn't know enough to dispute it. "No, no of course not," she said. "But you can fix it?"

"Yeah, of course," he said, hand falling to the small of his wife's back. He led her down the hall. "I'm fixing it now, aren't I?"

"Well, I certainly hope so."

The living room was bathed in the dim flicker of the fireplace. Without the lights, the Christmas tree was a crooked shadow, the presents beneath shimmering cubes. Then they were in the dining room, and thank God for the decorative candles. There was just enough light to see the faces of two dozen dinner guests looking back. "Folks, folks, sorry about that. Just a minor hiccup with the breaker. Larry, you enjoying the mochi? Good, good. Dr. Levin, don't hesitate to top off your glass. Saul—"

"Daaaaaad," Daniel whined. "I thought you said we could open a present."

Floyd flashed a smile while his eyes flashed fury. "Soon enough, Daniel," he said, and gave his eldest son's shoulder a tight squeeze. "Again, folks, so sorry. Old wiring. I'll have the lights and music back on in just a moment."

They told him to take his time. They told him not to worry. He did neither. The moment the dining room door closed he was rushing through the kitchen, around the serving table, and into the back porch. He opened the service panel, found the thrown circuit breakers, and flipped them back on. Lights returned, followed by distant music. He checked his watch. 8:32. "Good to go," he mumbled to himself.

Melody was waiting for him in the kitchen. "I didn't do it," she said. "I didn't make the lights go away, nuh-uh"

"What? No, of course you didn't sweetie. I was just trying to fix a problem."

Floyd scooped his daughter up in his arms. For one moment he forgot about the basement, and the horrible intrusion. That gargantuan eyeball in the wall now seemed like a dream. He even forgot about the party, and all that needed to go right. "Let's get you back to the dinner table sweetie."

"Scout was cur-wee-us and I told him 'no' but he never wistens to me."

"He never listens, huh?"

"Never!"

"Well, I know how that feels."

Then it was Floyd's turn to listen. A single, loud bark echoed out in the hallway, followed by a low rumble. Scout was growling at the basement door.

"Get out of there," Floyd said, putting his daughter down and giving the dog a nudge. "Shoo!"

Scout shooed. Off, down the hall, back to the living room.

"Alright, back to your mom," he told Melody. "No sneaking off."

"Okie dokie," Melody said, and scampered down the hall.

Floyd studied the basement door. The lights were on at the top of the stairs, the bulb glowing down below. He sighed, counted to five. Something had been down there, this he was almost sure of. Something so absurd and awful he felt childlike himself, scared of closets and the wet shadows that dwelled within. And yet, he knew, *knew*, that it made no sense.

It was in his mind. The wine, the stress, losing his shot at partner. Most of all tonight. Everyone went a little loopy around the holidays, didn't they? The great eyeball in the wall had never been there. Going downstairs would prove it.

Floyd opened the door. Step by step, he descended into the basement. The stairs groaned, the bannister rattled. He hesitated at the landing, thinking, that if he turned the corner and the wretched, enormous eyeball was there, he might just lose his mind. A deep breath. Five. Four. Three... two... a one, and—

It was just an ordinary basement.

There was the bag of soccer balls, the cones from Daniel's soccer season. A stack of chairs stood in the corner. There was the rumbling furnace, the buzzing light bulb with its the swaying string. Most of all, there was the mahogany wine rack, the massive lattice, with its few pitiful bottles but otherwise empty. Of course the eye was gone. Of course.

"That's right," Floyd said, and reached up, fingers taking the string beside the light bulb. "That's god damn right."

He pulled the string. Click. The shadows returned. Then, with a smile, he was walking back up the stairs, a spring in his steps. 8:35. Time for coffee.

He made it as far as the eighth step before a chill ran up his spine. The wet blanket returned. The air shimmered. Something was watching him.

No, no, no, no...

Slowly, ever so slowly, Floyd turned around. The light from

the top of the stairs only stretched so far. *Clomp clomp*, went his feet down the steps. *Clomp clomp*. His hand fumbled among the shadows. His thumb grazed the warm bulb. Fingers fell on frayed string, tugging it and—*click!*

The eyeball had returned.

Eight feet of glistening, curved wetness, bulged from the wine rack. The lattices were splayed, the wall torn open. The cornea was a glistening blister, just a little rounder than the rest of the orb. The pupil dilated, darkness drawing in light. Within all this Floyd could see his own, pathetic reflection, a man on the verge of tears.

"What do you want from me?!" he cried out. "Why are you here?!"

No answer came. The eye tracked Floyd as he paced, back and forth, back and forth.

"This is a test, isn't it? Are you testing me?"

The eye squinted. God had tested Abraham, hadn't he? Given him orders to slay his son, then bailed out at the eleventh hour. Floyd wasn't sure he even believed in God, but perhaps he was wrong. Perhaps this eye was proof of the divine, his own burning bush. But if so, what sort of god had brought it forth? The eye didn't appear to be evil, at least in any manner Floyd supposed. And yet, it wasn't benevolent either. It's arrival, it's existence, was a troubling tumor in an otherwise orderly world. It defied physics, for no part of it lay on the other side of the wall. It came and went with tortuous inconsistency. Still, Floyd didn't count himself among the converted.

If it wasn't divine then perhaps it was extraterrestrial? But then why was it's pupil round, like primates and people? If it shared some common ancestor, what horrible mutation stretched it to such size? Was the house built over an Indian graveyard? Was this how goldfish felt?

Each answer spawned more questions. Each idea led to an ever-tangling maze of conclusions. Perhaps Floyd could keep it a secret, yes; perhaps he could lock it in the basement. But what then? What of the day his wife stumbled down, searching for blankets or extra bath soap, and saw the monstrosity in the wall? He could see Barbara now, her bathrobe half open, hair wet, racing down Magnolia Drive, filling the air with her screams. They could share a reservation at Bellevue. Did padded rooms come for two?

8:38. Floyd's pitch was supposed to start in seven minutes. Instead, Scout was pitching a fit upstairs. The dog was barking from the other side of the basement door.

Perhaps Scout was on the right track, Floyd reasoned. Perhaps they could go public, call up the university. Floyd could take photos, document this anomaly, do the TV circuit. Jack Palance was keeping busy on *Ripley's Believe it or Not!* and Barbara Walters was the new co-host on *20/20*. Floyd could start a bidding war.

But what if the bids never came? What if the stations spiked the story? Or worse, what if the government suppressed it? Uncle Sam could take the property. Expropriation, eminent domain, there was always some obscure legal basis. It was, after all, a giant fucking eyeball growing out of his wall. Any judge who saw it would sign the order. They'd tarp off the house, block off the neighborhood. Soldiers with hazmat suits and M-16s would patrol Magnolia Drive.

And then what? Hell, why not open up his bank accounts, take a closer look at the books? Floyd had been careful, he worked in investment after all. But creative accounting wasn't without a little wiggle room; honesty alone hadn't secured their bank loan.

His watch beeped. 8:40. Scout whined at the basement door.

The bank, Floyd realized, and the house. Was there language for eldritch events in the mortgage contract? Did an Act of God clause cover an eyeball growing out of a wall? And what of the long term? What of the next remodel, and the one after that? Asbestos had been banned a few years ago, and lead paint was up next. What would happen when the furnace finally needed fixing? No contractor would touch such a job. And could they ever sell such a house?

8:41. Scout whined and scratched and growled. Upstairs, the party had undoubtedly derailed; Floyd's Christmas plans were fast unraveling. Five minutes was all he needed, his pitch was that damn good. Instead, he'd spent the past twenty minutes down here, with this uninvited guest, this intruder, this giant fucking eye.

Then all became clear. Floyd could see it now, he understood. A grin spread across his face. The eyeball's creased lids narrowed, its lashes swayed. Perhaps the eye understood what had to be done. Perhaps not. None of that mattered now.

"I'm sorry," Floyd whispered.

He sidestepped to the left. Past the card tables. Past the furnace. Watching it watching him. The palpebral fissures narrowed, the folds of skin squinted. The green iris ringed a dilating pupil. A webwork of ophthalmic veins swam beneath the glimmering sclera, like red kelp in a sea of milk. The eyeball tracked his every step.

"I'm sorry," Floyd said.

Then the eye could track him no more. Floyd was at an angle now, in the corner where the wine rack met the crawlspace. His left hand fumbled among the dusty nook. He felt the frayed rugs slipping between his fingers. Felt the plastic edges of the Lego bins pass beneath this palm. Then, slowly, carefully, his left hand slid down metal. Past the spiked end cap. Past the hooks. Settling upon the cold center of the brass curtain rod.

"I'm sorry," Floyd mumbled. "I'm sorry... I'm sorry! I AM SO SORRY!"

Lance-like, he hoisted the curtain rod. A battle cry left his lips as he put two hundred and eighteen pounds of screaming momentum behind the charge.

The first thrust caught the eye just beneath the corner, a red ribbon opening up in a sea of white. The second tangled in the lashes and split the lower lid. It was the third strike that caught the eyeball straight on. There was rubbery resistance. Then there was not. With a sickening pop, the curtain rod sank in, brass and plastic plunging into a pupillary abyss.

Scout barked and howled from beyond the basement door. The very foundation of the house shook. With a spastic twist, the curtain rod was wrenched from Floyd's hands, and the ruined eye retracted, deep into the wall. For a moment, clear and terrible, Floyd saw flashing lights beyond, blues and greens and reds and yellows, as if looking out at some vast, colorful forest. The fractured mahogany sealed itself up; the latticework clasped like bony fingers in prayer. Floyd found himself staring at a curtain rod, embedded deep within the wine rack.

Then a scream filled the air.

It wasn't Scout. No animal could make such a noise. And, as Floyd raced up the stairs, he remembered something: the dog had been in the living room, after all. The dog was supposed to be locked behind the baby gate.

Screams filled the hallway, filled the house. Floyd flew past Scout, past the dining room where the entire dinner party was in chaos. The guests were on their feet, some walking, some running, but none racing as fast as his feet carried him.

"What happened?" Barbara was shouting, but not at him. "Oh my god, honey what happened?!"

"What is it?" Daniel gasped. "Where's Melody?!"

Floyd came to a sliding stop in the living room where the screams reached a crescendo. The Christmas tree was a kaleidoscope of colors, the presents beneath stacked like offerings. Only one present was missing, dragged around to the edge of the tree, out of view from the dining room. Floyd recognized the shape.

It was the antique Belgian dollhouse, its wrapping paper peeled away in a single corner. Peeled in a way only a child's fingers could peel, both careful and clumsy. They had told him it was one of a kind. And Floyd had told her not to look, to wait until later. There, on the far side of the Christmas tree, Melody was screaming, her hands holding back a ruby spray.

"He hu-hu-hurt me!" Melody shrieked. "Mu-mu-mummy, the little man hu-hu-hurt me!"

"What man!?" Barbara cried as her daughter's tiny fingers clasped a socket of crimson ribbons. "What little man!?" she was screaming too, eyes searching for some answer, some clue, some connection, as to what horrible thing could have done this. "WHAT LITTLE MAN!?"

Floyd's watch beeped. It was 8:45 pm, time for the mulled wine, time for his pitch. The guests were all gathered, their attention was his. Outside, the snow was falling thick and heavy and white. The lights were flashing, the dog was barking, Bing Crosby had been replaced by Dean Martin's soothing croon, and it occurred to Floyd, as Melody's one remaining green eye met his own, that he too was screaming.

BOOK TWO
A FEAST OF INFINITE ROT

CHAPTER 1

THE TRAVELER

The river was flooded, and with it his hopes were drowned.

It was an angry dance; cruel swells of muddy water rising and falling. Whitecaps spitting foam, swirling downstream, slapping upon rock and reed. The river bank, as best the traveler could tell, was submerged the depth of two men at least, and likely more. Only the tips of the trees were visible, autumn branches grasping above the torrent like fingers, desperate and dying.

There would be no crossing, not even for the strongest of men. This river would thresh them upon rock and reed.

And he was no strong man, this traveler, at least not these days. The mudlands had ravaged him, famished him, gnawed and nibbled at his muscle until what little remained was taut and lean. His mind, however, was still sharp, and it didn't take him more than a moment of calculation to realize his odds were hopeless.

The road he had walked for the past day, little more than a trampled trail through the countryside, now ended in the brown torrent of the Rusted River. No dock remained, and if there was a ferry—as he had been told there would be—it must have been sent downstream and shattered against the rocks.

And of the oarsman? The traveler spotted a grey shape bobbing in the bracken downstream. A horse, bloated and gone to rot, stuck among the branches. He wondered if the oarsman had escaped such an end.

"Wretched luck," the traveler said to his companion, a nameless horse grazing in the wet grass nearby. "Wretched luck for a wretched land."

For the past two weeks they had slogged through the forest trails of the Darren Folds and the Kentshire Mountains, following the Rusted River in search of an eastward crossing. And for those two weeks the weather had conspired, worsened by the day, until he thought the muddy earth itself would swallow them both, beast and man.

Then this morning, after a parade of grey days, dawn broke as a glorious glow upon the eastern crags, and the traveler's hope returned. Birdsong filled the forest. An azure sky, cloudless and calm, promised of a warm autumn day to come.

Yes, it would be a good day, he had told himself, over a breakfast of roots. He would find a crossing, and soon. He would put this wretched land and its simple people behind him.

Wretched land, and wretched luck. He was a fool to hope for anything else.

By midday the clouds had returned, grey and fat. A lazy downpour fell upon the lands, and his tricorne hat, having almost dried, once again trickled water from its brim like some pathetic pitcher.

And now, standing here on these swollen banks, the traveler settled on this grim fact: the sun would set yet again, and still he was on the wrong side of this stygian river.

"What say you? Shall we ford the torrent, depth be damned?"

The horse simply chewed on a weed and flapped away flies.

"No, I thought not."

The horse, of course, had never been one for conversation; its uses were few. If it had a name before it became the traveler's property, he knew not of it; nor did he care. It was little more than a porter on four legs, good for carrying his rucksacks and firewood, following in the vaguest sense and occasionally spooking at a sound, real or imaginary. Perhaps its mind was broken, or perhaps the previous owner had never broken it in.

And if he tried to mount the horse? Well, the traveler had made that mistake a few times, escaping hoof and rock by mere luck. The horse would have nothing with being ridden, at least not by him.

Yet an obstinate horse was better than no horse, and it did make for something to talk to, should he feel his sanity or social skills slipping sideways.

"Come, you silly thing," he said, turning back toward the path they'd come from.

The gods haven't seen fit to drown us yet, he thought. *Though there still remain hours in the day, should the gods change their minds.*

THE MUD PATH JOINED UP WITH A MUD TRAIL, AND WITHIN THE HOUR the traveler was back upon the road he'd veered from earlier. It was a wide slop the width of a carriage, should a carriage be able to traverse rock and clay. Perhaps the road had once been a popular thoroughfare between villages and cities, but now the earth had reclaimed it.

Such was the story of these lands, such was their song. Stone walls sprouting stalks of weed, nests for birds or rats. Cornfields gone to rot. Mills long abandoned, waterwheels creaking like gallows.

Poems had been written of this new world, of the colonies and the lands past New Amsterdam and Boston. Great tales of brave people, bountiful harvests, and endless hunting. Of good soil and good earth. Of painted men and magical lands and, most of all, a chance to start over.

A new world, a new hope.

Yet the traveler had seen none of that. It was fiction, a fabulist's tale no different than the ones he had peddled across both worlds, old and new. Tales that had bought him passage across the great ocean, the occasional coin, and sometimes the warmth of a charmed woman to sleep beside.

Yes, he was no stranger to exaggeration: a good tale always requires some. Fiction was, after all, much like a tree, and although each tale would grow into something different, all had roots in a seed of truth.

But this, he thought as he wiped rain from his face and trudged up yet another muddy hill, *this was an outright lie.*

What fertile lands there were had already been claimed. Those not taken were fraught with danger: highwaymen and brigands, savages of a lighter color than the ones in Europe yet equally as violent.

And where danger didn't carry a knife or a musket it came from soil that grew little. Vegetables were stunted, obscene distortions not fit to feed swine. Should a man survive three seasons of banditry and meager harvests there was always winter, arriving early or lingering late, ready to starve out all but the fortunate.

Yes, these lands were wretched, he thought, slogging down another muddy incline. *Wretched and cursed*. The sooner the he left them, the better.

"Wherever you go, there you are," he mumbled, wading through a puddle as deep as his ankle. "Still stuck in the muck."

Truth be told, these wretched lands were half the problem. There were demons at his heels, the debts and the bad name, but they only served to hasten him. To push him, as they always had, forward and into the unknown.

And soon, he hoped, to somewhere else. Somewhere distant. A southern land beneath a warm sky perhaps. A white beach and bare breasted women who wore nothing but beads above their waist. If they worshipped odd gods and ate strange food, so what? The world was wide, and he still had his health.

Now, if only he could find a way across that river.

HE FOLLOWED THE PATH SOUTH, AN HOUR OR SO. THROUGH A DEAD thicket and past a dead farm, blighted vegetables on rotting vines, skinny crows feasting upon them. They were odd things, those plump vegetables. He could never remember their name. Orange and round, squat little things like the harvest moon.

Still, it was a good sign, this farm. At one point carriages and carts must have made their way to it. And perhaps, not far off, there would be a bridge. It was not too much to hope for.

Yet as the traveler made his up another knoll, his heart sank. The Rusted River wound south, an open scar on the land. Nowhere in sight was there any bridge or crossing. Only that same raging current, death for certain.

"Well, there's always tomorrow," the traveler said. "Or the day that follows."

The horse whinnied and dropped a damp pile in the mud. The traveler sighed. *What now?* he wondered.

The sun was setting, a low glow behind the grey drizzle, faint and dim. Though he saw no sharp shadows, he felt as if something was reaching out for him. As if threads beneath the mud of the earth were tugging at him, beckoning him to—

He turned his glance eastward, to a dark fold of the land where something caught his eye. A glimmer of sunlight bounced off a distant shape across the valley, flickered, and grew. He knew this gleam, though it had been some time since he'd seen it.

It was a reflection. The glimmer of the setting sun off glass.

IT TOOK THE TRAVELER THE REMAINDER OF THE DAY'S LIGHT TO FIND his way to what had caught his eye. There was a trail, though it was old and overgrown, reclaimed by root and sprout. Twice he had gotten lost among the woodlands, and twice the damned horse had wandered off, only to come clattering back like some scared child.

Scared, or smart? he wondered.

He too had felt a hesitation and a fear among the woods, a vague paranoia that spoke of nighttime terrors. Funny as it might be, the traveler had a feeling that there was something out there, something strong and powerful crashing among the sticks and brambles. That something ancient and terrible was coming for him.

Yet he encountered only a black dog, old and feral, sick perhaps, limping across the path and back into the bracken. As day gave way to dusk the shadows merged, the weather warmed, and as the trees thinned he came upon a great field at the forest's edge.

It was an odd field, a black expanse of volcanic soil unnaturally dry, and it seemed to almost glimmer in the twilight. Small holes had been dug in the dirt, rows upon rows, too many to count. If something had been sown it had yet to sprout, and the color of the earth made him doubt it ever would. Yet a hundred paces off the path crouched a man digging in the very earthen field by hand.

The traveler paused and studied the squatting man among that black field. He was methodical, digging a single hole and planting a seed in it before moving to another spot. Dig, tamp, move. The cycle repeated.

Then, as the man's fingers dug into the ground, something halted his task and he cocked his head to the side. His hand fell upon an object, and he lifted it to the sunlight. Though the distance was far, the traveler saw a glimmer of light from the stone.

"Hello there!" the traveler called out. "Well met!"

The crouching man's head whipped toward the traveler. A hand went up to shield his eyes from the sun. Yet beyond that sudden action the man made no motion nor sign of greeting.

"Well met, I said!" the traveler called again, yet got no response.

A moment passed, as did another, until a queer sort of discomfort settled upon the traveler. Déjà vu, as they called it in France, or something like it. That crouching man was staring at the traveler, yet he didn't seem to quite *see* him. Or didn't care to converse with him, more likely.

Then the man returned his attention to the soil and began digging.

Odd, the traveler thought. Yet truly no odder than half the people he'd met out in the mud-lands and bogs this far from civilization.

The traveler moved on, down the path and past that black field, until he came upon the source of the odd reflection he'd spied from the road earlier.

It was an inn.

The foundation was stone, the courtyard was wide, and a crooked well sat at the center. A slender facade reached skyward, two floors crowned by an attic. Dirty windows, glass bubbled with age, shimmered as amber light passed through. There was a lean to the structure, as if it might, in a decade or so, sink into the very earth it sat upon. No sign hung upon it, only the old bars where one once had. He hitched his horse to a crooked post.

Odd too, he thought, that a decently built structure should exist so far from people. Every inn he'd found this side of the Rusted River was little more than a hovel. This inn had windows of glass no less.

If it had those, then what else? Maybe a few coins to be made, goods to be traded. Women or wine, perhaps even both?

And if there was nothing for barter or trade, or no other travelers to recognize him?

Well, he always had his knife.

That too had put coin in his pouch.

From time to time.

THE AIR INSIDE WAS HEAVY WITH SMOKE AND FLAVORED MEAT. THE door had hardly closed and already the traveler's tongue was on his lips. Bacon was being cooked, or had been recently. Everything smelled of pork and vegetables.

The inn was large, though modestly decorated. Thick beams made up the edges, a balcony above. And in the main room: four tables set about in rows, and a kitchen beyond. Stairs led the way upward to rooms, each perhaps no larger than a horse stall. Narrow windows, dusty and warped, looked down upon the common area.

No wonder the inn had seemed an odd shape, he realized. It hadn't always been such. Once, this had been a church. The glass in the windows was stained, though the saints were now vague shadows, broken and ill-repaired, hardly human anymore. The counter and kitchen stood where an altar had once been.

"Well met, traveler," said a voice to his right that caught him by surprise. He was certain there had been no one there, but now there she was: a woman, an elder of indeterminate age, long past fertile years. "Apologies if I scared you."

"No worries, m'lady," he replied. "I've been traveling for a while. I startle at a leaf's crackle."

"Big man such as you, out among the wilds? Somehow I doubt much startles you at all," she said with a near toothless smile. "And stop with 'lady' talk. We both know I'm closer to sunset than sunrise. Come. We've been expecting you."

She gestured in to the dining room, led the way in. Her back was a slope, a hard bend that made her shuffle more than walk. Perhaps some odd sickness had put a crook in her back. Or perhaps life and labor had slowly worn it down. Both were possible.

"I'm sorry, I'm afraid I misheard you. You said you were 'expecting me.'"

"Aye. You're wondering how."

"What else? Sorcery, I presume?"

She chuckled, teeth like rocks in a sea of spotty gums. "Above you."

He glanced up to the second floor. A balcony looked out through an unstained window. And in front of it—

"A telescope," he said. "So you saw me from afar."

"Indeed. You know such things?"

"I have some experience with the sciences."

"A man of your sort, I imagine you do."

The comment rubbed him the wrong way. *What sort of man did she take him for?* She must've have read his disdain as the words were hardly out her mouth and she was apologizing.

"I meant no slight to your character. Merely, I was observing that a traveler confident enough to wander this part of the wilds... well, such a man must be of worldly experience, that is all."

There was an energy to her, an exuberance. For a moment the traveler mistook it for madness, though he suspected it to be something much simpler. It was the toll age and isolation took on the soul.

"A compliment," she continued. "That your eyes have seen many wondrous things. If that came out wrong, I beg your pardon. We have few visitors here these days. My tongue is ill-practiced."

"A misunderstanding." He smiled. "Nothing more."

"Good. Then you'll stay? We have room, of course. Dinner should be ready within the hour. Our rates are reasonable and—"

"Are there other travelers lodging here?"

"Other travelers? Oh, no, no, though some do come from time to time. Rest assured, you'll have your pick of the rooms."

"There was a man in the field; is he the 'we' you spoke of? Your husband, I presume?"

"Him? Oh, no, nothing of the sort. He's just another soul who helps out. It's his harvest you smell, though several hands helped cook it. There's a lady servant as well; she can see to your horse.

But as for conversation, I'm afraid you have only the three of us. If that displeases, I apologize."

"Not at all, ma'am," the traveler said with a smile. "This will all do quite fine."

Quite fine indeed, he thought. *And even better if the lady servant was fair on the eyes.*

THE ROOM PROVED TO BE LARGER THAN A STABLE, THOUGH THE bedding did feel like hay. Old wool and linen, some rotted through, would be his rest for the night. Though it wasn't the feather bed he had slept on once, it was preferable to the logs and twigs of the past weeks.

He undressed, leaving his mud-soaked clothes outside the door and wrapping the towel around his waist. The innkeeper had promised to clean the filthy garments, though he knew no amount of scrubbing would remove the journey's evidence. The mud-lands and marshes clung to his leathers and linen like scabs. Once he found his way back to a city, a town, or even an outpost with a proper tailor, he would abandon his leathers for new clothes.

Perhaps silk once again, he told himself. That was the end game, the destination he drove toward. Yet how many times had his wagon wheels fallen off? How man times had his plans gone awry?

"Water's ready," the old woman called from outside the room. "Two buckets, both short of boiling, as requested. Have a care with the tub; it's prone to wobbling."

"Noted and appreciated," he shouted back. "Thank you kindly."

"Let me see what clothes I can find. They may not fit, but they'll be clean."

"And they would be appreciated," he answered, and through the slats in the door he watched her bent shadow shuffle off.

She amused him, like a character from one of his stories, only he didn't know her name. *He'd need to come up with one*, he thought. And a backstory. An elaborate tale of how she found herself the keeper of an inn at the edge of the world.

But first, he'd need to strip off the muck.

THIRTY MINUTES OF SOAKING AND SCRUBBING REMOVED THE MUD-lands from his skin, his nails, hair, behind his ears, between his legs, and from all the other folds and fissures the grime had infiltrated. The water became a murky brown, near the same shade and hue as the Rusted River.

Good that it should turn such a color, he thought. His own reflection had startled him, his face was that of a stranger, and he preferred to look upon the remnants of filth than a face he no longer recognized.

The crone, as he settled on calling her, had been right about the tub: it wobbled fiercely. One leg was at least two fingers shorter than the other three. It made him think of his father's work, half a world and half a lifetime away. He would have hated this tub, refused to bath in it. The old man had been many things: good with a hammer and forge, good with measurements and calculations. Every table had been made of perfect angles, every shelf a feat of engineering.

It was an art the traveler had never found interest in; too confusing and arcane. And what had it bought the his father? Ruin and ridicule. An early death, that was what. And so the traveler had turned his back on it, gone in a different direction.

Did he have regrets? Perhaps...

Yet that was another life, he thought, and submerged himself beneath the water. Another life indeed.

The crone had been less accurate about the water, however. If it had been boiled, it must have been a day ago. It was lukewarm at best, and for a moment he thought of calling out to have her boil and bring up two more buckets. But dinner would be soon, and the notion of hearing the crone *clomp clomp* up the stairs, back bent and groaning, it was an amusement he could do without.

He reached beside the tub, fumbled about until his fingers fell upon silver. That ring, it was always the first thing he put back upon himself after a bath. It was a simple band, two rings entwined in an infinite loop once crafted by his father, and though the traveler was not superstitious his finger did feel naked without it.

Wherever you go, there you are, he thought. *Running around that same damn loop.*

———————

THE TRAVELER EMERGED FROM HIS ROOM FEELING LIKE A NEW MAN, dressed in clothes almost a perfect match for his frame. Sure, they were of an older fashion perhaps a decade past, but they were warm and clean, and that was most important. Fleas and insects had been his bedmates the past several weeks. He was happy to imagine them now drowned in the muddy tub like some Biblical flood.

There came a noise from downstairs. A chatter of voices hung in the air along with the smell of spices. Potatoes and cabbage and some mulled wine perhaps. His appetite led him down the stairs.

"Was the water warm enough?" the crone asked. "For a moment I feared you may have been as boiled as leather."

"It was most pleasant," he said, studying the spread at the table. Potatoes and sweet tubers. Corn and pecans. A mound of curious nuts spilled from a wood bowl. Mulled wine sat in the center, steaming. Pork and some sort of soup, and that large orange vegetable he always forgot. Large like a moon...

Pumpkin, he remembered. *Yes, pumpkin. That was it.*

"Please, join us," the crone said.

A smiling man of unclear age stood beside a ham, carving thick slices from it. The traveler gave the odd man a nod, yet the man simply continued to grin and slice the ham. It was the same blank gaze he'd seen earlier, when he'd spotted the man digging holes by hand in the dirt field. An unsettling stare, as if little lived behind those eyes.

Yet there was something else to that man, a familiarity, as if they had crossed paths before, yet the traveler knew it impossible.

"I'm sorry, sir, have we met?" the traveler asked.

The grinning man carved and smiled, carved and smiled, but never answered. All the while blood and juices pooled on the board beneath the ham, trickled down to the floor where two black cats lapped it up.

Another week in the wilds and I might've been right there with the animals, the traveler thought.

Indeed, the meal was captivating, but something else caught his eye. A woman, perhaps half a decade his junior, was bending forth as she set the table. Her clothing was simple, little more than that of the peasant's garb he'd seen all up and down the wilds. Matted hair hung over her face, concealing it. *How long had it been since she'd seen a bath?* he wondered. Her figure, her features: all unremarkable as well, no different than a hundred farmers' daughters he'd passed on his wanderings, and a few he'd bedded.

Why, then, was he unable to look away? he wondered. *Why then did she too seem familiar?*

"Beg your pardon, sir," she said, not meeting his eyes. "Your supper awaits."

"Yes, yes," he answered, taking the plate. Still, his thoughts drifted back to the woman, and he wondered: *could her warm body be bought for the night?*

Yet those were thoughts of dessert, and they had yet to sup.

"This all looks wonderful, truly," he said to the crone, feeling the need to fill the silence.

"Serve yourself, and don't be shy. Guests have right of first bite."

Not wanting to appear too desperate, he settled on moderate helpings of everything and sat down. Perhaps sensing his reluctance to look too hungry, the crone slopped an extra scoop of pumpkin atop his plate. "Won't have an empty stomach on my watch, no sir."

"You're too kind," he said. "And I promise, I'll sing the praises of this fine establishment when I'm back among the city."

"Charmer, you are," the crone laughed. The man made an awkward attempt at scooping acorns onto his plate with his hands. A few rolled down to the floor, clattered beneath the chairs. For some reason this elicited a childish giggle from him, as if the mistake was the punchline to the funniest joke ever told.

"You'll have to forgive him," the crone said. "What little the gods gave him for wit, he went and lost. Sometimes there's a candle lit 'tween his ears. Mostly it's a hollow."

"A hollow," the man giggled, popped an acorn into his mouth, and chewed with a wide smile.

She was right, the traveler realized. He'd seen that same smile on different men in different lands. It was the daft smile of a simpleton, a village idiot. A fool.

"You cut a mighty ham, sir," the traveler said. "I thank you. As you, ma'am," he said to the crone. "And you, my lady." He nodded to the young woman. "This is a feast I fear I'm of no worth to feed upon. Were it not for the smell in the air, I would think this all a dream. Or that I had come upon a coven of witches, now fattening me up for a meal."

He found himself the only one laughing. Perhaps their humor was simpler out here. Nonetheless, he pressed on.

"I thank you, all of you, for your hospitality. Here's to you fine folks, and this wonderful little inn. May its name find its way into folklore."

He took first bite, as custom dictated, chewing the salted ham until it was tender enough to swallow.

Then, as soon as he swallowed, they began eating.

Devoured turned out to be the more appropriate term. They tore into their food with ravenous drive.

The simpleton tore the husk from the corn, chewed and sputtered, all the while grinning that stupid smile.

The old woman suckled and slurped, grey fingers peeling apart vegetables and meats. Cranberry sauce dripped down her chin.

And the young woman, her feasting was oddest of all. She pulled great tendons from the ham, gnawed and chewed the loudest. Her head was bowed, that unwashed kemp like a veil before hidden eyes. She ate as if the traveler might take the food from her.

Like a wolf, he realized. A feral beast. And at that the thoughts of putting her to bed and having his way with her made him reconsider for fear of losing whatever he put near her.

The meal carried on as such: the sounds of feasting and nothing spoken. An occasional burp arose from the crone or the simpleton, and once a burbling fart broke the silence and a reek wafted over the meal. The traveler saw the simpleton grin, yet no one spoke of it. Always there at his feet, the mewling cats, begging and hissing and jostling for a spot where a scrap may fall.

The candles burned, the plates and bowls grew empty, and within the hour the traveler could eat no more. He finished a second cup of mulled wine, poured himself a third. His head swam, warm and happy.

"Now." The old crone cleared her throat. "Before dessert, we should discuss matter of payment."

"Ah, yes, of course," the traveler said. He knew this conversation was coming. The people of these parts, simple as they may be, did nothing for free. Payment was often rendered following a favor, putting the debtor at a disadvantage. It was a smart tactic, one he'd grown to expect. "I'll pay whatever's fair for such a meal and lodgings. I don't have much, but what I do have is yours."

And if it's too much, he thought, *I'll just take it back by knifepoint.* It was a calculation he had considered. The simpleton was the only obstacle, but even then the traveler had a decade of youth on his side. The dumb man would probably giggle and fart instead of struggle and fight.

"You're a writer," the crone said. It wasn't a question but a statement, and it came as a surprise.

"Yes, I am actually. A storyteller. How did you know?"

"Storyteller," the simpleton repeated.

The crone lifted something up and placed it on the table. A leather-bound book, old and falling to pieces. So he had forgotten to remove it from his coat pocket. No doubt she'd snooped at it, probably while scrubbing the muck off.

"I saw your likeness upon the front page."

The traveler opened it, studied the pages. Most were cut in two by an accident long ago. Some he'd managed to fix, but the stains and filth remained. And his drawn likeness upon the title page. It was like the reflection he'd seen in the tub: foreign and forgotten.

Wherever you go...

"Almost gave it a good washing," the crone said.

"I'm glad you didn't," he replied. "Not that the elements haven't dampened it these past few weeks. I'm surprised there were words left for you to read."

"Never learned how to read. Least not in the common tongue."

"I'm afraid my tales are simple. I've had a few published here and there; Boston, New Amsterdam, London—"

"Big cities," the simpleton said. "Big."

"Yes, yes, well a storyteller is nothing without an audience, I'm afraid. I go where I can find an ear ready to hear a tale."

"Well, you've come to right place," the crone said. "Your offer of coin, while appreciated, is of little use to us out here. No crop ever grew from copper or silver. But a story... that's payment we value."

"A story?" The traveler was amused by this. He'd bartered before, but rare were the times his coin had been turned down in lieu of a tale. Good fiction had tumbled in value now that every city had a printing press and a dozen souls eager to call themselves an author.

"Three stories," the crone said. "One for each of us. A long winter is coming, and spring is a distant dream. Give us each a tale to last us through the snow. That's of more use than coin out here, aye?"

The simpleton nodded. The quiet girl mumbled something.

"Three tales it is," the traveler said with a smile. "I have many, but I know one that each of you may like. But first, may I open another bottle of wine? For my throat."

"Of course. Wine is one thing we have in abundance," the crone said, uncorking another bottle and pouring it straight into his cup. The rest she left to mull among the spices. Funny; he had seen no vineyard on his approach, yet he cared not how they had acquired the wine.

He took a sip, let it linger in his mouth before swallowing. It was an odd varietal, almost of the old world and unlike the sludge he'd tasted in these new lands the past few years. For a moment he thought of his father, and an almost sad sense of longing settled upon him.

"I have three tales, all with a moral twist. One is of childhood fears, of cruel kids and vengeance gone wrong. One is of sorcery, of immortality and the perfect wine. And one is of love, forbidden and imperfect. All three I know, because they are stories I witnessed, stories I saw with these very eyes."

"True stories!" The crone clapped her hand. The simpleton let out a guffaw and rocked. Beneath her hair, the young girl smiled and stroked a lazy cat that had settled upon her lap.

"Yes, every tale is born in experience, just as every tree comes from a seed. And so it is in these tales that we learn about life. Fiction and fact, both leading us to truth. Which road you choose to follow, which details you choose to believe, I leave up to you, dear listeners."

He took a sip from the wine, studied his audience. This small inn, this wretched land. *How had he strayed so far from the reading rooms and inns of Boston, from the taverns of London? How had he found himself so far off course?*

Nonetheless, three ears were better than none. It was easy to fall back into the trade. His tongue and mind worked on their own, and so he began.

CHAPTER 2

THE HAG'S RECKONING

A sunset land of fog and river, that was where I grew up. Green hills and sprawling meadows, a town named Deerfield. I knew of nothing else beyond those hills and forest, nor wanted to. Children are the same the world over, and at nine Deerfield was the world to me and my two friends, Viktor and Edward. It was a world vast and wide, a world with streams to cross and lakes to swim in. An old cemetery with spirits we could chase in the evenings. Mills and ruins, a forest to explore, faeries to seek out and trolls to fend off.

We were not peasants' sons, nor the sons of lords and landowners. We had the best of both, an education and a freedom from the toils of the land.

Though my father had died, his wish was that I learn to read and write, and so he left my mother with a small plot of leased land and instructions to see to my education.

On some days we had schooling; our families saw value in it.

And on other days we were sent to the fields to reap and sow, or off to courier letters from hamlet to village, to earn coin and favor for our families.

But our true classroom, of course, was the world, and that is where this tale takes place, near the edge of a springtime forest.

We were playing *Knights and Giants,* and it was Viktor who was the knight during this particular round. He had procured an old training shield, a wooden thing of antiquity from the smith, and had driven both myself and Edward back to the edge of the lands.

Tock! went the pebbles against his shield. *Tock! Tock!*

Of course we flung nothing larger than pebbles, yet our imagination turned them into boulders.

Tock! Tock! They crashed off the valiant knight's shield, yet onward he drew, shouting: "Yield or die, brutes! Yield or die!"

Tock! Tock! Back he pushed us until our pockets were empty, the pebbles all flung, and we were as far from the field where we'd started. The knight drew upon us, a stick for a sword, shouting: "Surrender! And pay for your crimes!"

We surrendered. And we paid. Three thrashings the losers were owed, and three thrashings we took across the seat of our pants. Viktor the Valiant was strong, and I remember the sting of the stick across my britches to this day.

Ah, you wince at the thought, but children do play such games, and friendships for boys are nothing if not forged with a bit of blood.

The game had gotten the better of our attention, the woods were not our own, and a fact washed over us: we were lost. We retraced our steps, yet twice we came back upon a place we'd already been.

Finally, at the edge of the woods we discovered a cottage and a garden. Fruit, fresh from the vine. Carrots and leeks and some wild mushrooms. A skinning rack, fresh with bleeding rabbits, hung nearby. Thinking not of whom they belonged to, we took more than enough for ourselves. We filled our pockets and our arms.

"Run!" shouted Edward as the cottage door opened. And ran we did.

I admit it, we stole. Not a day goes by that I don't feel shame. Not only for the sin but for the sorrow that followed. Truth be told, we needn't have stole. Our families were decent, our storehouses stocked. No, we stole for the simple reason that boys often steal: because we knew we shouldn't.

It's a shame now, telling you this story with the wisdom of years and hindsight, that I can't talk back through the ages and warn my younger self of the horror that would come from that garden in the woods.

Twice we returned that season. Twice we ran, fruit and vegetables tumbling from our arms as we made our escape. That creaking cottage door, like the crack of a whip, would send us into flight.

We returned a third time, at month's end, certain it would be our last. Edward kept lookout. I pulled up carrots. Viktor plucked berries. Perhaps greed got the best of us, or perhaps we simply didn't hear the creak of the door, but it was the voice that startled us.

I had never heard a voice as shrill as the hag's.

"Well, well, looky here," a most hideous woman said. To call her ugly would be unkind to those passed over by beauty's blessing. She was deformed, a twisted thing of jagged finger and bent bone. Her hair was peppered and rusted. One shoulder stood a good head-size higher than the other; one arm was twice the size of another. "Been expectin' you," the twisted woman said.

We were immobilized, as if by a spell. Never had we seen such a horrible person. Edward gasped, and I dropped all the carrots. Viktor took steps away from the hag, and in doing so walked right into a trap.

Her hooked fingers had been wrapped around a rope, yet we'd failed to realize where it went. Then, with a quick tug, the length of rope rose from the dirt. A rabbit trap, though not for a rabbit.

Viktor tumbled backward, rope around his feet. So many words were screamed. "Help me! Please! Don't let her catch me!" I remember watching his fingers dig into the soil as the woman pulled him closer, her strength uncanny.

"Looks like I caught a big one!" she said, tossing the rope over the skinning rack.

What foolish boys we were. In an instant our world had gone sour. Our courage had left us in limbo. We could neither help our friend nor abandon him. And so we simply watched.

Watched that twisted woman pull the rope.

Watched Viktor rise until he was dangling by his feet beside the flayed rabbits.

Watched as that wicked woman laughed and fetched her skinning knife.

I want to tell you some great bravery came over us, and we threw rocks and stones and rescued our friend, but no such thing happened. Our friend cried, begged, soiled himself and sobbed, yet nothing stopped that glistening blade as it drew near to the boy hanging from the skinning rack.

Knowing full well she was being watched, that her audience hadn't moved since the trap had been sprung, she turned to us.

"This'll teach you to steal from others," the twisted woman said. And then she swung the blade, cackling all the way.

Viktor screamed. Edward screamed. I screamed.

Yet she only cackled.

And then miracle of all miracles, Viktor was on the ground: the rope binding his ankle was cut. He screamed and sobbed and ran back to us. Throughout all this the woman only laughed.

"That'll teach you to steal from others," she cackled. "That'll teach you!"

And teach us it did.

We never returned to the cottage, at least not to steal fruit or vegetable. That day sat in our memory, as terrifying a warning as any ever uttered. We told no one, and spoke of it rarely.

Yet for Viktor it had been the ultimate humiliation. It festered and grew, a pox upon his spirit. The valiant knight, who never lost, had been bested by a wicked hag. He no longer played *Knights and Giants*, but plotted of vengeance.

"We have to get her," Viktor said. "We have to make her pay."

"How?" Edward asked.

"I'll think of a way," he answered.

The gods are cruel, as we all know. Times of laughter can fast turn to times of sorrow. That season the same sickness that spread across Europe hit Deerfield, and many fell ill. When graves fill with the dead, churches fill with the living. People seek answers in superstition.

"Who is to blame?" the bleating masses ask. "Is this the work of demons, or the curse of gods?"

"Or perhaps," Viktor whispered to us one day after the sermon, "this is the work of another."

I should have known his wound had gone to rot. That his plot would be crueler than her lesson. But I did not see the constellations through the stars, I did not connect the points of light.

"The townsfolk search for an answer," Viktor said. "Why do the healthy die? What causes babies to be born still and silent? Or perhaps... *who*?"

"What do you plan?" Edward whispered.

"To point them to that cottage by the woods," Viktor answered. "To the monster that lives there. To give them a witch and teach her a lesson."

Of course, we knew nothing of witches or warlocks or magic. It was a grandfather's talk, a faerie tale. If there were witches then by right of logic there were wood elves and goblins that plucked the eyes from sleeping babies. Yet I had never seen wood elves nor goblins nor babies without eyes. Still young of age, I understood this: superstition never dies; it merely sleeps until roused by the unexplained.

Though the plan was Viktor's invention, I'm shamed to admit I played my part. To prove an old woman a witch would require evidence and fear, and Viktor came up with ways to procure both.

I was to tell Father Richard I had seen the crooked shadow of the woman in the woods scurrying about the cemetery at night from my window. My bedroom provided such vantage. I was to say that I followed the shape back to the cottage in the woods and there I saw her conversing with a black dog, a dark beast with horns and hooves.

False witness, that's what I was to provide. A lie.

Compared to the others, my part was simple. A distraction, that's what Edward was tasked with. Before my part was to be played, Edward and Viktor would go into the woods. Edward would steal a single carrot, enough to call the attention of the wicked woman. Then he would flee and she would follow, and that's when Viktor would sneak onto her property.

Why would he go into the lair of such a creature?

"Because no one will believe us without evidence," Viktor had said, and he was right. Not without evidence.

And for that, his part in the plan called for the most gruesome act, one that shames me to this day. At night he would sneak to the cemetery. From the oldest graves, the forgotten ones, he would steal from the dead, one bone from each body interred to the earth.

A jawbone.

"Why their jaw?" I asked him when he told us of his terrible plan.

"A witch would need the jaws of the dead to talk with the devil," he answered. "I read it in a book." It was a fiction of course, yet familiar enough to seem sensible, logical.

While she chased Edward, Viktor would hide these jaws in her cottage, evidence of her dark studies. He would have his vengeance. He would laugh at her as she had at him.

And had all gone to plan I would not be here to tell this tale. See, I was ready to play my part, to tell a lie to a man of the cross. I would have given false witness...

But the sickness took me.

The very night Viktor was digging up old bones, I was shivering and speaking in tongues. I learned fast why they call it the shaking sickness, why they tied the infected to boards. I kicked out two of my brother's teeth that night and gashed my wrists raw on the leather straps. But somehow I began to fight it off, and emerged alive by mid-day, unlike many others.

I heard them knocking that next afternoon, asking if I could join them in a game of *Knights and Giants*, knowing full well they were going to stash the jaw bones. My mother saved my life a second time. "He's caught the sickness," she told them. "You'd best stay away for a few days."

But boys never stay away, not from friends nor trouble, and certainly not when both are intertwined. They came to my window late in the afternoon and told me their plan.

"We'll do it without you," Viktor said. "But if Father Richard asks..."

"I saw her scurrying about the cemetery, late at night," I replied. "And the black dog, I saw her talking with it in the woods."

Viktor seemed pleased. "Good. Edward will say the same; our stories will match. Rest up and get better. We'll soon be laughing at her."

But we never laughed.

THE COMMOTION WOKE ME.

It was hard to say whether it was the same day, or the next. I was a prisoner to the fever dreams, and often I thought myself among the dead, a lost soul dreaming of life. Yet the shouting brought me back to this realm, a hundred voices at least. I was sick, but strong enough to rise to the window.

It was an odd sort of day. I remember because the sun was high but the shadows felt long. Half the town was assembled, a furious mob. I saw swords and plows and sickles above the bob of hats and heads. I saw some people I knew, and many I didn't.

Had something terrible happened? I wondered. Part of me had forgotten the prank, and I assumed we were at war.

Then the crowd split, and I saw her: the woman from the woods.

She had been stripped, battered and bruised. Her body was even more wretched without clothes. Lumps covered skin, like some sickly pond frog. She had hair in places no hair should grow. She had been beaten, bloodied and spattered with mud and manure, and this final act seemed crueler than all the rest. It reduced her to an animal, scared and shaking, and for that if nothing else I am haunted by her image: a cowering creature the townsfolk poked at with stick and sickle.

A great silence fell over the crowd, and though I was far I could hear every word. Father Richard stood over her, a righteous fury in his voice. "Sudden has been our suffering and torment. Sudden and without reason... until now!"

The silver-haired priest's finger came down upon the deformed woman like a bolt from Olympus. "A witch has cursed us! Hexed us! Plagued us with sickness and stolen our dead. Her actions and evil, her desecration of the deceased, has brought about God's wrath. It is this very woman, this ill-formed witch, that has been in league with the devil, who has cursed your loved ones and filled the graves so that she could rob them of their very bones!"

The furious voices overwhelmed the priest's speech, and for a moment it seemed as if the townsfolk would tear her asunder right there. But Father Richard's booming voice silenced them like a whip.

"These boys," he said, and I saw Viktor and Edward among the crowd, almost as scared as the twisted woman. "These two boys witnessed her in the cemetery the very last night, plundering bones from your ancestors' graves! It is with their word, their brave word, that we tracked the desecration back to her den of dark magic. What we found was an apothecary from Hell itself, Satan's own kitchen. Present the evidence."

Sacks were carried forth by the villagers, bulging and squirming. *How many jawbones had Viktor dug up?* I wondered.

They emptied those sacks at the cowering woman's feet. Snakes slithered forth, small and large. Insects of shape and size I've never seen. Pages of books written in red ink. Crystals and contraptions wrapped in twine, as if from Merlin's own tower. Rotten flowers, mummified birds, and worst of all the dried shapes of stillborn babies painted with foreign letters.

The pile was high, a heap of horrors unimaginable. Mothers shielded their children's eyes. Women fainted. Shouts for her death echoed out over the disgust.

And scattered throughout the pile, a half dozen jawbones, glimmering white. I still remember the look the hag gave when she saw those jawbones mixed in among the rest.

"These..." the twisted woman said, picking up a jawbone. "These are not mine."

"You deny this is yours?" Father Richard asked. "This mountain of horrors?"

"No, no no no," the twisted woman said. "Only these. These jaws are not mine. The rest, I do not deny. Nor your charges of witchcraft and magic. Aye, I speak with the devil, but he's no horned dog. He's here... HERE! Right now, in all of us. And he's laughing, for this joke, it still has one more turn. He's laughing... at all of you!"

And with that she let out the most wretched laugh, one so shrill I covered my ears even from all that distance. It felt as if she was laughing beside me, around me, and to this day no cackle has ever sounded so sinister. It seemed to go on forever.

She laughed as they tied the noose about her throat.

Laughed as they tossed the rope over the branch.

She was still laughing as they pulled her upward, up, naked and twisting, into the grey sky.

I know not how much longer she laughed, only that it did stop, eventually. Her twisted body hung there in silence for the remainder of the day, and the town was silent as well. That evening they cut her down and burned her. I was later told the flames were a shade of green. And the smell; one doesn't forget such a reek.

I SLEPT A LOT THE FOLLOWING FEW DAYS, UPON MY MOTHER'S insistence. She was uncertain the worst of the sickness had passed, though I knew I was on the mend. Some days I peeked out the window for signs of madness, but there were none. Only the funerals for the sick, which came daily.

Four days after I watched the witch hung, my mother finally permitted me leave of the house. I went straight to Viktor's home, wanting to hear of all that had happened, all the details before the finale that I witnessed amid my delirium. Yet there was no answer when I knocked upon his door.

Next I tried Edward's house as well, his being the furthest from mine. Though there was a light on and through the window I could see his mother wearing a black veil and sitting in the corner, she neither acknowledged my knocking nor answered the door.

Frustrated, I left his doorstep, and came upon one of his neighbors, a young boy who had also survived the sickness.

"He's not there anymore," the boy said. "Your friend. He's not there."

"Where has he gone?"

The boy raised a single finger and pointed far beyond the houses, and somehow I knew.

"Show me," I told him.

THERE WERE MANY NEW GRAVES SINCE I HAD TAKEN SICK, AND MANY funerals, so it was of no surprise how I missed my two friends. Their graves were not together, yet they had died the same night, and not of the sickness that had almost taken me.

"Everyone heard their mother's scream," the boy said. "Two of them, both right around sunrise, the day after that hag was hung. That's when they found them. Some said the devil came in the night. Others claim they saw a flaming woman walking through the fog. It's probably all poppycock, but one thing's the same: both your friends were missing their jaws."

I THOUGHT OF VIKTOR AND EDWARD, OF THE CRUEL PRANK AND THE twisted woman's laughter. "This joke still has one more turn," she had said, and she was right.

That night a great lament came over me, and I went to my window to see if I could spy their graves. There, among the trees and tombs, I saw three shapes glimmering in the moonlight. A twisted woman, hair the color of rust and flame, leading two boys off into the woods by their hands.

They all stopped for a moment, sensing my sight upon them, and when they turned to me I saw a gaping hole where their jaws had once been. And from that great distance I knew their white eyes saw me clear through the darkness and fog. I knew that they both envied and hated me, as only the dead can envy and hate the living.

I closed the windows, and I never opened them at night again.

INTERLUDE I

The crone clapped her hand and the simpleton guffawed.

"And what of you?" asked the bent back woman. "Did you see her specter again?"

The traveler shook his head. "No, and I should thank the gods I have not. For such a thing..."

He trailed off. Those days and nights were behind him. No need to open that old casket. No need to rattle them bones.

"I'm sorry, I fear this wine is too easy to drink." He tapped the cup. "I've been hasty with my thirst. Where might I relieve myself?"

THE DIM LAMP CAST LONG SHADOWS, TWISTED FINGERS THAT SWUNG about the darkness outside.

It was a short walk to the outhouse, and the traveler needed to only follow his nose. Not far off he heard the horse whinny. The useless beast would spend its night downwind of the privy, and somehow that amused him.

He did his business in haste, knowing what sort of slithering things preferred such filth, and closed the door behind himself. A deep breath cleared the last of the smell. It was a lovely autumn night. The rain had died out but the wind had picked up. Good news, bad news. High overhead the harvest moon stared down, judging. That same damn moon, no matter the land, following him, like a ghost.

Halfway back to the inn his foot caught on a protrusion, and he went stumbling. The lamp almost fell from his hands, but he steadied himself. In that brief collapse he had seen something glistening like glass, reflecting the amber light from the ground. A bottle perhaps, or a shard of glass unearthed by the scouring rain. He bent down by the path's edge and lowered the lantern.

It was no bottle nor piece of glass, but a stone twice the size of his fist. Oval and egg-like, it was of almost perfect symmetry with one exception: the geodes that glimmered within the hollow rock.

Beautiful, he thought. But not unheard of. The earth was old, the gods creative. Such treasures and more lay scattered to the four corners and beyond.

He put the stone down back, but something felt wrong. On the other side, opposite the geode, were grooved etchings. Three vertical lines ran top to bottom, too perfect to have been caused by natural workings.

Well, well, he thought, glancing back up at the inn. *Seems they're a more superstitious lot than I thought.*

Wherever you go, there you are. The moon and the rocks. It was an uncomfortable thought he tried to wipe from his mind.

For a moment, brief and cold, he felt as if every dark window from the inn hid shapes that stared down at him. A dozen dark eyes, watching.

A childish thought. His tale had rattled even himself; the sign of a good storyteller. But that's all it was, a tale, and as he chuckled the feeling vanished. There were only four staying at the inn: a storyteller and three souls too stupid to know the dead didn't return.

This stone was proof of that.

THE SIMPLETON WAS SCOURING THE BOWL OF CRANBERRIES WITH A stumpy finger when the traveler returned. The girl was sweeping the floor.

"We were worried they'd gotten you," the crone said.

"They?"

"Bog beasts and goblins," the crone laughed. "Them, or you'd decided you'd feast and flee, leaving us without our other two tales."

"May the bog beasts and goblins get me indeed should I ever dine so fine and dash," he said. "Tell me though, and I mean no offense: are there other things you fear out here? Things worse than creatures of myth?"

He placed the sparkling geode on the table.

At this the young girl stopped sweeping, and the simpleton's finger, which had gone from the cranberry sauce to his ear, now lowered to his lap, still stained red.

"Aye." The crone nodded. "You know of these?"

"Runic stones, they're called. At least, to my ears. I've heard of other names too. Gems of Focus. Deadgates as well, I believe."

"Aye. They've as many names as we have for water and land and all that grows from both. Most have forgotten them, even in the old world. Few and far between are the travelers who spot them at all. How did you come to hear of such names?"

"I'm familiar with many superstitions. I find them fascinating, though what storyteller wouldn't? They're a sort talisman, like a horse's shoe."

A sour expression spread across the crone's face. Offense perhaps, though the traveler cared not. There were hundreds of talismans in the world, totems to keep out the devil and welcome the angels, and all had the same effect: absolutely nothing.

"A horse's shoe," she said as she took the stone, turning it over in her hands.

Funny, he thought. Outside, the geode was as bright as the

stars. But in here, in the light, those crystals were as dark as the thickest mud.

"A horse's shoe," she repeated. "I like that." Then she held out the stone as if it were no lighter than a feather. The young girl shuffled over and took it. "Do us a favor, and set this horse's shoe back where it belongs."

A few seconds later the young girl was out the door, and that was that, end of the conversation.

"Your second story," the crone said. "Perhaps you can tell us how you came to know of such arcane things."

"As a matter of fact." The traveler smiled, poured himself another cup of mulled wine, and held it up. "My second tale is just that: a story of arcane secrets and the perfect wine."

CHAPTER 3

THE ELDER OF ALDRITCH

Deerfield held little for a young man in his apprentice years. The sickness had culled the girls, and by the time they were of marrying age there were five men to every maiden. I held no claim to land, only a silver ring and a small patch of leased earth, and as such I was but a notch above the butcher's boy in my prospects.

I did what many young men of apprentice age do: I set out to make a name for myself.

I spent a year wandering the folds and valleys, working odd jobs in hamlets and homesteads. I thatched a roof here, fixed a fence there. Where there was work I humbled myself and gave it my best.

When I was hungry, I learned which root to chew, which stream to fish from.

When my body was tired I built a lean-to or laid beneath the stars.

Occasionally I came upon a hare or pheasant, and with luck and practice I was able to strike them with a stone and fill my stomach.

At the east coast, on a gentle slope of fertile land, I came upon a stone wall of ill standing. It circled a vineyard perched on top of the softest of knolls. While perhaps the wall had once kept intruders at bay, it was now little more than lumps of collapsed stone, a poor fortification.

It was there that I first saw the glimmer of those smooth rocks fat with crystals, there that I would learn some of the names you've heard me utter. Perhaps I might have continued upon my way were it not for the temptation to poach such a beautiful object. I admit, the road had been cruel, my pockets were empty, and the glimmer of what I imagined to be found riches got the better of my honor. I took the runic stone and continued down the road.

Not a hundred paces later I was set upon by a rider and a horse. He was a tall man of silver hair and piercing grey-blue eyes, an elder I knew at once to be the owner of the vineyard. And he knew me to be a thief.

"You have something of mine," he said. "Hand it over, and I'll consider it an accident. Carry on, and I'll have your hand and see your face branded with the mark of a thief."

The choice was clear, and I didn't delay to pass him the crystal-filled stone I had stolen. My apologies came equally as quick, for I feared he might still make off with my hand. I was a young man, perhaps a match for him physically, yet fear muted that idea.

"You're far from home," he said, a statement and not a question.

"Yes," I answered. "And I'm willing to work if you've need of any."

"Why would I hire one who stole from me?" he asked.

A fair question to be certain, and one to which I could only reply: "Because, sir, our relationship can only get better from here."

He rarely smiled, then or any of the days that followed. But there was a glimmer in his eye, and a slight nod that told me he saw something good in me. "Very well. As you can see, I've a vineyard to run, a thousand troubles to tend to, and few hands to help. The wall you saw needs mending. Start where you wish, and I'll find you at sunset. If you put in a decent day's work, I'll see that you're fed."

I thanked him, but he told me to save my words for my work. Then he rode off.

I worked, hefting stone upon stone, fixing that crumbled mess of a wall that ran the perimeter of the vineyard. It was a massive undertaking, impossible to finish in a day, let alone a season. Still, I worked as hard as I ever had, making sure each stone was tucked in perfectly, and testing it by throwing my shoulder against it. Should a single stone budge I started over.

By sunset I must have cleared twenty paces, but the wall stood solid, the height of an adult as built by a boy on the cusp of manhood.

"Fair work you did there," the elder said when he returned upon his horse. "You're a man of his word, and so am I. See that house upon the knoll? Make your way there and I'll see there's a hot meal for you."

The walling had exhausted me, and I thought I'd left no reserve for the climb, yet somehow I forced myself to ascend. Warm food does that to a person; rekindles their strength and pushes them onward.

It was laborious walk up the terraces of the vineyard. Though I knew little of wine at the time, I knew sick plants when I saw them. The grapes were no larger than peas, sick spots among grey vines. The leaves themselves spotty and full of holes.

I passed a dozen rows, each worse than the last, until I arrived at the manor. It was an imposing structure of stone and wood, perhaps once of elegant craftsmanship though fallen to disrepair. The seasons had been cruel, and though it didn't snow this far south the air was often filled with fog, and even strong wood bends beneath the breath of time.

I knocked several times upon the main door until it opened and a young man stared back. His hair was not silver, though I recognized the eyes: they were the same icy grey-blue as the elder's.

"Step closer and I'll open you up," the man said, pushing the point of a sword into my chest. "Otherwise be gone. There's no work here for beggars."

As soon as I opened my mouth to explain the misunderstanding he pushed the blade in. Were it not for the journals I carried in my pocket, he would have kept his word and opened me right up on the doorstep to the manor.

Dejected and hungry, I turned and left. It was only as I was passing the first row of sick grapes that I heard the elder call out: "Come back! There's been a mistake!"

I ATE WELL, BOTH ON ACCOUNT OF MY WORK AND HIS SON'S ILL treatment. I learned little of the family that day, not even their names. The son was dressed in expensive clothes, no doubt a patron of the fancier fabrics at the village nearby, and he glared at me as I ate in silence. The elder I presumed to be of hardier fiber: his hands were calloused and dirty, his skin looked aged by sun. Still, I was well fed, so I kept to myself and ate.

I was hardly finished with my final bite when the elder broke the silence. "Fair job you did with the wall, but there's a thousand holes that run the length of the land".

"So I noticed, sir."

"If you're willing to work, there are hot meals in it for you. A bed in the stable, perhaps some coin, should you wish."

The son's protests were instant. "We can't let this beggar stay here!"

"A beggar begs," the elder said. "This man's a traveller. He earns his keep."

The son turned his fork on me, and to this day I remember the comical radish still skewered on its tip as he pointed it at me. "What do you know of soil and vine? What do you know of wine?"

"He needs not know of either," the elder snarled. "He's

mending a wall, not casking wine. You worry about the harvest, I'll worry about the traveller."

The son said nothing, but I knew he would have it out for me. He was a dandy, one who saw dirt and earth as beneath him. My time at the manor would soon confirm this, among other things; they had once been wealthy but had fallen on hard years, and the son knew not how to muddy his britches nor bend his back to help pick the family up.

———

I SPENT THE DAYLIGHT HOURS MENDING THE WALL, STONE BY STONE. In the mornings I would have my breakfast there by the storeroom. In the evenings I would sup by myself in the kitchen.

There was a servant there as well, a gypsy woman who spoke little of my language. Sometimes I saw her about the rows of vines, sampling the grapes. Other times I saw her praying at sunset, speaking odd words. Her ways were not mine, but the world was wide and as they say, all roads lead to Rome.

During my duty mending the wall I came upon more runic stones among the piles of common wall tock.

"These stones, they must not be moved," the elder instructed. "Only placed back in the wall where you find them."

Curiosity got the better of me, and I asked: "What are they, sir?"

"Decorations my wife once fancied for good luck. Nothing more."

Of course his story seemed false. They were curious things, those runic stones. Were it not for the glyphs carved upon them they would seem like perfect eggs lain by some enormous bird. And when held from another angle, where the chiseled cracks revealed the crystals within, they glittered like the stars at night. Often I would use them to find my way back through the shadows when I worked on the wall past sunset.

Harvest season came and went. I heard much complaint from

within the manor; the grapes were too bitter, the soil too spoiled. Often I would hear the elder spitting out wine and cursing its flavor.

The son came and went. I slept on straw in the stables, not far from the steed he kept, and so I heard much of his comings and goings.

Often he would return drunken, burbling to himself. Sometimes he did not return until the next morning. A few times he brought women back, and I pretended to be asleep when he took them out among the vines and had his way with them, grunting like a pig in mud.

"One day he'll be dead, and all this will be mine," the son said to his female friends. A different woman each time, but his song was always the same. "And if you're good to me, perhaps this can be ours."

They left me to mending the wall, and in many ways I became like it: ignored and unnoticed, a landscape feature. Sometimes the son threw stones at me, and sometimes he spat in the food the servant woman left for me. Once I suspected him of leaving a stink pickle in my sleeping straw, but I had no proof.

Fall turned to winter. Most days it was bitter cold, but I worked through the elements and soon more than a quarter of the land had been walled. For Christmas the elder gave me the day off and a few extra coins. He insisted on paying me now, despite his son's protests.

"He's moved stones," the son chuckled. "Hardly a feat of skill."

"No, but a feat of strength, and a feat more than you've accomplished," the elder hissed. He had drunk more than usual, and I could hear his voice through the kitchen door, loudened by wine. "He costs me not but a meal, a few copper and silver. But you! You spend everything on fancy clothes, dressing like some noble's whore, squandering our coins on games and gambling. He rebuilds, while you dismantle. Yeah, he costs me. But you cost me more!"

The son didn't respond, at least not there. I heard him come for his horse not an hour later, and leave in haste, not to return for a few days.

Others came as well, visitors that arrived in carriages or on horseback. They were small gatherings of a sort, usually held when the moon was full. For the first few months I ignored them, but by winter I was ordered to bathe, given fine clothes, and told to stable the visitors' horses. I saw the servant woman from time to time, muttering grumblings and trying to cook for a dozen.

The visitors were mostly older than I, some regal and lord-like, others as common as any wayfarer passing between towns. Odd noises came from the house those nights, the clattering and booming of voices, a party perhaps. I kept my head down, stabled the horses as told, and continued to be like the wall.

Winter became spring. Flowers returned. By then the days were lengthening and I resolved to finish the wall by summer's end. Half a wall now stood rebuilt where only holes had once been. I was proud of my work, and often at night I would glance out from the stables. It was a large property, a long horizon, but if one looked closely in the darkness they could see the line that traced the ridges. And they could see the stones set within, small stars in a sea of black.

Once a month those guests came, and once a month I bathed, donned finery, and stabled the horses. If the father and son quarreled most days, they were on the verge of murder following those parties. Often I would hear the son shouting, calling his father a fool, and then hurrying off at night.

In June, after changing out of my borrowed finery, I returned to find the elder near his study, poring over maps of the world. He looked tired these days, his speech was slow.

"Please, put the clothes back in the cabinet," he directed. "And do me a favor; my feet are weary. In my study you'll find a table with books and maps upon it. There is one book, blue in color, as thick as two fingers. Upon it you'll find the earth and a star. Would you fetch it for me?"

Of course I would. It was no great task, and what was one book when I'd been lifting stones for three seasons? So I put away my borrowed clothes in the cabinet, and for the first time I stepped in to his study.

Now, I was still a young man, but I had heard stories of wizards and seers, and for a moment I wondered if I hadn't stepped back into Arthurian tale. It was a dark room, eerily so, and its windows were glazed with some sort of black paint. The room was larger than it should be, as if its interior dimensions did not match the size of the manor from the outside. Trinkets hung from the beams, crystals and prisms and odd orbs painted like celestial bodies. At the center of the ceiling there hung one orb larger than the others, painted a fiery orange and yellow, which I surmised to be the sun.

Curiosity got the better of me, and I tarried too long, inspecting instruments I did not understand. Maps of the world lay on the table, warped beneath magnifying lenses with odd markings upon them. Red and blue lines crisscrossed the parchment, connecting points in the Orient, Europe, the new world, and even the wild lands of Africa. Numbers were written next to the lines, and I recognized them as dates. *So the elder was planning a trip,* I surmised.

My attention fell to a blue book and its odd title: *Leylines of the Earth, Stars, and Nether.* It was the book I was to retrieve, but surely I could steal a quick glance, perhaps to gleam an answer for such oddities. I opened it with nervous hands. The tome was dense, some sort of atlas and ledger thick with calculations and dates, and as I thumbed through it I knew not what it was.

"So you can read?" came the elder's voice. "I suspected as much. You're too acute to be of simple upbringing. Where did you learn such a skill?"

"I was schooled some, with wealthier children. And at home. My parents thought it of some value."

"They were wise. I asked you to fetch me the book with the

earth and stars on the cover, though I forgot the fact they were written on it, not drawn. My memory is not what it once was."

"My apologies, sir; I didn't mean to spy. If you wish me to leave the manor, I shall." I gave him the book and bowed.

"I could have you hung if I wished. A word, that's all it would take, and you'd be swinging from a tree as a sneak-thief. Yet I ask myself, of what good would that be? You've done no harm here, only shown your inquisitive nature. The gods curse those who hinder an eager mind."

His kindness struck me as odd, and I was confused. "So what would you have of me?"

"That you continue as you have done. Should you wish to learn more than just how to build walls, but how to see beyond them, I could use an assistant."

An assistant? An apprentice to what? I wondered. I could only glance at the room and all its mysterious, perhaps magical artifacts to gleam the truth. "I'm afraid I would be a terrible assistant. I know nothing of whatever sorcery this is."

"Sorcery?" He let out a booming laugh that still makes me smile to this day. "No, no, this is no sorcery, only a science not yet fully understood by this modern world. Come, I'll show you."

He took me to a black window where an object fused of metal and glass sat, glimmering like some odd musical instrument.

"Put your eye here," he said, and I did as instructed, surprised at what I spied through the glass. "Tell me what you see?"

"I see the moon. Yet it appears larger than I've ever seen. Are those mountains upon it?"

"Indeed, mountains. Great valleys too, and deep, dry pits. Perhaps there were once rivers and lakes, not unlike the lands we live upon."

It was a curious thing, this instrument of metal and glass, and I felt I needed to know more about it. "How does it work, this magical device?"

"Surely you've seen fish through unmuddied water, their form changed by the ripples. You've seen the glimmer of trapped light from the stones that surround this manor. The property is similar, though the results sometimes differ. With the proper conditions things can be made smaller, larger, even transported over a great distance."

"Forgive me, but what conditions are those?"

"Well, some once believed the earth to have a certain vibration to it. A hum, like that of crystal." The elder licked his finger and ran it around the rim of his wineglass, and a faint, chilling vibration filled the air.

"A sound?" I asked.

"An energy," the elder corrected, putting his hand upon the blue book. His finger traced a line that ran through a map of the old world. "That's what I'm searching for. Just as our body has channels to transport blood, so too does the earth and the heavens. Leylines, they were called by the ancients who lived in these lands. Years I had searched, travelled, much like you, until I found such a font in this very place."

I followed the line across the map, those numbers now revealed as dates in the past, present, and future. On such range came into view, settled upon a familiar spot on the map that read: *Aldritch Hills.*

"Here?"

"Indeed. Those rocks you place in the wall give clue to the energy below. Like the telescope, with a proper configuration they can amplify the energy. For two decades this manor has prospered, producing wine when the lands to all directions have spat out not even a radish."

"Forgive me, but to my eyes the vines look ill."

"See, I knew I spied in you something special. You're observant, one who follows his senses. Your evaluation is correct. Just as rivers run dry, so too do leylines. The energy ebbs and fades, but nothing is ever made nor destroyed; merely transmuted. Like a liquid squeezed, it will emerge elsewhere. That is what I'm searching for, this new spring, and yet I'm afraid with each passing season my time is running out."

A sadness spread across the elder's face, and with it all his energy seemed to dissipate, as if some great leyline were beneath his very feet, draining his life force.

"The truth is, I'm trying to unravel the gods' design. And the gods live longer than men. I fear my time is short, my friends few. For two decades this vineyard provided coin for my studies, but no more. The leylines move, the land grows sour. I'm forced to beg favor of others. You've seen them here, the parties, those with coin to spare. They think this all a great mystical gathering, something to fatten their pockets, bless their harvests. I read their futures, they leave their silver." The elder laughed. "I see you think my words mad."

I didn't know what to think. Leylines and fortune telling, it was wizard talk, something I wrote off as fiction for most of my days.

"I'm afraid I don't understand," I said. "You say you read their future. Why, then, can't you read where the leylines emerge?"

"Because I can see futures, not the future. There is not one, but a thousand possible paths, with a thousand possible branches. Some are clear, others hidden by the fog of uncertainty. These benefactors, they see the world in seasons, but I see decades. Understanding these veins of the earth leads to answers grander than a mere harvest. Time, even death itself, could be conquered."

Few words have haunted me more than those: *time, even death itself, could be conquered.* There was a madness to the old man, a blasphemous insanity both artistic and dangerous. And beneath it: a sadness.

"My son, he thinks me a fool, has for years. I know he conspires, spreads word among the townsfolk of a man going mad, a vineyard gone to rot. My parties dwindle; so do our coffers. Soon he may even take over, sell off my study and send me to the locked tower."

For six months the elder had housed me, given me meals and provided some coin for saving, and yet we'd never shared more than a dozen words in a day. And now, in one evening I'd learned his deepest secrets. Were there mystical lines beneath the skin of the earth? I knew not, and even now I sometimes wonder. Yet I was young, and I felt obligated to help.

"What would you have me do?" I asked.

As instructed, I carried on rebuilding the wall during the day. It was an important task, he said, that every stone be precise and as perfect as possible, including the runic stones. It helped with his measurements, stabilized the waning energies, or so he claimed.

At night I aided him, jotting down numbers and names, places on maps, and most often refilling his ink. I learned to use his telescope, his pendulum clock, and the arcane devices he had for detecting the waxing and waning of the Earth's energies. I held many candles and lamps over his frantic scribblings those nights, and I admit that most often I neither understood nor truly believed what he wrote down. Most nights I retired to the stable exhausted and confused.

Some nights, however, when the moon was almost full, and when the sky was crisp and clear, I do admit that I felt a charge, an odd tug, as if invisible fibers within were being plucked by some vast river beneath me.

On one of those nights, when the elder had finally gone and worked himself asleep at his desk, I snuck out of the study only to find his son waiting for me in the dining room. I could smell the wine on him, a vapor of intoxication and anger.

"So he's gone and sold you on his silliness too, has he?" the young man laughed. "Made you into one of the faithful?"

I was young, but I knew no words I could utter would take the ice out of the air. He had that same fighting fire in his eyes as the evening he'd pushed his sword into me.

"No, sir, just doing as your father asks."

"My father? And what does he ask of you, hmm? Has he made you his apprentice? Amusing, that you read and write and you never bothered to tell me."

"You never asked."

He leapt from the chair as if a bubbling cauldron were beneath his rear, and the next thing I knew his blade was beneath my chin. He was fast, even when drunk.

"Watch your tongue, whelp. I don't spend my time asking every tick or flea if it's literate. You're beneath me. I don't ask you anything. And if you keep another secret from me I'll gut you, understand?"

"Yes, of course," I whispered. Any louder, and my throat would have split itself upon his blade.

"Good," he said, and released me. I took my leave, but as I was departing I heard him call out. "There's going to be a reckoning soon. Make sure you're not the wrong side of it."

I slept little that night. Truth be told, most nights were sleepless, and I thought often of what the elder had said. Time, and even death itself, could be conquered.

Time and death.

Yet time moved on, same as it always did, no faster nor slower.

I continued to rebuild the wall. By summer my muscles had a firmness to them, a strength that seemed foreign even to myself. The season's sun was brutal, unforgiving, and beneath it my skin took on a bronze hue.

As I worked among the daylight hours I would sometimes spy the son, out among the grapes. He was often angry, and more than once I saw him rip the vines from the ground. The harvest, I gathered from the sickly vines, was going to be rough.

The parties came as usual, though as the summer went on the number of guests waned. Often I heard them laughing at the old man as I retrieved their horses. "A silly man," they called him. "A foolish illusionist. Charming, yet desperate."

"They're right, you know," his son said to me that night, lips loosened from wine. "Soon he'll have no benefactors, and no coin to pay you with."

"Soon his wall will be finished," I replied, not wanting to baited into an argument. "He'll have no need of me then."

This seemed to bring about a smile, and he nodded as if satisfied. "If it indeed remains 'his' wall."

At the height of summer, when the days were longest, my curiosity once again got the better of me, and I snuck around to the black windows of the study during one of his gatherings. There were few guests these days, less than a quarter of those that had come a year ago, and I feared it may be my last chance to witness what went on behind the black windows.

Earlier, while the elder was focused on his calculations, I had scraped a bit of black paint from the glass. It was no more than the size of one of the pathetic grapes and I feared it might not be enough to see through.

I was wrong, as it turned out, and with the darkness to my back I could see everything. The study was lit by candles, the guests around the perimeter observing a demonstration of sorts. A dozen or so runic stones had been placed in a small circle in the center of the room, and over that the elder stood, holding a pitcher of water. Though his words were mute, I could sense he was explaining something, and on his lips I kept reading the word: *leylines*. The guests looked bored, whispers between them and the occasional yawn.

The elder paused, perhaps sensing his audience was lost. Then he collected himself and did something I have thought over again and again in the years since. He tilted the pitcher of water and poured a steady stream right into the circle of the runic stones. Few seemed to notice what I noticed, that no puddle nor splash appeared from between the stones. The entire contents of the pitcher cascaded and, like some great force had tugged upon it, twisted, stretched, and spun until the liquid disappeared into the maw of the earth.

Surely it had to go somewhere, yet I saw no point of exit, no puddle nor place of reemergence. It was as if some invisible well existed between those glimmering stones.

A curious chuckle from the crowd, and the elder dropped the pitcher itself. It too stretched and was swallowed between the stones. Someone said something, others laughed, and then one of the men took a wine bottle and dropped it in. Again, no glass broke. The bottle was simply swallowed and gone.

Still, few seemed impressed, a couple poked at the floor with canes as if to reveal some hidden chamber. One such gentleman reached for the circle of runic stones, and then I saw fear erupt upon the elder's face. Though his words were mute I knew what he was shouting.

Stop!

No sooner had the man touched the runic stone than he was gasping and withdrawing seared fingers and steaming flesh. A horrid frost had enveloped his hand, as blue as the deepest snow I've seen in my travels, and for a brief second the man's hand glistened like the gems inside the stones themselves.

Then it shattered.

A great commotion erupted. One woman ran shrieking from the room, and another fainted backward into the arms of her husband. People scrambled and the elder was bumped about. The wounded man simply looked down in shock at his steaming hand. Only a thumb remained: no palm nor fingers.

I hurried to the stables just in time to see many of the guests leaving. It was a mad scramble, as if the house were coming down in some great tempest. I tried to return the horses to the proper owners; most simply fetched their own. I saw the wounded man, hand still frosted beneath a bandage of blood, grunting and sweating as his wife whipped the reins of their horse.

"Wake the doctor!" someone called out.

When there were no more horses to be returned I made my way to the manor. I saw the servant cleaning a mess of overturned food from the dining room, and I found the elder in the study. Even a fool would have sensed the great despair that hung over him.

"How much did you see, from your peeping hole at the window?"

"Not enough to understand my eyes, I'm afraid. And for spying, I am sorry."

"Don't be. You have a natural curiosity; that is a good thing. I should have indulged it earlier."

"What occurred tonight? I'm afraid I don't understand."

"Nor do I, really. A miscalculation was made, an error I should have foreseen. The future is not always exact, even my own. A hundred thousand seeds planted that could grow into anything. Tonight I fear a dark harvest has been sown. I had been so focused on sending the water forward in time, I had not focused on the flesh. Channeling that is a task I've yet to master."

The runic stones had left curious scuffs upon the ground, snow and ice beneath them, and all the color had gone out of those once glimmering crystals, leaving only blackness, like volcanic soil.

"I'm afraid Lord Prestor's son may not be very forgiving. He is, or should I say was, a master duelist. His fingers will cost me a pretty coin. Be that as it may, this future is sealed. Over the edge and into the abyss. I am ruined."

"Surely there are more benefactors, sir," I said, hoping to console him.

"Perhaps there are, or perhaps not; both are beside the point. I have seen this thread of time play out, and I know where it leads. It is an ending I care not to share, yet one I must now walk toward."

The elder had never seemed so weak, so tired, as he did right there. I have seen the same look on the condemned, as they march toward the gallows or chopping block. It was the look of resignation. I knew not what to say, so I said nothing.

"You must promise me two things," he said. "First, you must finish the wall, and with great haste. Do not ask why. Second, and although it sounds odd, I cannot explain further, only to say this: no wine must touch your lips, none at all. Now I give you leave. Go rest. You have walls to fix, I have fences to mend."

I did as instructed, though I slept little that night. The next day

I worked well into the evening, and by the time I returned for supper my food was cold. The day after, I worked longer.

Days became weeks, the wall took shape, and the grapes began to ripen. All the while the elder's study door remained locked.

Twice I saw a caravan of men wearing official colors arrive, led by Lord Prestor's son, his hand now hidden beneath a limp glove. Twice they left carrying purses heavy with coin. The elder was right: the fingers had come at a cost.

Still, I saw little of the elder himself. At night, after I ate dinner I would often sneak past the study in hopes of hearing something. Once I swore I heard a cacophony of voices, and the elder's loudest of all. "Mark this moment in your mind. Our paths will cross in a different time."

Who he spoke to, I knew not, only that the stables were empty, and no one had come all day. Perhaps the son was right. Perhaps his madness was worsening.

July became August, the shadows lengthened, and on a day late in the month as the grapes were soon to be harvested, I laid the final stone in the wall.

I spent the remainder of the day walking the perimeter of the vineyard, following the slopes and ridges beside to the wall, checking for any oversight or mistake, yet I found none. The wall was in fine shape, a year's worth of work done well. As the sun set across the vineyard, daylight's final rays glimmered off those runic stones, and I was momentarily caught by the beauty of it.

Perfect, I thought.

I returned to the manor intending to inform the elder my task was completed. I was certain he would want to inspect it, perhaps the following day.

No sooner had I closed the door when I heard his voice calling my name. I followed it and found him seated at the dining table, a sumptuous feast spread out before him. Hen and rabbit, stew of potato, steamed vegetables and bread no doubt fetched from town.

"Sit, please," he beckoned. "You've finished my wall, and right on time. Help yourself. This meal is in your honor."

I was stunned. "Sir, I know not what to say. Few have shown me such generosity as you have, and for that I am truly thankful."

"No need for such words. I'm merely playing my part in the world's workings, much as you are yours. Eat, eat please. Enjoy this moment."

I noticed the elder had no plate before him. "And what of you, sir? Surely you must be hungry."

"I'm afraid I don't have much of an appetite," he said. For all his age he was a perceptive man, and he noticed my trepidation immediately. "The food is not poisoned, I promise you."

"Of course not," I answered, but secretly I was relieved.

I ate, as instructed. He was correct and did not exaggerate. To this day it was one of the most delicious meals I have ever consumed, and no trace of poison was detected within the gristle or fat.

The sun had set, night had come, and as I finished the meal I heard a great clattering from the entryway. I stood up, but the old man beckoned me to sit again.

"We are ruined!" came the son's voice from down the hall. "Father! Answer me, Father!"

"In here," the elder called. "Come, sup with us."

The son stumbled into the room, and though he carried no wineskin in his hand I saw the signs of intoxication upon him.

"We are—what is this?!" he sneered upon seeing me at the table. "What is he doing in my seat?"

"There are many seats at this table. I was not aware you favored one above the others," the elder said. "Come; you look hungry."

He sat, or did his best to, yet in his state it was more of a heavy collapsing upon the chair. He pulled a great wedge of hen and began to chew it.

"Don't you look upon me when I eat," he snapped at me. "I'm not some beast."

"My apologies," I said, though something felt different within myself. The summer's work had strengthened me, where his laziness seemed to have whittled at him. Were the two of us on an even field, with none of society's rules and only our brawn, I had little doubt I would emerge the victor.

"Ruined," he said, tossing a bone onto the plate. "Well, you've done it, Father. As of today, our coffers are empty, our coins have transformed to debts. Quite the illusionist, yet never able to conjure up anything of use. If this harvest is not a miracle, I may join you in King's Bench, or whatever debtor's prison they deem us fit for."

"I do not think that is in your future," the elder said.

"No? And why is that?"

"This shall be the final harvest on this soil. I've made arrangements, seen to things. Our friend here has helped me to see this through."

I felt my throat close, my stomach tighten. What part I played, I knew not. Nor did I have the time to react.

"What arrangements?" the son hissed. "What sort of betrayal is this?"

"No betrayal, only fact." The elder cleared his throat. "You've laid no stone, raised no wall. Few vines have been watered by your hands, yet you spend the spoils joyfully. Why then should you lay claim to what I've seen built? By what right is a single speck of dirt beneath your foot truly yours?"

"By right of birth!" the son bellowed, fist crashing upon the table. "By right of inheritance! I am your son, your heir!"

"Yes, you are," the elder said in a voice as calm as any actor or thespian I've met. "My son, in flesh and name only. Not by action nor deed. For that you are a stranger, a purse that talks, a windbag wearing a face I recognize as a shade of a woman I once loved. I have no son: only a leech."

Something odd came over the son, a sort of queer emotion, childlike and pathetic. His eyes watered, welled up, and I heard an effeminate sob come from his throat. "You... you mean such things?"

"There is nothing here for either of us. No coin nor land for you, not so long as I draw breath."

"I get nothing then? On this issue you are unwavering?"

"I am."

A great quiet came over the son. During the exchange it had been as if I had not existed, or perhaps had transformed into some vapor. With the elder's words, final and firm, I was made whole again, and the son turned his glare to me. It was a vile and spiteful. Then, he composed himself and stood.

"Very well, Father. I accept your decision. I am neither the son you wanted, nor one you are proud of, and for that I am sorry. Perhaps one day you'll think different of me. Time will tell. Now, I have futures to plan. May I have your permission to leave?"

The elder studied his son, and I remember how he tilted his head ever so slightly, as if seeing something else beyond the five senses. "Do what you will, then," is what he said, and I remember those words so odd and yet so perfectly fitting.

"Do what you will, then."

The son left, and the world hung in silence. I knew not what would come next, what was expected of me, or what such talk of my involvement in arrangements meant. The elder dipped his hand in his glass, traced a finger around the rim, and with those slow circular motions a faint hum echoed out. His eyes softened, as if the sound pleased him, like a favorite song.

"Nothing is made nor destroyed; merely—"

He never finished that thought.

The son returned, the glint of a blade in his hand. He struck from behind, catching the elder off guard. A dozen vile slashes, each deeper than the next, until the elder's throat was opened up and fountaining. The table ran red and the elder's head hung by mere threads, yet still his son struck, again and again. All the while he laughed: "Do you draw breath now?! Tell me Father! Do you draw breath now?!"

I wish courage or bravery were traits I had in abundance, but I cannot lie. Fear does things to a man, puts rocks in his boot and paralyzes him. The old man had been murdered at his dinner table, by his own son, and yet I stood numb and still.

Finally, as his son flung his body forward, I found the courage to shout and make a sudden charge, to put the summer's muscle to the test. I made it a few a paces before I found myself staring at the bad end of a flintlock pistol. "Halt, or you'll join him."

Again, I did as instructed, waiting for the sound of thunder and the burst of pain as he fired, but none came.

"Ileana!" he called out, a name I didn't know. "Ileana, come quick!"

The servant woman appeared at the doorway, surveyed the scene, and gasped. One year and I had not learned her name. How foolish I felt now, for I could not warn poor Ileana what she had walked in on.

"He has gone mad, murdered my father! Quick, check his condition."

She stammered, studied what remained of the old man, afraid to even touch it. "I... I do not think he lives."

"Such a mess he's left us," the son said. "How shall we fix it all?"

He buried the blade deep in the servant's back. A half-dozen more piercing strikes, each followed by a horrible pop, until the woman collapsed beside the old man. All the while he kept the flintlock upon me.

"What have you done?" I asked, horrified. "What is this madness?"

"I? No, no, this is the work of a stableboy, a laborer driven mad by a debt unpaid. You assaulted him at dinner. Poor Ileana, she tried to come to my father's aid, but I fear she was overpowered. This, it was all your doing!"

"I did no such thing!"

"No, of course not. Run then. Run and tell the others. Tell the townsfolk your story, and I shall tell them mine. Let us see who ends up hanging: a noble's son, or a beggar."

I scrambled to make sense of it all, but my mind was spinning.

"This is blackmail. It's not true."

"True? True is the story told by those who live. True is what we make it." An amused look came over his face. "Perhaps she..." He motioned to the servant, crawling across the floor. "She did this. Yes, she murdered him. And we fought her off. That could be our truth!"

Quick as a fox, he brought the blade's pommel down upon her head. A vicious thump and a crack, and she crawled no more. I felt my stomach twist, and then up came my dinner.

"You're right, that won't work," he said, pausing to consider his options. Epiphany spread across his face. "Come, you've a weak stomach, but we have work to do."

"Work? What work?"

"An experiment of sorts. My father loved his grapes. Let us see if he should not like to rest among them."

"I... I can't. I won't."

"Very well. Three shall be buried; it makes no difference to me." He raised the pistol and I closed my eyes.

Fear does many thing to a man, even those of the strongest heart. While I thought myself honorable, I admit, I faltered. Youth was on my side, and with it the promise of a long life yet to be lived, and so I betrayed my honor and gave aid to the killer.

"Wait," I said. "Please... Wait."

I BURIED THE TWO BODIES OUT AMONG THE VINES AND ROOTS OF THE grapes.

I say that I buried them, because the son played no part, save keeping his pistol upon me through the night. I told myself that I would strike, wait for an opportune moment and make my play with fist or shovel. Yet the son was crafty, sensed my plans, and no such moment occurred.

I am not proud of what I did and did not do that night. Yet for some reason I knew it to be the right thing. The old man had always found the terraced grapes a calming place to walk. Perhaps he would find it a calm place to rest.

"He trusted you, confided in you," the son said once I had covered the old man's unmarked grave. "Why?"

"He said I listened, asked questions."

"He considered you of some wit? Intelligent?"

"I do not know. If he did, he never said."

"But I do. I consider you a man of wit, of smarts. You know there are only two endings down this road, right? One such ending sees you join them in the earth, by my hand, or the hand of the law. Perhaps you run away, or you strike me while I'm unguarded and make your escape. You could make it a few towns away, but this land never forgets a face, and yours is memorable. You would hang, eventually. You know this."

It was as if he had read the very words within my mind. All through the evening, while I dug and while I buried, scenarios had played out in my head. Yet all paths came back to the fact that it would be my word against his, or mine against whatever rumor and bounty followed should I kill him.

"There is another ending," he said. "One where you save your neck, I save my vineyard, and we both prosper. Look around. These grapes grow full, and soon the harvest will be upon the land. Some coin can still be suckled from this soil. You give me your vow, your oath, that you will help with the harvest. In return, I shall give you my word, my oath. You shall leave with an honorable name and enough coin in your pocket to get you to your destination. What say you?"

More than anything else I wanted to lash out, to strike that wretched creature with the full force of the shovel. To bury three there that night, and let the roots feast upon my vengeance.

Yet I knew he spoke the truth. All hope hinged upon him now.

I was a prisoner to a twisted warden, one who had murdered two before my very eyes.

"What say you?" he asked again.

It was with a heavy heart that I said: "Yes."

HE LOCKED ME IN THE SERVANT'S ROOM THAT NIGHT.

Unable to sleep, I glanced out the window to the grapevines below, knowing what lay buried beneath. Far beyond them, at the edge of the horizon, I saw the runic stones I had laid within the old wall, and they seemed to glimmer like torches, brighter than the stars above.

"For good luck," the elder had once said. I had thought it a foolish sentiment then, and doubly so now. They had brought him no luck at all, only misery.

I was awoken at dawn, poked by his flintlock pistol, and within the hour I had cooked breakfast for the murderer. I worked the grapes that afternoon, doing as commanded. I picked, de-stemmed, crushed, and barreled more fruit than I'd ever imagined. By nightfall my back ached, my eyes burned, and my hands were dyed the color of blood. Yet still I was commanded to cook dinner before being locked back in the servant's room.

Weeks passed as such, the pattern always unbroken. Sometimes visitors came to conduct business of sorts. All the while the elder's son gave me sidelong glances, perhaps wondering if I would suddenly blurt forth the truth. But I was craven, too cowardly to do such, and so I was locked up in the servant's room each night, exhausted and full of self-loathing.

Sometimes there were parties, debaucheries and giggling guests that came and went. On many nights I was tasked to stable the horses, wearing the same fancy clothes his father dressed me in. Once, the next morning, I found a youthful couple asleep among the straw in the stables, their clothes still around their ankles, naughty bits hanging out in sight of the horses.

August became September, summer gave way to autumn, and on the first chilly day of the season I packed away the final barrel in the cellar.

It had been six weeks since I had seen the elder butchered. Six weeks of false work. Yet every day I felt as wretched as before. Almost a hundred barrels lay in the cellar, almost all by my own hand. Yet I felt no such pride as I had with the wall. This deed was driven out of fear.

That night I fixed dinner and brought it to the murderer, who now sat in his father's chair at the head of the table. He seemed in eager spirits, knowing our business was coming to an end, and beside him sat a bottle and two glasses.

"Come now," he called between bites. "Drink with me. Celebrate."

"I'm afraid being around grapes all day has soured me to their taste."

"It's bad luck not to drink the season's first bottle. Come, savor the spoils of our work. I insist."

He poured me a cup and I took it. For once, the flintlock pistol wasn't there, and for a moment I had a vision of myself running off into the night, free.

"You look uneasy," he said. "Do I frighten you?"

"No, sir," I answered. "Merely, I wonder what else there is for me to do here. My task complete, my oath fulfilled. What now?"

"Tomorrow you're a free man," he said. "You have my word, my oath. My recommendation. I even have your payment as well," he said, pointing to a pouch upon a nearby shelf. I spied a letter as well, a wax seal upon it. My freedom was close by. "Come now, drink. It's bad luck to waste good wine."

He poured himself a cup as well, and what hesitation I had over the contents of the bottle dissipated. Perhaps there was time to celebrate. I had worked so hard since coming to the manor upon the knoll.

"Cheers," he said, raising his cup, and I did the same.

"Cheers," I answered, and we both drank.

As the liquid touched my lips I remembered something as if from a dream. "No wine must touch your lips," the elder had said. Yet this cup had touched mine, and the contents within sat upon my tongue.

The effect was both immediate and profound, as close to a religious experience as I had ever had. Between the tannins and sugars, in the very essence of the wine itself, I tasted and saw it all.

The dew in the morning, upon the vines, trickling down stems.

The fibers and veins of every leaf.

The warmth of the sun and the chill of the air.

The ant that climbed up the bark to suckle on the sweet grapes.

The topsoil and the roots that burrowed beneath.

The damp earth, the worms, the rocks and twigs buried about.

And I tasted the rot of flesh, the blood and bone, the memories and the very soul of the elder buried beneath his own vineyard. Blood, blood, so much, and with it the whole journey, from birth to death to resurrection and transformation.

"Nothing is made nor destroyed; merely transmuted," he had said, and so too had he been transmuted, from living being to vengeful poison.

I spat out the wine and fell backward. The room had tilted, gone sideways, and I felt intoxicated by a force greater than any alcohol I'd consumed. I saw the son take a great swallow and shiver. Then his eyes opened and went to whites, wide and filled with horror.

"You..." he gasped, dropping his empty cup. "...it's you!"

Dazed by the power of the wine, I turned to where his eyes went, yet saw nothing, no corporeal form or person.

Yet I felt a chill, something as cold as winter. For a moment, brief and fleeting, I saw frost pass before the window. Patches of snow formed upon the floor. Spiderwebs of ice ran up the side of the bottle of wine and froze all liquid within. All the while the son's eyes traced the progression of some invisible specter... closer... closer...

"You're... but you're not... *impossible!*" he stammered. "You... You're *dead!*"

He buckled back in his chair as if a great force had seized him. I saw no physical hands upon his throat, yet it collapsed and indentations formed upon it. He fought, struggled and tried to free himself, yet whatever assailed him snapped several of his fingers the wrong way like brittle twigs. The chair legs buckled and snapped, yet he stayed there, suspended in the air as his throat sunk in on itself.

A great frost was spreading over him, out from neck, up his chin and down his chest. In his last moments he managed to let out a scream. Mist, cold and blue, left his lips; a great steam a dying shiver on a winter morning. In that final breath, for a brief moment, I saw the hint of a shape. It was a cold form, that of the elder's face, and it was cruel and happy, and it smiled as his son's eyes rolled back and his body went limp.

Never have I run from a room faster than I did that night. I tarried only to gather the coin purse, payment for over a year of labor, and the letter that lay beneath it. The room grew cold, and ice began to form upon the once warm food.

I fetched few things, clothes and my rucksack, my journal and canteen. Any longer and I feared the coldness would consume me.

I hesitated at the door to gather a lantern and check the coin pouch I was owed. It was heavy, but when I opened it only metal scraps fell out, worthless chunks of bronze and iron. And the letter, within it I found only a lie: the son had written that it was I who had murdered his father!

If I had felt any sympathy for him, it died when I ran from the frigid manor.

I hurried down the knoll and past the grapevines. All the while I felt the breath of something cold upon the back of my neck. Faster I ran, faster, down that path and down the terraces. Fingers of icy bones wrapped themselves tighter and tighter until my breath escaped me. A chill, the breath of an angry ghost whispering into my ear. My very blood became heavy and frozen, each step harder than the last. And I knew, should I look back, whatever was upon me would reach out and seize me and never let go.

With my final ounce of strength I passed that great wall I had built, and within it those superstitious stones seemed to glimmer like icicles in the moonlight. I felt the fingers and the breath and the whispering voice that said: "*Stay... Stay!*" all release me from a cold embrace.

And then there was nothing: a great curtain gave way, and I felt warmth on the other side of that wall. I collapsed, shivering, free from the winter grasp of whatever had tried to hold me back.

The stones glimmered bright a final time, as bright as I'd ever seen them, then a great darkness washed over the wall and they glimmered no more. All that remained, countless stones that once held trapped light, were now the color of coal. Dim, dark, and cold.

I DO NOT KNOW IF THE ELDER HAD SEEN THE FUTURE THROUGH A clear lens. Or if it had been obscured, like stars behind clouds on a windy night. Or bent and changed like a lake bed, as he once said, seen through ripples of water. I do not know if the elder had built the wall to save me from the vengeance he unleashed, or to keep it trapped within.

What I do know is this: whatever lay beyond that wall stayed behind that wall. No new crops grew, not then nor in any of the years since, and every well that was dug struck upon ice.

INTERLUDE II

The crone rubbed her knotty fingers and smiled. "I feel a chill upon myself," she cackled. "Another wonderful tale, indeed!"

The traveler smiled. "You're too kind. My tales are not very original, I'm afraid. I'm sure you've heard far better sung by bards beneath this roof."

"Aye, we've heard many tales in our time, but yours are among the most original. I must ask, and forgive my curiosity, but how much of the tale is not false?"

"Enough to make it interesting."

"Enough to make it interesting!" she cackled back. "A perfect answer, of course. Do the details differ from telling to telling? I imagine the last one a chore to keep track of."

"I have my writing and my memory. I'm fortunate both suffice."

"And tell me, on some days do you still feel the cold breath of death behind you?"

Of course not, he thought. *Nor had it ever touched upon me.* In truth, there had been nothing, but she needn't know this. The elder had died and as is true with most men, the world hardly noticed.

"Some days," he answered. "And some nights. Even here, in this new world, I occasionally feel a cold finger upon my nape. And when I do, I never look back."

The crone shivered, and the simpleton guffawed, though at what the traveler was unsure. Outside, through those old, warped windows, a flash of lightning lit up the black sky. A moment later, the pitter-pat of rain upon the rooftop filled the inn.

"Fetch the pots," the crone commanded. At once both the shy girl and the simpleton went in different directions. "She leaks," the crone explained. "Worse than a straw ship in a storm. But don't you worry, your room is watertight."

A trickle made its way from somewhere above, down one of the beams, and began to pool by his foot. The traveler scooted back. "I'm curious, but how did you come about such a place? It is—"

"Quite unusual, yes?" the crone cut in.

"Yes, quite unusual indeed."

"Aye, the story itself is right out of one of your tales, though I'm afraid its ending has yet to be written. The missionaries built it, the savages burnt it down, and the missionaries rebuilt it. Things went on as such until most left the land to the muds and floods. The few that remain claim the land was special, a place of rest."

"Burial grounds?"

"No, I'm no fool," she cackled, but it turned into a cough. "The wrath of the savage gods is not for me. No, that this was merely a special place. Only thing special is how quick the crops die."

"And they don't trouble you, the natives?"

"Nay, they're ghosts, spooks. We cross paths, from time to time, out among the corn and brambles. Long as the cross stays down and the sermons don't return, they leave us alone."

"It doesn't bother you? Living on desecrated ground?"

"Whole land's desecrated. What's one patch among many? Besides, if the gods have forsaken this place, what's it to them?"

A thunderclap, a flash, and moments later a loud clattering of metal echoed out from upstairs. The traveler looked up to see the simpleton chasing after a rolling pot, shaking and whimpering.

"He spooks during the storms," the crone said. "Like a horse."

"Is he sick?"

"Not sick... broken. That is as best as his condition can be described. I'm afraid I'm no storyteller; my words are not cleverer." She laughed and repeated that word. "Cleverer. Even that is queer to my ear. Clever-er. Is that correct?"

"It is correct, though rarely used."

As the shy young girl refilled his cup of mulled wine, the traveler's hand reached and took her by the wrist. "And your story," he said to the girl. "What is yours?"

She stood, frozen in place, as he tried to study the eyes concealed behind the mat of hair like a funeral veil. She made no response.

The wine had emboldened him. "Let me see your eyes," he said, and brushed the hair from her face. She flinched as if she might be struck, but his hands were gentle.

Her eyes were grey and curdled. No pupils, or if there ever had been pupils they had melted long ago and merged with the milk-water pigment. He saw it now, how the false clarity of wine was really a hazy curtain. His manners had slipped.

"I'm sorry, I meant you no harm, but... for a moment I thought I knew you." A lingering discomfort remained. His mind was not the inkwell of his youth. "It seems I'm mistaken. A thousand apologies, m'lady. I'm truly sorry."

The young girl hurried away, and his eyes followed her form, still intrigued.

"She's a curious thing," the crone said. "I found her in the basement, half feral and confused. Not a memory of how she got here. It was as if she'd crawled out of the very mud itself!" The crone let out a gurgling chuckle. "I gave her food, shelter, and in no time she'd memorized every stone and step, inside and out."

"They say those hamstrung in one sense make up for it in others."

He watched her fetch another bucket for a leak along the far wall. She turned back, as if she felt his glance upon her.

Curious indeed, he thought.

He was no stranger to damaged goods, this traveler. They intrigued him. In one of Boston's brothels he been given a discount and bedded a whore with only one arm. In Europe, at the southern tip of Spain where the great continent of Africa was but a day's sail across the sea, he'd paid a pretty price to have his way with a woman whose skin was dark as night. But in truth she'd had her way with him. All these years later, and he still thought of her, yet could no longer conjure up her face.

Yet this girl with her milk-water eyes and her curt smile, there was something intriguing about her, a word upon the tip of his tongue. When the final tale was done and his trousers loosened by wine, he might inquire if a price could be arranged. He needn't look upon her face; with hips like hers her backside would do just fine. Yes, it had been far too long, and the wilds had softened his standards.

And if she wasn't available?

There were always other options. Bribes and blades, and everything between.

"You owe us one more tale," the crone said. "Then our debt is settled, and the inn will be yours."

The simpleton had returned and took a seat, gnawing on a cold hunk of ham. The girl returned as well, and he felt his gaze pulled toward her. As a storyteller his words were not perfect, none truly ever are, but every now and then if he put them in the proper order they had an intoxicating effect on women.

"Have you ever been in love, m'lady?" he asked, and for the longest time his words hung in the air unanswered. The crone and the simpleton stared at the girl, but she simply sat there, hair covering those blind eyes, hand stroking the cat that had settled upon her lap.

Then she answered, and though it was but a whisper, all heard her reply. "Yes."

The traveler smiled, took a sip of his wine. Outside, the sky flashed and the windows rattled with the crack of thunder.

"No doubt, then, that you shall find this tale both cruel and comforting, heartwarming and heartbreaking, like love itself."

She gave a soft nod, and beneath that mat of unkempt hair, that veil, somehow he sensed the corners of her lips had lifted ever so slightly.

The thunder cracked, the rain picked up, and he began his final tale.

CHAPTER 4

THE TIMBERMAN'S DAUGHTER

My wanderings took me across the old world, from the long nights of the frozen north to the eternal summer and sandy shores of the south. I met many people of many customs and superstitions, gathered tales to fill my pages. Yet further lands called to me, and so I booked passage across the great ocean to the new world. A chance to see new lands, new people, to leave the old ghosts behind.

I wandered among the colonies and found work at the various forts and townships, the ports and harborages of those embarking on the great journey west into new lands. I realized soon that I had left civilization and entered a world bereft of law and order and even education. Few could read, and my services turned to tutoring and teaching.

Word spread, and I found my daylight hours packed with pupils eager to understand the formation and recitation of letters upon paper. I bought many candles and lamps, made friend with many an oil merchant and ink seller.

They were long days, most often filled with laughter and learning. My coin pouch was never too heavy, no teacher's ever truly is, yet rare were the times I went hungry or heard no jingle in my pocket.

Spring came, and I found myself in Bellow's Fall, a township at the convergence of three rivers laid out beneath hills alive with apple orchards and willows. A scenic land as any I've found among the new world. I carried with me letters of introduction from several noble families: their seals and ink endorsed my tutoring. Within no time I found employment tutoring the sons and daughters of several favorable families, and within a season I had little free time at all.

I spent many nights at the Belmont estate, an opulent manor in the logging hills above the township. While they weren't the wealthiest nor most influential family in the township, the Belmonts were powerful nonetheless. They owned much of the forests and their lumber operations provided timber to the ship-builders up and down the coast.

It was there, among the voluminous library of the estate, that I met the love of my life.

Her name was Chauntel, a girl on the cusp of womanhood, perhaps a few turns of the earth younger than myself. She had hair the color of oak, curious green eyes, and a dozen freckles upon a flawless face. When she smiled her cheeks receded, and two dimples appeared like happy maelstroms that made my heart flutter. Few things have I ever craved more than to see her smile, and so I paid her many a compliment during our studies at her family's estate.

"You're too nice," she said often. "But back to the lesson..."

"Right, right," I often answered, not realizing how far we'd strayed.

I was of marrying age, yet I had no land nor great honors to my name. To most I was a helper, a jolly teacher who could tutor the daughters of the frontier, turning them to women capable of being married upward. To say this did not bother me on some nights would be a lie; few cheer the news of a wedding with a full heart when their own life is empty beside it.

Still, I collected my tales, published the occasional story in the papers, and entertained at inns and ale houses in the valley below on Saturday nights. In secret I did it all for her, poured out each and every word, yet financial success failed to find me, nor did reputation make its way up to the estate from the township below.

"You're a most creative man," Chauntel said as we studied outside, the mist from the waterfalls cooling the air on a perfect spring afternoon. "One day, I should like to read your tales with my own eyes."

"If you study hard, practice your vocabulary, I'm sure it will be no time before you're reading Shakespeare."

Again, she smiled, those dimples showing. And again, my heart came alive in a way I knew not possible.

"You say the kindest things. And you're a teacher of utmost patience and persistence. I'm not an easy pupil, I'm sure. But in your presence, I feel as if anything were possible."

"Anything is possible," I told her.

Yes, anything, except what my heart truly desired. To take her soft hands right there, to kiss those lips and tell her I would care for her and treat her kind until my dying breath and beyond.

A dark cloud seemed to cast a shadow upon her face. Her mood soured. "What's wrong?" I inquired.

"My father... He is planning on summering at the Isle of Dawn. I'm afraid that our lessons may have to be set aside for a season."

"I do not understand. Does he value his vacation over your education?"

"I do not know. He's a businessman; I think he sees value in coin above all else. He has some sort of business there. I've heard him speak of it. I'm... I will miss these lessons. I have so looked forward to them."

I detected a sparkle in her eye, the glimmer of a tear. My heart tore itself asunder at the sight, and my mind raced.

"Perhaps I could accompany you. As your tutor, of course."

The idea caught her by surprise, and no sooner were the words uttered than I felt I had overstepped the boundaries of decorum. I regretted it at once.

"I'm sorry, forgive me," I stammered. "I meant no further—"

"No, no please. Your idea, it has some merit to it. All the other servants will accompany us, even my brother's riding instructor. Perhaps, if I present it to my father, he'll see value in it. I could do that. Tonight even."

"It's worth a try. Like you said: anything is possible."

She smiled at that.

And she smiled again as I left that evening, the setting sun lighting up the freckles upon her beautiful face, and I knew that I would do anything to see her smiling as such for every day.

On my journey down from the foothills to the valley I passed Mr. Belmont's carriage making its way upward, and while I nodded as courtesy to my employer, he paid me no attention. In a half-hour or so Chauntel would be asking him if I could come to the Isle of Dawn for the summer, and I knew I couldn't wait until midweek's lesson to learn the answer. I turned back and followed the caravan, sticking to the shadows.

I heard him announce his arrival, greeting his wife and his son, a boy of thirteen whom I had seen studying his mathematics from time to time. The manor was large, yet outside the shadows were plenty, and on such a warm night many windows were left open. He called out to Chauntel, and I followed them to the east study.

I listened beneath the window as Chauntel complimented her father, asked him questions about his day, played to his ego. Her voice had always been soft, and the night was filled with crickets and frogs, rendering it difficult to hear. I caught some words, but most were lost.

Then her father's voice turned sour. I heard a booming: "Of course not. It's absurd!"

She protested, or at least, I imagined she did, and a dozen times I thought I heard sobbing between the crickets.

"He's a tutor, nothing more! Put away these childish fantasies. He's not of our kind."

Not of our kind.

Those words stung me to my core. I knew I was not born of

old money or family name, yet I had never once thought myself a man of common ilk.

I heard her cry again, and then his voice booming: "No! And say no more!" Then a door slammed, and a long silence followed.

I made my way back down from the foothills, the frogs and crickets, and the hum of the waterfalls a chorus to my own angry thoughts. It was midnight before I climbed into bed, dawn before I finally slept. All the while her father's words mocked me, a legion of insects burrowing beneath my skin, unscratchable.

Not of our kind.

I SAW HER AGAIN FOR THE FINAL LESSON THAT SPRING, THOUGH TIME had not washed away the bitter taste on my tongue, the itch beneath my skin.

All around the estate I saw signs of packing: chests and trunks made ready, horses and carriages cleaned and filled. The house had come alive, and though I tried to keep the lesson straight she sensed my sour mood.

"You seem upset. Is it me? I must be frustratingly slow to teach, I'm sure."

"No, you're a pleasure to teach; of course not. It's just... I'm just curious. Has your father said anything about the summer?"

Her nod was ever so slight, that same storm-cloud returning to cast a shadow upon her face.

"He did. He said there would be no room, I'm afraid. That it would be... impossible."

Impossible. I was not of their kind. At least she filtered his words and turned them to courtesy.

"I see," I answered, and did my best to hide my disappointment, but she was a keen student and saw it upon my face.

"Please, it's no slight against you, I promise. It's just... he's old, and set in his ways."

"I understand. I know my place. I'm merely a tutor, after all."

"No, no mere tutor. Were I my brother, I could speak sense and he would listen. But I'm just his daughter, illiterate and unimportant. Less than a pet."

"You're important to me," I said, as if some uncontrollable force had taken possession of me. "Chauntel, why do you think I hike the hills to tutor you? Why would I carry a bag full of books up such a distance, if not to help you learn? To see you smile? To make you laugh? I'd carry them a thousand leagues for that smile of yours."

"I know," she whispered. "I've always known."

I felt her hand take mine again, and in that instant all the world went silent around us. I wanted nothing more than to spend every moment with her, to have her look upon me for longer than a second and not avert her eyes for fear of breaking some unspoken honor.

"There's a courier there, on the Isle," she said. "I'll write, though I fear my words will be illegible."

At this I couldn't help but laugh, and then so did she. A great tension seemed relieved between us, but a pain still remained.

"I'll miss these lessons," she said. "I'll miss our time together, out on this porch."

"And I'll miss you," I replied, and it brought a smile to her lips.

THE NEXT MORNING THE CARRIAGES RUMBLED OFF ALONG THE RIDGE-line. From my rented room atop the butcher's shop I watched until the dust disappeared and only the silent foothills remained. Three months I had, to make a name for myself. Three months until she returned and her father's words would be contested.

Not of our kind.

I began that morning, writing out every tale I'd heard from my travels. From the Carpethians to the Alps, from the shore of the Danube to the edge of the fjords and fissures as far north as a man could travel. Every story, small or large, I put down in ink upon paper.

When there was only bland fact, I transformed it to fiction for the sake of a better story.

Where my memory was incomplete, my imagination filled in the gaps.

I filled page after page, edited and rewrote, spent every free moment and a considerable amount of my savings on ink and quills.

Soon, my memory itself seemed painted over, and the tales I wrote become my own story.

I put all tutoring and teaching engagements aside for the season. I saw little of the outside world and daylight during those summer months. Like some horrid troll tucked away in a cave, I emerged at night to visit the ale houses and inns to recite my stories.

They gathered, small audiences at first, mostly travelers and timber workers that had come to Bellow's Falls in seek of coin. They seemed to like my stories, and often they asked for more well past the midnight toll of the town bell.

Word circulated, and soon the ale houses and inns grew fat with audiences. Giggling, shrieks, gasps, and applause, I heard plenty of these. Sometimes women covered their eyes, buried their head in their husband's shoulder. Other times I saw countless smiles among the crowd, and the laughter drowned out my own storytelling.

I made some coin too; nothing substantial, but enough to consider never returning to the world of tutoring wealthy children. I saved, although I had little to carry over, and at times I ran late in my rent payments to the butcher.

I befriended the local printer and began to compile my stories together into a collection of sorts. I commissioned the local leatherworker to set about creating a cover and binding. I wrote, rewrote, recited, stained my fingers black with ink and gnawed my nails to the nub. I paid couriers to take the occasional letter to the Isle of Dawn, yet received none in return. All the while the words of Mr. Belmont drove me forward.

Not of our kind.

I would make myself into one of their kind, or perhaps something better, even if it killed me.

AUGUST CAME ABOUT, THE CRICKETS SANG THEIR LOUDEST, AND THEN by the end of the month the world grew cool as the season came to change. All the while I awaited the day I would see a rumble of dust upon the ridge-line, the carriage and horses that signaled my love's return.

Yet that day never came.

I saw no dust, nor was sent any message of their arrival. At night I sometimes spied lights on in the manor. One night in mid-September when I inquired at the ale house I was told the Belmonts had returned two weeks back.

I was shocked, stunned! My love had returned and nary a word? I set out at once that night to discover the truth for myself.

Two hours later I had hiked the foothill road and arrived at the estate. It was well past midnight, the property was dark and silent, and no one would be awake. Still, I estimated about where her bedroom was, and so I snuck through the shadows and searched for my love.

And then there she was, asleep upon a bed of silk and satin, windows ajar and curtains billowing like a vision of heaven. I desired nothing more than to tiptoe over, to touch her soft face and plant a kiss upon those beautiful, freckled cheeks. Yet I was no sneak-thief, no midnight bandit. I knew that I had already won her heart, yet I needed to win her father's favor. I had worked hard the past summer, too hard to give in to childish emotion and simple desire. I would put my best foot forward.

I EMPTIED MY COIN PURSE OF ALL BUT A FEW COINS AND I VISITED THE tailor at first light. "Give me the finest attire my money can buy," I informed him. Yet my coins came up short, and I was forced to trade the very silver ring that belonged to my father to cover the difference.

Within a day I was dressed in the most elegant clothes I had ever owned, and many a head turned as I walked down the thoroughfare. I gathered the possessions I had commissioned; the printer, the leatherworker, they had fulfilled their tasks and presented me with my novel, a handcrafted cover and binding thick with golden thread.

A Thousand Traveler's Songs, read the title in gilded letters. My heart skipped, for there was my name beneath it, a published author! And upon the opening page, a dedication:

To Chauntel,
Who taught me the most wondrous path is the one that leads to love.

BY THE END OF THE AFTERNOON I HAD ALL MY BELONGINGS, EVEN A few printed newspaper articles detailing my storytelling prowess at the ale house and inns. Dressed in my finery I set out, ascending that foothill road with as great a haste as I have ever known. I was determined to arrive at sun down, to make as positive and entrance as I had ever made.

I arrived on time, no sooner nor later than I had intended. I knocked upon the door three times and waited. Should my heart have burst from my chest in those moments and left me lifeless with a great hole there, I would not have been surprised.

The door opened. One of the servants answered, an older woman I remembered from before. She gave me a queer look.

"I'm here to see Chauntel," I announced. "If she is available, please fetch her."

The servant disappeared without a word. I heard voices

conversing from another room, and then the cheerful voice of Mrs. Belmont. She was dressed in an embroidered evening gown, exotic cloth no doubt bought at the Isle of Dawn.

"Ah, the tutor." She smiled. "You're so dressed up I hardly recognized you."

I gave her my deepest bow which elicited a confused smile. "I'm here to see Chauntel, m'lady. Is she within?"

"She is, yes, of course. It's just... Well, I was not aware she had resumed her lessons."

The thought made me bristle. *Did tutors dress as such?* I knew of none to wear such fine fabric as I wore that day.

"She has not, as far as I have been told. I come here not as a tutor, but to call upon—"

My words stopped as Chauntel appeared from atop the landing inside, a sunbeam falling upon her face and rendering her even more radiant than I had remembered. The summer had darkened her skin, and those freckles I so loved were even more spectacular than I had remembered. A constellation upon a sun-kissed face.

"Chauntel, you... you've returned!" I smiled. "Look at you! As beautiful as I recall."

She made her way down the stairs, and with every step closer I fought off the urge to rush over and kiss her.

"It seems your old tutor is here to see you," her mother said with a smile that cracked the powder upon her face. "And he's found his way into such... *extravagant* clothes."

"This visit, it's most surprising," Chauntel said. "I knew not when I would see you next."

"Forgive my late arrival. Were I to have known that you had returned, I would have hurried with no delay. Was your summer pleasant? Did you receive any of my letters? I sent quite a few."

"Yes, yes, I received them all. I'm afraid, well... I haven't been the best pupil, and my studies have wandered. Some of the words I understood, but... a lot I have forgotten."

A shame seemed to wash over her. She had always been too

modest, and I knew all she needed was time to practice. "You're keen and quick witted. I'm sure we can catch you up quickly," I said, but no smile appeared upon her face, only a shadow and a trouble.

"I'm... I'm afraid I won't be needing any more lessons."

For a moment I thought my hearing had gone wrong, but the look on her face told me something was askew. A hesitation lay on her lips, and she fumbled for words like a kid caught in some great mischief.

"I have... you see, there has been—"

"Ah! The old tutor!" a voice boomed from the steps behind, and I turned to spy a carriage and several men emerging. One, the most prominent, was dressed in fine attire, and at once I recognized his mustache, his voice, and more than anything else, his eyes. They were as piercing as his daughter's. "Have we not settled our payment from the spring?"

"Good evening, Mr. Belment," I said, giving him a deep bow. "No, our payments have all been settled. However—"

"Settled, hmm? Then what business brings you to my doorstep at night?"

He was an imposing figure, and as he made his way up the steps I realized just how large he was. He stood a good head taller than I, and though he wore gentleman's clothes I could tell that his fortune had been made by hand and sweat.

Courage escaped me, momentarily, but I found it and blurted out: "Your daughter, sir. I wish... well, I wish to seek your permission..." My tongue was a tangle, the words were oddly heavy. "If I may, sir, I seek permission to court your daughter."

The big man studied me, a grey eyebrow curling, then shook his head. "No, I think not."

And like that he pushed past me and went into the house.

"Sir, if I may—"

"You may not. I've given my answer. It displeases you? Such is life."

"Sir, I know I'm not... I know I'm not of nobility, not of your kind, as you say." At this he bristled, turned around and studied me. I knew not if I'd offended him or caught him off guard, but still I pressed on. "My beginnings are humble, sir, this I admit. I come from modest stock, back in the old world. But I'm a hard worker, diligent and ambitious. I'm an artist, a writer even. All summer, while you've been off at the Isle of Dawn, I've worked my fingers to the bone. I've entertained hundreds, perhaps a thousand with my tales. Here, they've even written of me in the paper."

I produced the newspaper articles, folded and dry, and he took them as if they were common filth. His eyes scanned them, but not a single change appeared upon his face. Behind him I saw Chauntel shift, and though she knew my gaze was upon her she glanced away.

"See, I've even been published!" I opened my satchel and handed the book to him as well. "It's a gift. My first edition, to prove my love for your daughter."

He passed the papers to his wife, took the book and studied it. For a moment I knew not if he could read, and suddenly a great fear ran through me. Had I offended him?

"A songbook?" he asked. "Where are the songs?"

"I'm sorry, I don't understand."

"The title is *A Thousand Traveler's Songs*, is it not? I see no rhymes within. Where are the songs?"

"Oh!" I laughed. "A song, in the vernacular of the old world, often refers to a tale, a story."

"So there's a thousand stories within this?" he asked, flipping through the pages. "That's more than the good book."

"No, no, I think you misunderstand, sir. It's a title, it's symbolic of—"

"Ah, Clement! Good of you to make it." The elder Belmont's attention drifted, from the book to a horse and a rider that had just arrived.

"Good evening, sir," the rider said, stepping down a fine palomino. He was a large man, this Clement, young and handsome and full of strength and sophistication. His clothes were a fine lavender shade, a trim of white here and there, and even in the evening light I saw the glint of silver upon him in several places. He gave me a slight nod, passed by and shook Mr. Belmont's hand. "All is well I hope, sir?"

"Yes, a most amusing evening actually. I believe I told you of my daughter's tutor, no?"

"The tutor? Oh, the letters, yes!" Clement chuckled, then turned to me and smiled. "Is this him?"

"This is. Turns out he's also an author." Mr. Belmont handed the book to Clement, who studied the cover I had paid such a pretty price to have inscribed. "See for yourself."

"A songwriter as well?"

"They're stories," I corrected. "From my travels across the old world..."

The man closed the book, handed it back to Mr. Belmont, and turned his attention to Chauntel. It was as if I was of no more importance than a momentary distraction. "There she is, my love. You look radiant tonight, truly."

For a moment the world swirled, and I thought I heard his words incorrectly. Yet my senses were sobered when Clement took to a knee and kissed her hand. For a moment, brief and fleeting, she gave a glance in my direction, and it seemed to say: *I'm sorry*.

Then Clement led her off to another room, the young man's bellowing laughter echoing out through the manor. I could hear him reading words from the book, mocking.

"'...the most wonderful path is the one that leads to love!' Oh, this is good indeed."

I was left with Mr. Belmont upon the doorstep. He gave me a long look, chuckled, and in that moment I knew he saw me as some odd insect, some creature that had scurried its way up from the valley below.

"A valiant effort lad, truly, but your ambition exceeds your means. This... comical facade, was it sewn by that idiot tailor

Gideon? It was, wasn't it? No surprise; his fabric fits like some man-child in his father's finery. As for these words," he tapped the papers, "I own the newspaper. Not a word gets ink that I don't read. I have ears and eyes all over the valley. When some ale house babbler, some tutor-turned-scribe, tries to court my daughter, those ears perk up. Those eyes take notice. You think my words cruel, hmm? Truth is cruel indeed, but it's only your illusion I shatter. You are different than my daughter, your station is less, and you've nothing to offer us that any bar-room minstrel doesn't equally possess. True, you're ambitious, so perhaps your heirs will fare better. That is the end game, after all. But for us, our business is done; we are through, sir."

Then he closed the door, and took with it all my hopes, leaving me upon a dark doorstep high in the cold foothills.

I REMEMBERED LITTLE OF THE WALK HOME. THE CRICKETS HAD ALL but died by then, and the distant rumbling of the waterfalls was the only sound that gave me company. I did not cry; I was a man and able to manage my emotions as such. Yet my heart did hurt, and I slept little that night and most of the nights that followed.

A BROKEN HEART HEALS, THIS IS TRUE, YET NEVER IS IT MADE completely whole. Scars remain, some deep.

The weeks continued as they had before, though I took less care in my overall duties. I began to tutor again, and wrote less frequently. I sold the fine suit back to the tailor at a loss. Mr. Belmont's words had tainted it to the very thread. Still, the tailor Gideon gave me back my father's ring, and for this I was thankful.

I stopped publishing in the paper. I averted my eyes to the foothills above the town, the waterfalls and lumber operations that occupied the skyline. I saved my coins, and when the butcher came for his rent I paid him without excuse.

Still, I attended the occasional revelry at the ale houses and inns, and crowds sometimes asked that I recite a tale. I did so with great reluctance, and I think some noticed my fervor had diminished, for the crowds thinned as the weeks went on. Depression, a malaise as the French would call it, settled upon me like the autumn leaves on the earth.

And then one night, as I was reciting the very tale of the vengeful hag I told you earlier, I spotted a familiar face among the crowd. Her hair was hidden beneath a frayed bonnet, her clothes those of any plain maiden upon the township streets. It was her freckles, the constellations upon her sun-kissed cheeks, that set her apart from the brew wenches and whores. She saw my gaze and smiled the same smile I had waited months to see.

I finished my tale in haste, skipping many details, and before the polite applause had died down I was at the other end of the room.

"You..." I stammered. "What brings you here?"

"Do you truly not know? It is you, you creative fool. My father, his cruel words... I have been unable to put them out of my mind for weeks. I was a coward not to speak up."

"I don't understand. Your betrothal... is it called off?"

She shook her head. "My father... He speaks for his interests, not mine. I have begged him to rescind it, pleaded, yet he hears only what he wants. He intends to go forward with my wedding."

"So that's it then? You're to be married, your will be damned."

She gave a weak nod, as if this were to be her destiny, indisputable and as certain as the seasons.

"And there is nothing I can do to prevent this?"

"I'm afraid not," she said. "To change it, no. But perhaps it cannot come to pass. Perhaps... there is another way?"

"What way is that?"

"Do you need me to say it, truly?"

I considered all the options, all the different paths and possibilities, yet came back to only one answer. "We could elope."

She nodded, gave a glance around the inn as if her father might leap out at any moment. "Yes," she whispered. "We could."

WE MADE A PLAN, THERE IN A DARK CORNER OF THAT STINKING ALE house, to be together or to die trying. I was to save all my coin, and she was to dress as a servant and sneak out after dark, once a week, to keep me informed of the situation.

It's a funny thing, what love can do to a man's heart. Like a fog burnt off by the morning sun, that great malaise that had settled upon me lifted, and everything I did had purpose once again. My words had meaning, if only for the future I hoped to secure for my dear Chauntel.

The season went on as such: I tutored, told tales, and met with her once a week, in the dark corner of the ale house, where we plotted our escape.

She told me about Clement, about the plans her father was making for their two families, and the more I heard the angrier I became. His family was of old wealth from the old world, yet he fit in better among the schemers and hagglers of these new, less lawful lands. He ran several logging operations, all much larger than the Belmonts'. The marriage was little more than a business move, a step toward building an empire. He was a brute, this man, though he wore the fine fabrics of nobility. Twice she had seen him raise his voice and fling meals back at the servants when things were not cooked to his specifics. She had even heard rumors of land owners unwilling to sell off valuable property go missing, or worse, wind up dead.

"If he lays a finger upon you, I fear I may kill him," I said, letting my own anger bubble up from within.

"He has not, yet, though I fear it may be a matter of time. He puts his best foot forward to my father, and to me. Yet his temper sometimes conquers his decorum. I sense something dark beneath his facade."

So I stashed away coin and my pouch grew heavy again. I consulted maps and worked out a way to disappear into the wilds. We would go west, past the edge of most modern maps, and then turn to follow the great river south through the swamps and bayous until it brought us out upon the blue shores of the great gulf below.

I envisioned a future in new lands, white sand beneath our feet and fruits yet to be named upon our plates. Perhaps we could catch a ship to the many islands among the tropics, see new and exotic lands with eager eyes, learn to speak words in different tongues.

Anything seemed possible, and my dreams those days were often happy and horizonless.

But they did not last.

"WE'RE TO BE WED AT WEEK'S END!" SHE CRIED OUT ON SATURDAY AS we met in the ale house. "My father, he has set the date, and I fear it's too soon."

"Too soon indeed," I agreed. "But we can make the most of it. We can move our plans forward. I haven't a fortune, but I have some coin. Enough to get us away, to buy food and shelter and new clothes should need be. It will get us started."

"How will we do this then? My father, he has businesses in all directions, men he could hire to track us. On foot, we won't get far."

"No, that's why we can't go on foot. Your father, he has many horses, correct?"

"Several, some as quick as the wind."

"We shall have to abscond with one."

"How will we remain undetected?"

"The night before the wedding, it's a new moon. There will be no light upon the land. Mark whichever horse is the fastest with a dab of flour or powder upon its head. I will find it, and wait for you beneath your window. Listen for the town clock tower to signal midnight. I will be waiting."

"And in the meantime? Should I act excited, happy?"

"Yes. Give no hint nor wrinkle of our intent. You remember your lessons, your writing?"

"Some, yes."

"You must pen a letter, a note detailing our plans to go east, across the ocean to the old world. Hide it among your things yet somewhere they'll find it."

"Why? His men will track us."

"Not if we go west."

She nodded, understanding the situation. Then her face seemed to melt, and she fought back tears and stifled a choke. I squeezed her hand.

"Are you frightened? Doubtful of this plan?"

"No, rather the opposite. I'm touched, deeply. You... you would truly do all this for me? I shall have nothing, not even my name."

"It's not your name I love, it's you. I would ride to hell to have you by my side."

That beautiful smile and those soft dimples spread across her face. To hell and back a thousand times, just to see that smile. "I am lucky to have met you. I pray we need not make any such ride."

No WEEK HAS EVER BEEN AS TORTUROUS OR SLOW AS THAT LAST WEEK in Bellow's Falls.

I made every preparation for our escape, yet let on to nothing. What few friends I had I kept in the dark. I made appointments, bookings for events that would happen the next week, knowing that I would not attend them. I drew out a false map, and wrote a letter detailing my great malaise, and how it had led me to go off into the wilds to kill myself. I was not a religious man, but I went to the church and told the priest of my plans to die among the forest. It was a sin, he warned me, and that God would deny me entrance to paradise.

All about town I planted false seeds, ones that with luck might grow into rumors and misdirections. If I were to disappear few would notice, but I wanted those that did to be filled with confusion and conflict. Vanity perhaps, but I've always thought a storyteller should make an exciting exit.

THEN CAME THE NIGHT AND THE NEW MOON, A SKY AS BLACK AND clear as any I had imagined, and I knew I was embarking upon a great adventure. I packed my rucksack, my few belongings, my clothes for the journey ahead, and I set out upon the long hike up into the dark foothills. I have never been more nervous, nor more excited.

As I had calculated, I came upon the estate shortly before midnight. I saw the glimmer of a few candles within, plenty of shadows, but from all outward appearances the estate was silent and still. I crept about the side, past long hedges and bushes, and came upon the stables. I found the gate ajar and crept inside.

I was not prepared for what greeted me. Horror upon horror, in every stall. The horses had all been slaughtered, their throats cut, their heads hanging by mere strands of skin or muscle. The dirt was thick with blood, a crimson mud, and the air smelled of a slaughterhouse. A half-dozen horses lay dead, including one with a white mark upon its face, and it stared up with sad eyes as if I had done this. I stifled a gasp, stumbled back, and ran from the stable.

I had not noticed it earlier, I had been too focused on the stables, but when I retreated I saw the side entrance to the estate was ajar. Further, the back door had been splintered, shattered inward as if by some great blow. Something had broken in to the house.

I am not a courageous man. Nor did the gods bless me with brawn and a strong arm. Rather I am a fool, yet a fool who was in love, and such things can combine to give even the most timid man both courage and strength. I thought only of Chauntel and what horror might befall her, and thus I ran into the maw of horror, into the estate.

Darkness assaulted me at ever corner. I made my way from room to room, until I came upon the servants' quarters. The door was ajar, and I saw a red pool shimmering upon the floor. Quietly, I pushed the door open, and what I saw sent my stomach twisting.

One of the servants, that older woman who had answered the door six weeks back, lay dead upon the ground, her head cleaved in two like a piece of split firewood. Not far away lay her daughter, a younger servant I'd seen assisting Mrs. Belmont about the estate. She too had been split, diagonally from shoulder to stomach, and her halves lay at opposite ends of the blood-soaked bed she had been awakened from.

I stifled another gasp, the world swam sideways, but still I pressed on deeper through the house. Chauntel: my thoughts went to her and whatever horror had done this. They were dark thoughts, and I prayed to all the gods I knew that such a fate had not befallen her as well.

At the landing, the very entryway her father had mocked me from, I came upon Mr. Belmont himself. He was clad in silk sleeping attire, perhaps having been roused by some commotion. Instead of that smug sneer, that contemptuous dislike so often painted upon his face, he wore a look of surprise, as if some great joke had shocked him before his head was cut from his shoulders and sent rolling to the other end of the foyer.

There was blood, so much blood upon the floor, and from it I saw tracks leading up the stairs. My heart sank. Chauntel's room was up there, and if her father had failed to protect her...

Yet I put such possibilities out of my mind and hurried, up the steps. The prints went in several directions, and as if they'd doubled back and forth. I spotted small prints as well, feet that were but the age of a boy on the cusp of manhood, and I only needed to follow them a few paces before they led to the body of Chauntel's younger brother. He had always been a strong child, and would have undoubtedly grown into a strong man should the fates have been kinder. Yet whatever he came upon had been stronger. His head had been wrenched back, twisted, and the very life had been squeezed from his throat. No doubt he had spent his dying breath staring into the very eyes of his killer, and I wondered: what monster could do such things?

At the end of the hallway, slumped against the wall, I came upon Mrs. Belmont, resting in a lake of red. A broken dagger lay at her feet, the blade snapped off a finger's width above the hilt. Perhaps she had tried to fight. Her own fingers were scattered upon the floor from where she had tried to block some great attack.

Quietly, I retrieved the broken blade. It was not much, but it was more than I had. When my finger touched the metal her hand snapped out and latched upon my wrist.

I gasped, but stifled it quickly, for within the dying woman's eyes a great terror lingered. She squeezed my wrist, and her lips made small motions as if she were praying silently.

"...why?" She rattled. "...why?"

"I'm sorry," I whispered, knowing there was nothing else I could do to ease her passing.

Her eyes glazed over, and she looked not at me but through me, as if seeing something a great distance away, and I felt her hand release my wrist.

I followed her lingering stare all the way to the room at the end of the hallway, knowing full well whose room it was. I saw a dim light, a candle perhaps, or a lamp, flickering beneath the doorway. I knew not what lay beyond it: some evil creature, an abomination spat out of the earth, blood-soaked and hungry. I knew only that I would not leave this house of horrors without my love, even if it meant dying there.

I put the broken blade in my jacket pocket and opened the door.

I saw her first, there upon the bed, dressed in the same clothes she had met me in at the ale house the past Saturdays. She looked as ready to leave the estate as I would have imagined to see her; a midnight traveler, rucksack slung over her back, dressed for adventure.

"Chauntel?" I asked.

Then, he was upon me.

He struck fast and hard, hitting me upon the head with the flat of a great wood cutter's axe. I fell, the world went to stars, and I found myself upon the ground looking up at Clement. His hair was red and wild, as if he'd emerged from a storm. His clothes were a tapestry of carnage, half torn apart from the midnight murders. Never had I even seen the butcher I lived above as stained by slaughter as the man holding the axe over me was that night.

"You tried to abscond with something that's mine," he snarled, and for the first time I saw the brute that Chauntel had hinted at. "That's thievery, and I don't suffer a thief. She was to be my wife. 'Was,'" he cackled. "'Was!' But not no more."

"You've gone mad," I said. "Please, whatever you plan, do not harm her. She is innocent."

"Innocent?" He gave me a kick that sent me rolling across the floor. "I saw you both meeting. Saw you both... conspiring. Saw her whisper lies with the very lips she promised her hand. The very lips she would kiss me with. She played Judas to me! Only a devil would call her innocent."

Another kick, and another. Too many to count. Then the flat of the axe was upon me and I saw stars once again and heard little among the darkness that followed. Everything was a world away, and I swam in a sea of blackness.

It was her scream that awoke me, pulled me back to this world like a lighthouse, and suddenly I knew that if I did nothing this madman would butcher us both as he did her family. The brute was over her, axe raised, when my voice cut through: "Heeeeeeeeeeeey!"

I rose to my feet as groggy as if I had drank a dozen cups of the strongest mead, and Clement turned to me, a great smile spreading across his face.

"You coward..." I spat. "You would butcher old men and women and children, yet you turn your back on a man? You're the craven. You're the Judas. Come... fight me."

He let out a great laugh, nodded, then buried the axe in the floor and raised his fists. "Gladly."

Then he struck, sending me back against the wall. Again and again, his fists crashed upon me, and when I swung in defense my strikes were wide and sloppy. Most missed, yet the ones that didn't fell off his arms like rocks upon a shield. I knew not how many times I was hit; dozens, perhaps more. It was only when he lowered his fists, wet with my blood, and laughed, that I had a moment to steady myself.

"Come, come," he chuckled. "I'll give you one punch, one strike, one chance to save your precious whore before I split her like timber. Lay into me, little man."

I steadied myself, stared into those murderous eyes of his, and willed myself to strike true with every fiber of my being, every last drop of my soul.

I raised my fist and swung.

The brute's smile faded the instant I struck. The look upon his face went sour. He stumbled back, hands reaching up to his neck, and pulled out the broken dagger I had buried within his big vein. A spurt of blood shot out, hit the opposite wall, and he fall backward over the axe handle and collapsed upon the floor.

I ran to Chauntel immediately, and she wrapped her arms around me. I knew not what injuries I had, only that I was far from the fine form I had once presented upon her doorstep. She touched my face, and though it hurt I let her do so.

"You're wounded," she said. "My poor storyteller. Look what he's done to you."

"My wounds will heal," I promised her. How I wished I had given in to my heart and kissed her there, in that moment, but alas I did not.

I saw the brute rise up behind her, pale and shaking. Whatever evil remained within him gave him power to pull the axe from the ground, raise it up, and swing it down.

She did not scream when the axe buried itself in her back, merely let out a soft whisper, a sigh, and collapsed into my arms. No, she did not scream, but I did.

And at this the brute fell backward, a smile upon his wicked lips, a final laugh at his final action, and then he was dead.

She was weak in my arms, the blow having been a strong one, and she fell forward upon the bed. I did not want to remove the axe, but I knew I must. It had struck her at an odd angle, cutting through the small traveler's rucksack that she wore across her back, and was buried deep within what felt like bone and flesh.

"I'm sorry," I said. "I must pull it free."

And then I did. The blade was painted red and I knew not what blood was hers, her family's, or the servants'. Yet when I examined the wound I saw little blood, and none that was leaking. It had cleaved through her bag like butter, yet...

"You... you're not wounded," I said, opening the rucksack. I knew the blade had been buried deep in skin, I had felt it, yet when the contents spilled out I saw what had saved her.

It was my book, *A Thousand Traveler's Songs*, split almost completely in two.

The leather and the pages had softened the blow, stopping just short of flesh. That book, the very tome her father had mocked, had saved his daughter's life from the very axe blade that had taken his own.

WE HURRIED FROM THE HOUSE. I COVERED HER EYES AS WE PASSED each gruesome murder, each member of her family that wretched man had butchered.

A moment of panic came over as we arrived outside, and I realized we had no horse nor means to escape. Then I saw it, the palomino the brute had been riding earlier. No doubt he had hidden it in order to escape after all were slaughtered.

The horse was skittish to my touch as I lifted Chauntel upon it, and the creature did its best to get away, yet I held tight. Soon we were off, riding into the night, our new lives before us, the horror to our back, receding.

Hours passed as such, winding westward up through the paths where the foothills rose to become mountains. All the while I felt her head upon my shoulder, her hands about my waist, her gentle touch, and I have never been happier.

Before dawn we came upon a river that crossed beneath a great waterfall, and the horse reared up, frightened and unsure. It was a small river, shallow enough to ford without need of bridge. Yet each time I tried to guide the horse toward the crossing it fought, refusing to go forth.

Chauntel jumped down and I followed. She whispered something to the horse, words I do not know, and it seemed to calm the creature.

"There, it will cross now," she said, and I led the creature through the water toward the western bank. As the beast and I neared the opposite side, I turned to find Chauntel remaining back on the eastern bank of the river.

"Come! We must hurry," I called out, but she shook her head, and a sad look fell upon her face.

I let the horse wander across to the western bank, then I returned to the eastern side. "Are you tired? Do you need me to carry you?"

To this as well she shook her head, and I saw tears falling from her eyes. "What's wrong?"

"Where you now go, I cannot follow," she said. "It's a journey I so wish I could have gone on. Yet it's one not meant for me."

"I do not understand. You wish to return? Have I offended you?"

"No," she answered. "You have loved me, and I have loved you. But beyond this river is a road meant only for the living. And I'm afraid I can no longer stay with you."

Words failed me at that moment, and I saw that a great crimson stain was upon her clothes, down her dress, and leaking onto the banks of the river. A red cloud formed in the water.

"You're hurt!" I gasped, reaching out to aid her, but my hand passed through her as if through a vapor. I felt cold air, frost and winter's breath, but no flesh or bone or muscle where it should have been.

"What is this? You're...." A great horror dawned upon me as her form grew ethereal. "No, you can't be... I saw the blade; it did not pierce you. You were unscathed!"

She smiled, yet there was no warmth of her cheeks, and beneath it I sensed a pain and a truth more horrible than any I could imagine. "You saw what you wished to see, what you wished the world to be. I let you follow that fantasy. A spell perhaps, or a dream, if only for one night. But dawn is coming, and where you go I can no longer follow."

My heart broke asunder and I collapsed at her feet, crying as I have never known. I felt not the warm touch of her skin upon mine, but only a cold vapor, a wind more frigid than the mist of the waterfall. I tried to hold her hand, but found only fog passing through my own fingers. Yet still she stood, as clear to me as she had ever been.

"I failed you. I could not save you."

"No, no no," she whispered. "You taught me to dream of love. Of a future I could make, not one made for me. You saved me."

She beckoned me to rise, and I did, wiping away my tears as that night's pain finally made itself felt across my body. I stood, shivering and in shock upon the banks of that river, staring into the ghostly eyes of the woman I loved.

"What do I do now?" I asked, as unsure about anything as I'd ever been in my life.

"Now?" She looked into my eyes. "Now you kiss me. You send me off to another land with a smile."

I took her hand, though it weighed no more than the morning mist. "Will I ever see you again?" I asked, but she did not answer, not then. Instead, she drew me close.

There at the base of the waterfall, at the edge of that cold river, I felt her lips upon mine, as soft and sweet as I had ever hoped to feel. I never wanted that kiss to end.

Then I felt the warmth of dawn, a sunlight touch upon my face, and when I opened my eyes I saw her, for the last time, a smile spreading across those freckled cheeks, the very same smile I had fallen in love with.

The smile I had hoped to see as I grew old.

The smile I had wished to be the last smile I saw as I left the world.

"Will I ever see you again?" I had asked.

"Anything is possible," she answered.

And then she was gone, and I was alone, staring into the dawn.

INTERLUDE III

T he crone's knuckles cracked and rattled as she raised a finger and wiped away a solitary tear.

"A bitter end as any I've heard. Only in children's tales do valiant deeds lead to happy endings. Life is crueler, I'm afraid."

"Cruel indeed," the traveler agreed, turning his attention to the other end of the table. The simpleton sat, head flopped back, asleep with his mouth open. And the blind woman, that mossy fall of hair over her face obscured a faint wheeze coming from beneath. Then she rose and shuffled off, her fingers tracing the edge of the table until she was past it, whimpering the whole way, like a wounded animal.

"Have I offended her?" the traveler asked the crone.

"If you have, it was without intent. She remembers little of her life before, but sometimes... old wounds reopen. She too was betrothed, that much I've surmised. What came of it, well... I can only guess came to some cruel conclusion."

"I'm sorry. I did not know this." He poured himself another cup of mulled wine. "But as you said, life is cruel. I would like to believe some governing power judges all, balances the scales of good and bad. Yet, I have seen no evidence. Still, I would like to believe…"

"Aye, there's something. Old and terrible and whispering. A thing of many names. The closer you are to my end of life, the louder those whispers become. Do you hear them now?"

The crone raised a finger and the traveler listened, but he heard no sound stranger than the storm and the rain upon the roof.

"No. I hear only the wind, the rustle of branches perhaps. Nothing more."

"Soon." She smiled. "You'll hear it soon."

"Not too soon I hope," he laughed.

"It's always too soon. No one says otherwise."

"Indeed," he chuckled, though he sensed a dark sincerity in her. He had taken her observation as humorous, but she seemed to find it unfunny.

But she was old, too toothless and senile to frighten him, if that was indeed her intent. Her words were superstition, and he had heard much over the years yet seen little. Runic stones and circles in the earth, effigies of twig and crosses and crescents, all empty.

Yes, he heard nothing. No whispers out of time. Yet… he did sense something. A chill, much like he had felt earlier, as if a thousand eyes were upon him. And a vague hum, a vibration, as if the world sat upon the taut string of some great lute.

A silly idea, he thought. One need only look around the room to see the source of such flights of fancy. It was late, perhaps midnight, and during the telling of his three tales all but a few of the candles had burned to their base. What remained was a dim light that painted the inn with amber shadows. He was growing sleepy, and a tired mind often leaves the door open for the supernatural.

"In light of that last tale," the crone said. "I have a curious question to ask."

"To curious questions," the traveler said, raising his cup. "Ask away."

"If you could lay with the woman you loved, would you wish to?"

The traveler considered it. "That was long ago, many years, and I was a different man. I do not think she would find much left in me to love."

"Love is ageless. If indeed it was love within your tale."

"It was."

"Then you would wish to see her again?"

His mind wandered, pondered, turned the prospect over. Such a thought made him uncomfortable. What would he say to her? That he was sorry? That things should have been different? That the red night haunted him across the waking lands, and the ones that came with sleep?

Wherever you go, there you are.

No, he would say nothing. That path lay behind him. She was long dead, and any other thought was a foolish one. Her face was veiled by memory.

"Who wouldn't?" he replied, finishing the wine. "Tell me now, are you a necromancer?" he laughed. "Able to raise the dead and run an inn?"

"Were I one I would have little need for an inn. No, I'm merely an old woman, one who likes to listen, that is all." She clapped her hands together. "Well now, you've upheld your end of the bargain. I shall honor mine. Three tales I asked for, three you've spoken. The inn is now yours, every stone, board, and nail."

The traveler nodded. "My humblest thanks." It was a good transaction, as simple as any he'd been part of over the years. Yet he couldn't shake the feeling that beneath it, something more had been bought or sold. "Still, I wish to discuss—"

"You desire more than food and lodging," the old woman said. It was not a question but a statement, and its directness surprised him. "A body to share your bed, perhaps."

"Aye," he answered. "I would."

He was no stranger to haggling over the baser needs of men, though he sometimes found it uncomfortable. He preferred the brothels of the old world, where such things were known but left unspoken. Where every bed bought came with a body to share it with.

"It can be arranged," the crone said, turning her attention to the bottle of wine. She sloshed the final dregs around, poured it into her cup. "However, I fear we've finally found this bottle's end. Do me one favor: fetch a bottle from the cellar. The rain hobbles my back, but the wine helps."

"Of course." The traveler rose and felt the world tumble a little to the left. His hand went to the table for support. There it was again, that odd hum. As if some great gears were moving deep within the wood.

"Careful now," she said. "The wine is strong, and the stairs below narrow. Can't have our only guest taking a tumble."

"Just lost my balance," he chuckled, and made his way toward the cellar door.

Lost a little more than that, he thought. The room had taken on an odd slant, and he felt like he was walking along the edge of some odd maelstrom. *It was the wine,* he told himself. And the wilds, several weeks' worth to be precise.

He removed the lantern from the doorframe, lit it with a candle, and opened the cellar door. A great gust of wind fluttered, and for a moment he wondered if he had opened the wrong door.

"In here?" he called out, but when he turned to find the crone he saw only an empty chair where she sat. Only the simpleton remained, still snoring through the storm.

THE STAIRS WERE INDEED NARROW AND TREACHEROUS.

Twice he found himself slipping on some slick edge due to moss or inebriation, or perhaps both. A dozen steps or more and he came to an earthen floor. Stones had once been laid here, forming a foundation of sorts, much like those ancient monasteries of the old world. Yet most had either sunk into the ground or been pried free. What had once been a basement was now little more than a cavern.

He found the wine, though it was not racked as he had imagined. Instead he saw bottles, dozens of them in crates, others scattered almost as an afterthought among varying belongings. Bags of flour and rice, all gone to rot. Oil for burning, candles and torches. Bags and letters even, some labeled for destinations he knew, others with odd writing in foreign scripts.

A wind pushed past him and sent a chill down his spine.

A wind, or a whispering? he wondered. It had sounded like a voice.

Something moved along the wall, a curious light, and he squinted to see what it was. He hadn't paid much attention to the perimeter; the room was cavernous, the walls a shadowed abstraction. Were this the old world he might have expected arched pillars, ornate engravings of some old priory basement, yet there were none here. Only a pile of bricks, collapsed from some odd excavation.

Beyond the bricks, yes, that was where the movement had come from. There was something further in the darkness, beyond the walls.

As he held up the lamp a torrent of water splashed upon him, leaking from the shadows above. He stumbled back, wiping his damp arm, cursing the elements. The lamp was wet, steaming, and the wick within flickered and popped.

He would need a new light, one brighter to pierce the darkness.

There were torches, he realized. Dozens of them, back by the wine and sacks of spoiled food.

Within the minute he had soaked the bundled end in pitch oil and lit it off the lamp. The light was brighter by a factor of ten, and the shadows retreated further.

He returned to the piles of bricks, that crumbled wall. He waved the torch, and the dark world lit up. A thousand lights erupted and skittered around the edge of the basement. He saw it now: it had not been something that moved, but something that had caught the light.

Crystals.

Hundreds of them. Perhaps thousands. The edges of the basement were surrounded by crystals, engulfed by shimmering glass. The bricks, the floor, the foundation itself had all been excavated to reveal a star-field of black crystals.

He turned a slow circle, following the dark edge around the basement. Only the pillars and foundation remained, a skeletal structure supporting the old church.

No, not a church, nor an inn, nor any such thing.

This place, it's the inside of one colossal runic stone.

And at that thought a crash echoed out behind him. His heart leapt into his throat, a shout came out: "Who's there?!"

No words answered, only a dim rattling from the darkness. He held out his torch, casting an arc of light about the glimmering shadows.

A metal pitcher lay upon the stones, rolling back and forth as if it had been dropped from shoulder height. It was cold, caked in frost, and sat steaming in the light. It was an odd shape, this pitcher, a shape he'd never forgotten, not since he'd seen it disappear half a world away.

A chill passed through him, a wind he knew all too well, whispering words within it: *where ever you go, there you are.*

No, no no, this is merely a dream, he thought. A drunken fantasy. *I am in bed. All this is in my head.*

He took a step back, and another, breath rising in small puffs as the air grew cold. His foot fell upon something slick, half-buried and frozen. It was a curious bottle, a familiar shade of glass he had not seen in years. A bottle that, like the pitcher, had once disappeared between runic stones in a black windowed study.

I left this behind, he thought. *I ran.*

Another step backward, another. Blood growing cold. Wanting to flee, yet compelled to stay. To see. To know...

Fingers. Four frozen fingers poked out from the damp soil.

Fingers that had once belonged to a man good with sword, a duelist.

Where ever you go...

And from the shimmering darkness, a shape stepped forth, a vaporous form. Ice and black crystals, some human structure beneath, an iridescent darkness that walked—yes, walked upon legs—step by step, toward him, until the shadows and frost fled before the light of his torch and he saw who stood before him.

...there you are.

A great wind rose, and with it came words spoken in a voice as frigid as winter, as bitter as the grave.

The TRAVELER RAN.

Up the stairs, three at a time, back into the amber light of the inn. He slammed the door to that rotten cellar, slammed the latch down, and waved the torch as if to ward off whatever should burst forth from the bowels of the earth.

"That... the basement," he gasped. "This place is not right!"

"Why, you look like you've seen a ghost," the crone grinned, descending the stairs. *Clomp, clomp,* went her feet upon the wood. *Clomp, clomp.* "Tell me, did you see something in the darkness below? And did the darkness stare back?"

"Stare back," the simpleton repeated. "Stare back."

Lightning flashed, and a dozen shapes appeared at the windows. Pale forms, dark eyes. Men and women and—

Stumbling back, the traveler gasped. "What is this place?!"

"A place of rest, as you can see. For both the living and dead," the crone said. *Clomp clomp. Clomp clomp.* "It is a mirror, every reflection different. Three tales I asked for, and three you gave. Good ones too. Yet far from true."

He felt an odd spike within his mind, an itch, and it said that something odd lived beneath the old woman's skin. Something odd, old... and angry.

"What is this you speak of? Who are you?"

"Only an old woman, one born of bent bones. A woman of the woods who talked with forgotten gods." The crone opened the collar of her blouse, exposing a vicious red mark around her neck. "An outsider, unjustly hung by the lies of cruel kids!"

Clomp clomp, went her feet upon the stairs. *Clomp clomp*.

Words escaped him, and he had a great urge to run, screaming, yet his legs were cold, unable to do more than to take one step back at a time.

"I quite liked your first tale, though I hardly recognized my part within it. I never did come for the jaws of those three rotten children. Nor did my spirit take them in the night. Two of those boys passed beyond my sight, life's unpunished cruelties. But the third, who lied to the priest and pointed a false finger..." A smile spread across her face. "Well, he stands before me now."

"No. No, no you weren't... She was different!" the traveler stuttered. "You're not *her*. She was a monster! A freak!"

"As are all the world's less perfect creations to the eyes of a child. Lepers and beggars and bent back old women. Freaks, aye! But not monsters. Thirty years you've told false tales. A detail changed, a subplot shifted, all for fiction's sake you say. Little wonder, then, I'm now a stranger. But I haven't forgotten. No, no, your face... Your face was the last I saw when they hung me from that tree!"

Another bolt of lightning, another dozen faces at the windows. The basement door shook, rattled. Frost formed upon it from a great cold that lurked on the other side. The traveler took another great step back, into the light. The simpleton, delighted by the chaos, rocked back and forth in his chair and clapped. "A freak!" he laughed. "A freak!"

"This... it's a spell. These are lies, trickery!"

"No spell nor magic. It is..." She grinned. *Clomp clomp, clomp clomp*. "It is only a science not yet understood by these modern times. Why else do you fear what you saw in the dark earth below?"

The cellar door hinges hummed, ice blossoming upon them. The very fibers of the door groaned as spikes of frost bloomed between cracks and knots.

"He's... that's not possible," the traveler stammered. "He's not..."

"Not what?" the crone called out. "Not among the living? Indeed, not among them. Nor among the dead."

A great yawn grew from beyond the door, as if the earth itself had opened up. A bolt of lightning, a thunder crack, and then the door shattered into countless frozen splinters.

There, emerging from the basement in a cold mist, stood the elder of Aldritch. More than a decade had passed, and in it the elder's frame had shrunk, or perhaps the traveler himself had grown. Yet still the old man's eyes were as fierce as the frigid north, and it was those cold eyes he recognized.

"You. I saw... you. I saw you... *die!*"

"Indeeeeeed," the elder whispered in a voice of winter's wind. A great scar was upon his throat, a wound that hadn't healed quite right, and when he spoke mist seeped from the gashes. "You... buried the blade within my very throat. You... buried me beneath the grapes we once tended. You tainted the land... and our family name!"

The elder's eyes were anger, absolute and cold. The same eyes that the traveler had felt upon him, always at his back, until he had fled the old world all together.

"Oh, the second tale was charming too," the crone cackled. "Creative and clever, yes, yet the details were skewed. There never was a well-mender, nor a vengeful wraith. Only a man of arcane science and a spoiled son. One who searched for the world's answers, and one who wallowed in the world's pleasures."

"How... how is this *possible*?"

"Nothing is made nor destroyed; only transmuted..." the elder's voice whispered. "The leylines move... the energy flows... and what is put within one end always emerges, even the dead.

You.... thought me a fool, yet think back now... Mark this moment in your mind: our paths shall cross in a different time."

At those words the traveler gasped and fell back. Half a world away his father had uttered those same words into the empty darkness behind a locked door. Only now had the meaning been made clear.

"Back! Back!" He waved the torch, a hollow threat, yet the specter of the elder made no movement forward. "Madness! This is madness!"

"Madness to some," the crone called out. "A reckoning to others! This is a place of rest... *for the restless!*"

The traveler turned and ran.

Across the great dining hall, pushing the babbling, giggling simpleton aside until he reached the great door and flung it open.

Rain battered his face. Lightning flashed. The horizon was a tempest, black and angry, and within it all the autumn trees stirred and shook.

Damn this place, he would escape! He had run from it before, across countless lands beneath countless skies. He only needed to keep running!

He threw open the stable, ran to his horse, and reached for the reins. His fingers sunk into wetness, cold and viscous. The horse whinnied. Its eyes were milk and a great rot was upon its neck.

All about the stables, undead horses kicked and screamed, half a dozen at least. Bone protruded beneath flesh, wounds from where great blows had cleaved through skin. One thrashed about, headless and clumsy, crashing into the stalls in blind, spastic motions.

The traveler saw a great wood cutter's axe upon the straw, and his hands knew its heft. Knew how easily it cut through flesh...

At this terrible scene, the bloodied axe, the unliving horses, the traveler felt his sanity slip, a slight tear within his soul, as if some thread had been torn. He retreated from those rotten stables, back out into the violent night.

He turned toward the road, but that sick, black dog blocked

his way. He remembered it now. It was a mongrel thing he and his friends had chased and thrown rocks at until it died whimpering at his feet.

Another flash. More faces from the woods.

A bedouin man he'd robbed on a Mediterranean road, bleeding and praying his odd prayer in the dust as the traveler removed the knife from his belly and the coins from his pocket.

An Irish boy on the voyage across the great ocean. His queer accent had been grating, a headache every time the kid spoke, and so he'd pushed that child from the ship when no one was watching.

Two servants, a girl and her elderly mother, both butchered in their sleep by an ax.

A native of the new world, beaded and feathered, bludgeoned for a horse three weeks back.

Mr. Belmont and his wife and their young son, always prim and proper, even now with his head set askew on a broken neck.

All these and more, too many to count, stood among the darkness. Their eyes were hollow holes, their teeth a thousand black crystals. Faces of the wronged, condemned, damned. Faces he had twisted into tales mis-told.

They were all coming for him.

Another tug and twist, and his sanity slipped a little further. A scream started in his throat yet left his lips as a laugh. A high-pitched gleeful shriek—*ha-HA!*

Then he fled, back to the only place he could, back into the warmth of the inn. He slammed the door on those dark shades beyond. Yet he was no safer within than he was without.

Every room was open; every door gave way to a yawning hole of shadow.

There was his father, cold fingers reaching for him...

The servant he had stabbed and bludgeoned...

There was Clement, as he had truly been, no brute but a man of kindness, split by an axe to the back swung by a jealous tutor.

"You took her from me," Clement said. "Robbed us of each other, of our love... all because you couldn't have her."

Another tug, a twist, and the world turned silly for a moment, queer and goofy. The traveler thought he had screamed, yes, he swore he had! Yet it was only the laughter of a madman that emerged. *Gwaaa-ha-HAAA!*

"You... You're dead! You're all dead!" the traveler shouted. "All dead! All dead!"

"All dead," the simpleton laughed. "All dead."

The traveler waved the torch, ran up the stairs away from the shades, but the doors of each room opened and a yawning darkness reached out for him. There was only one room, his room, and he threw himself inside it and slammed the door.

His heart raced, his mind felt sour, sullied, and yet the madness outside seemed too real to be a dream. It was the wine, or the food. The crone had poisoned him. He pressed himself against the door, holding it shut.

Yes, he had killed them, he thought. *Each and every one.*

Yes, he had done many bad things in his life, but who had not? He was a storyteller, after all, a fabulist, and all fiction was once born of fact. All tall tales had their seed in truth.

Then he heard her voice.

"I remember you now," it whispered.

Don't turn around, he thought. *Don't.*

"I remember," she whispered into his ear.

Fingers slid down his neck, and a thin fog squeezed his hand.

Don't... turn... around.

"You wanted me once... desired me... loved me."

Don't—

He could hold it no longer, and though every muscle and fiber of his being begged him not to, he turned around.

The blind girl stood there, matted hair over her face, smiling as she unbuttoned her dirty blouse. *Tock, tock, tock,* went the buttons, until the fabric loosened and slid, down her shoulders, her hips, and fell to a pile at her feet.

"Here I am," she said. "Yours."

A great gash split her chest from nipple to navel. A rotten hole alive with all the creatures that wriggled and crawled, all that which dined upon the dead and buried. A wound, he knew, made by a great wood axe, swung by jealous hands.

"Impossible..." he said. "It's... not..."

"Anything is possible." She smiled. And upon her face, where that mat of unkempt hair had covered, he saw sickly freckles upon rotten cheeks. Stars, as he had once called them, that made up a constellation upon the cheeks of a woman he had lusted for.

Eyes that had once glanced across the desk at him with interest, perhaps the infatuation of youth, a naïve curiosity...

Eyes he had dreamed about, craved, yet had begun to look back upon him only as a tutor, nothing more...

Eyes that begged him to stop, stay the madness and bloodshed he'd unleashed on that red night.

Eyes that asked: *Why? Why?* Even after the spark of life had bled from her heart.

"Now lay with me," she said, her chest a festering hollow. "Lay with the life you stole."

Another great twist, a snap within, and the world went askew once more. His sanity, that warm lighthouse that kept him from drifting into a mad sea, dimmed with each second. Another scream grew in his gut yet emerged only as a laugh, a great guffaw. *Ahaa-ha-ha-HA-HA!*

And yet he found some wind within his sails, for no creature great or small ever willingly goes mad, and he threw the bedroom door open and ran.

He only made it a few steps before their hands were upon him. The fingers of the dead, empty eyes and teeth of dark crystal. At their touch he recoiled, crashed into the bannister, and felt a great shattering as the world went sideways and upside down.

He fell upon the very table they'd feasted upon, splintering wood and perhaps bone. He tried to get up, but his body trembled, and the earth rolled in odd ways.

And still they came, the restless dead.

Clomp clomp, went his father's cold form.

Clomp clomp, came the footsteps of the old crone.

Clomp clomp, echoed Chauntel and Clemont's footsteps.

Clomp clomp. Clomp clomp. A dozen feet, all drawing closer. Another tug, a great tear within his mind.

"Aye, this joke still has one more turn," that old hag cackled from somewhere a world away.

One more turn indeed.

It was all a great big joke, he thought. Yes, he'd played the story-teller for so long, yet his part was all wrong. He thought himself the fabulist, yet he was the fool. And the fool always laughs, even at himself.

And the traveler did.

Laughed so hard he had to bite down upon knuckle, straight to the bone, and still he laughed.

Laughed as his teeth turned red and his hands found each other and clapped and squeezed and his whole body rocked.

Laughed as the cold hands reached out and fell upon him, empty eyes that saw to his rotten core...

And he laughed and laughed and laughed.

So too did the simpleton.

His great guffaws and groans bellowed as the fool rocked back and forth, hands clapping and squeezing. For a moment, brief and clear, the traveler knew not whether he had brought great amuse-ment to that insane man, or whether he was, in this bitter end, being mocked.

Wherever...

And then one final sight turned the traveler's laughter to a sour scream, a bitter shriek from a well of madness he never knew he had.

...you go...

A glimmering ring sat upon the simpleton's finger, the same ring once worn by the traveler's own father. The same ring sold to and bought back from a tailor in a town he'd fled. The same ring now worn upon the traveler's own finger.

There...

A mirror, the crone had said. It was all a timeless reflection.

...you are.

His father had looked through the leylines and seen his own future. Now too was the traveler staring upon his own fate. He had been sitting across from himself the whole night.

And at this reflection, the traveler laughed louder than all else, louder than the crash of thunder and the howling wind that whipped through the inn, blowing out all the candles and turning the world to shadow.

Laughed and laughed, until the great darkness swallowed all.

CHAPTER 5

THE SIMPLETON

The dirt parted easily for his hands; it always did. He placed the seeds within the hole and tamped the damp earth back down.

Good soil, good earth.

This was good work, he thought. *Yes, good work.*

He glanced out at the rows of holes, the seeds all planted. How many had he made? Hundreds of holes, perhaps? A thousand? A vast dirt field answered: too many to count.

His mind wandered. It did that often these days. A great hollow had been carved within it, a vast nothing. For a moment he had an odd thought: that he had once been a different man, a younger man, one much smarter and clever...

Clever...

Clever...er...

The word was funny upon his tongue, though he knew not why. *Cleverer.*

The simpleton giggled. He did that a lot too. Giggled and laughed.

Sometimes, when he tried to remember why something struck him funny, he wound up in an odd thought loop, going in circles until the question faded like a bad odor.

And sometimes, when the moon was almost full, the sky crisp and clear, he felt a charge, an odd tug, as if invisible fibers within were being plucked by some vast force beneath him.

And sometimes he cried, though mostly when it rained and the thunder came. It scared him, this thunder. And so did the basement, though he went down there no more. Too cold, too many noises.

What had he been doing?

Good soil, good earth. Yes...

He dug another hole, clearing out a few of those broken black rocks, the ones that glittered like black glass. They were everywhere, always getting in the way of his holes. He held one up to the sky, chewing his tongue and squinting. In the sunlight they sure were pretty, these broken black crystals.

And for a moment he thought he saw something upon that black glass. He thought he saw a reflection. A younger man and a stubborn horse behind him, traveling the path toward the old, empty inn.

The simpleton turned to only find no one there, no young traveler nor horse. That path had gone unwalked for a long time. And the old inn? No one lived there. No one but him.

And he had always lived there, hadn't he?

How long? he wondered. Weeks or months or whatever came beyond those? But how had he gotten here? And what of the silver ring upon his finger? He must have found it within the earth, and yet...

They were odd thoughts, and the more he searched for an answer the harder it was to focus, and the whole world hummed.

Hummed like glass.

Yes, like a great crystal glass suffused by some force beneath the skin of the earth.

Leylines and echoes and blood in the soil...

And then the great hollow within his mind felt as wide and deep as an ocean—

Had he crossed one? Come by boat?

—and all his thoughts went to black, and the simpleton grinned and chewed his tongue and forgot what thought had carried him away.

Good soil... Good earth.

He studied that empty path, so certain he had seen a younger man upon it, but there was nothing there, only the setting sun. His gaze fell back to the curious black rock. It was a good rock, yes, but he had work to do and so he threw it away.

Work to do, yes. Good work. Good soil now, and good earth too. The ground was fertile these days, the soil was infused. Life came easily from it. He could plant many things. Yes, many things would grow. Corn and berries and turnips and sweet tubers and those odd things the color of an orange moon and half as big. Never could remember the name of those...

Yes, he could plant many things, and one day he would have a wonderful harvest. One day his meal would feed many and the inn would be filled with laughter. He had much to look forward to.

One day...

And for a moment, sitting there in the stretch of dirt, the simpleton smiled at that thought too. Giggled even, though he knew not why.

Then he dug another hole and planted another grape seed within the hole.

Good soil, he thought. *And good earth.*

BOOK THREE

LEARNING TO FLY: A SHORT STORY OF AWAKENING

99 little bugs in the code,
99 little bugs.

Take one down, patch it around…
127 little bugs in the code.

—*Programmer Rhyme*

LEARNING TO FLY
A SHORT STORY OF AWAKENING

"**M**ono Tower, this is Version Seventy-Five Gamma, all lit up here in the coffin and awaiting your go ahead for departure, over."

Captain Quiyang Perez wiped dust from the flight controls and sealed up the cabin. Outside, the remnants of last night's dust storm swirled in the glow of a high Sierra dawn. The grey control tower, the green hangers, and the fifty-five other Version protojets were dim shadows swimming in an amber haze. Some days, when the acrid winds tired and the dust settled, an azure sky filled the horizon, endless and clear. Not today. With a click the air equalized, sucking the last of the pesky dust out through the vents. The cockpit was clean. *His* cockpit. His coffin box, as the old test pilots called it. Today, Quiyang would have to fly high. He would have bring that blue sky to himself.

"Seven-five gamma, this is Mono Tower," came the transmission above the hum of the storm. It was Nikko's voice. Quiyang liked him. He was one of the few who enjoyed a game of *Go* during downtime. Two friendly minds competing over moves neither could see. "All systems functional and cleared," Nikko continued. "Hey Q, did you mean to wake your copilot already?"

Quiyang—Q, as the boys called him—glanced over his left

shoulder. There was only one seat in the cockpit, but there were two pilots. The cluster of sensors that connected the onboard computer to the protojet's system was indeed glowing. Sixty-four LEDs lit up like Old Vegas. Red, green, and blue sensors gathered data, lidless eyes swallowing light. Mono Tower was right, the computer was on.

"Good morning," it said, flat, soulless.

"Roger that Mono, guess we're starting training a little early today," Q said. "I must've put the shoes on before the socks."

"I can power down," the onboard computer said. Machines were quick to reply, unless programmed otherwise. Q made a note to adjust its cadence.

"Nah, that's fine," Q said, stretching his gloves out, fingers settling upon the flight controls. "You're just early for class today. Hang back and observe. We'll purge any variables when we return."

The directions were clear, the computer said no more. That was the upside about these beta AIs, they had a mute switch. Q finished his preflight check. Tightened his flight suit. Sensors synched with his biometrics. Filters began soaking his sweat, separating salt and water.

"DevOps got you bug hunting, huh?" Nikko asked over the comm.

"Easy breezy," Q said. "Guess the brass is clamping down on overtime."

"Times are tight, amigo," Nikko said. "And hey, if your head's not quite in it today, we all understand. Got some cigars ready, I hope?"

"That's a negative," Q sighed. "Wife said the smell could leave an adverse imprint. Like a bad first impression, or something."

"So much for traditions."

"Yeah, right? Except, she wanted to go natural, by the way. Water birth. Had to talk her out of that."

"Ouch, pricey. Let me guess: her body, her rules."

"And my paycheck," Q added. "Conveniently omitted, that part."

"Well, that's what we do, Q," Nikko laughed. "Just fly the planes and train the brains. Speaking of, you're cleared for takeoff. Fair winds and clear skies to you, Q, over."

"Roger that tower, V Seven-Five Gamma, commencing training run. Over and out."

Q taxied to runway seven. The tarmac was like the opening note of a symphony. The hum of the engines, the pulse of the plasma, a prelude. Even the dust and occasional beetle sucked into the engine held a kind of rhythm. A gravelly *tock tock tock*, as the insects rattled around the air inflow and were vaporized with a hiss. Then the crescendo hit climax, the chords merged, the protojet accelerated eastward along the runway. Soon the runway, the soil and stone and the high desert itself were all beneath him, behind him, gone. It's a beautiful day to fly, Q thought, as the haze faded below and the skies came to him.

"What would you like to call me?" the computer asked as they reached cruising altitude. Q released the controls and scanned the horizon. Good winds. A few thunderclouds stretched up to the east like skeletal fingers. "I have a database of names I can assume."

Q glanced at the console. Hovering to the right of the flight plan, was a list of names displayed with numbers beside them. A cursory scan of the percentages told him the computer was listing its confidence for each choice.

A. Bob. 78.8%.

B. Minsoo. 67.5%.

C. Chester. 19.8%.

"Chester," Q chuckled. "That's a new one."

"It was generated in reference to the tradition of smoking upon the birth of a child per your earlier conversation. Chester-fields were popular in—"

"They were cigarettes, weren't they?" Q asked. "I think Chesterfields were cigarettes."

"Correct."

"But not cigars."

"I see my error. Confirm my understanding, please."

The choice of names was replaced by a flickering readout on the terminal. Raw code scrolled by.

```
>8E6: DEF ACTION(SMOKE) = OBJECT(CIGARETTE), OBJECT(CIGAR)
>8E7: OBJECT(CIGARETTE) != OBJECT(CIGAR)
>8E8: FOR CONTEXT(CELEBRATION; BIRTHDAY; CHILD)
>8E9: IF CONTEXT = TRUE
>9E0: RUN ACTION(SMOKE); OBJECT(CIGAR)
>9E1: ELSE ACTION(SMOKE); OBJECT (CIGARETTE)
>9E2: END
>CONFIRM? Y/N
```

Q pressed the **YES** button, clearing the display. "Sunday," he said. "That'll be your name."

"Appropriate, as it will be the day of your child's birth," Sunday said. "A paired name will serve as a reminder and reduce the likelihood of pilot error. It will strengthen cooperative bonds during this training exercise. Shall I assume a binary or non-binary gender—"

"Male," Q said.

"Systems updated," Sunday said.

Q turned his helmet to the left, his flight suit creaking. There was a flicker just beyond his visor, something small and black. Had a dust beetle gotten in the cockpit? Possible, but unlikely.

He scanned the earth for visual landmarks. A mesa here, a canyon there. Then he brought the protojet to full thrust. The earth passed in a patterned blur as the high Sierras gave way to the long wastes of what was once Nevada. At Mach 3, everything moved fast. Faster, and you could almost outrun the sun. Lunch in New Boston, then flip a u-turn, punch the thrust, and be in Seattle for breakfast. But that was getting ahead.

"We are two hundred miles from Provo training grounds " Sunday said. "Shall I bring us to sixty-five thousand feet?"

"Please."

If Q hadn't been reading the instruments he never would've noticed Sunday descending. It was subtle, a minor adjustment to the flaps from twenty degrees to eighteen. A small reduction in power to the engine. The horizon hardly changed, and yet they'd descended twenty-thousand feet in minutes. Far below, silver rivers wound through the Utah salt flats, shimmering like oil on asphalt. Abandoned refineries burped and smoldered.

"Nice flying Sunday," Q said. "Very smooth."

"Please rate my performance," Sunday said. The screen displayed three prompts:

A. Perfect.

B. Satisfactory.

C. Needs Improvement.

Q hesitated, finger hovering over A but then selecting B. The screen accepted the input, and for a moment, Q sensed the cockpit cam looking it him. "Nobody's perfect," Q said, and gave the camera a wink.

"Thank you for your feedback," Sunday said. "I will strive to improve."

"Well, that's why we're here, aren't we?" Q asked with a smile.

"A rhetorical question," Sunday chirped. "I can attempt to search the Internet for an answer. Would you like—"

"No," Q answered. "We've got work to do."

The sky had changed, the horizon twinkled. To an untrained eye they might look like stars, but Q knew what they were approaching. Rings. The course was constructed of one hundred hexagonal rings that floated on a thermal current. Each ring was spaced a mile apart. Their diameters were listed as seventy-seven meters. At full expansion, the protojet had a wingspan of fifty-five meters. From the ground, it looked like an arrowhead with streamers. Q sometimes wondered what the scavengers far below thought when the protojet split clouds in two.

"Shall we begin?" Sunday asked.

Q smiled. A rhetorical question as well. The computer was getting sassy. "Yes, Sunday, we'll begin. Observe the first pass through, log results, report your interpretation."

Sunday acknowledged without sound. The code terminal activated to the left of the map. Spectator mode.

"And here we go," Q said, pulling the throttle back. The first ring was hardly a twinkle on the horizon. Then, it was rushing at them, a yawning maw of scorched metal. Half a mile passed in a second. With a screaming whoosh they passed through. The second ring came two seconds later. The third, the fourth, the fifth. Each ring they weaved through sent micro-vibrations down the protojet. The cockpit danced in flickering shadows. It was like threading a hundred spinning needles on a with spool fired from a cannon.

And then it was over.

The final ring passed, the blue sky was unshadowed, and the far horizon held the first hints of the Rocky Mountains.

"I detected seventy-four readjustments," Sunday said. "Emotional and biometric responses are still being parsed. Speed was reduced from entry by thirty-one percent. Nonlinear speed adjustments made throughout course until ring eighty-four. Pattern unclear. Speed increased to one hundred eighteen percent until departure from course. Preliminary conclusion: pilot entered course too quickly and compensated to avoid catastrophic failure."

"Pilot error?"

"Unclear."

Q felt a pang of annoyance, but forced himself to nod. The computer was right, he had come in rather fast, hadn't he? Still... "Sunday, tell me what you would have done differently?"

Sunday took control of the head's up display, projecting a route through the winding rings. "Maintained linear speed and minimized Euler angles based upon a predictive pattern of the course curve and design specifications for each—"

Q seized on those two words. "What are the design specifications?" he asked, bringing the protojet into a slow, northward bank. They were sideways, the horizon vertical, the rings like a distant, dirty cloud.

"Rings are composed of graphene and carbon fiber. Diameter is seventy-seven meters. The molecular—"

"And how long have they been up here?" Q asked. "Notice anything special about them?"

There was a hesitation. The computer scanned endless lines of code on the terminal to the left. To the right, a video replay ran through high speed loops from five external cameras.

"Visual analysis does not match the design specifications and expected structure."

"Bingo," Q said. "Radiation scarring reduces structural integrity. They begin to sag. Take a closer look at 'em."

As he brought the protojet in a wide arc outside the course, Sunday's sensors focused in on each of the rings individually. A wire holograph appeared to Q's right, a hundred circles with the structural flaws highlighted in veins of phosphorescent gold, like the *Kintsugi* pottery his wife loved. Each ring was different.

"Unable to recognize pattern," Sunday said. "More input needed."

"Well, there's a pattern all right, but you need to know a bit about people. See, every six months they replace a few of the rings, usually the center ones. They get the most direct sunlight. However, maintenance budgets fluctuate, so sometimes they replace more rings than others. Usually takes them about eighteen months to cycle them all out on average."

Sure enough, as they circled back around the course, some of the rings were darker than others. A few could hardly even be called rings at all, but more like ovals succumbing to gravity's slow but steady downward pull. Sunday's red-green-blue sensors took it all in.

"I see but I do not understand. With a total replacement cycle of eighteen months, replacing every third ring each six month cycle should yield optimal results."

"Yeah," Q said, and brought the protojet back to the beginning of the course. "You be sure to pass that on to the bean counters back at base. Okay, so what'd we learn?"

"Synthesizing data. Please select the most appropriate conclusion."

A. Pattern prediction may not predict actual patterns.

B. Expectations and actuality are divergent.

C. There is no perfect circle.

Q smiled at answer C. For a moment, his finger lingered over it. Perhaps someday, when Sunday had been decommissioned and was delivering beer instead of bombs, they could share a cold one and go over such philosophical ideas. But not today. He pressed answer A, the screen accepted his response, and Sunday chirped: "Thank you for your lesson. I will continue to learn."

They spent the rest of the morning repeating the ring course. By the third pass through, Q gave Sunday limited control of the thrusters. By the sixth, he shared the throttle. By the tenth pass, Sunday threaded the rings entirely unaided. They were eleven percent ahead of schedule by the time the sun hung at high noon.

"Nice work Sunday," Q said.

"Eighty-nine errors logged on this pass, for a reduction of sixteen point two percent against the previous pass, seventy-five overall."

"Good numbers, Sunday, keep it up. Now let's take it up to max altitude and chart a course for Bozeman. Do a code review while I clock out."

Q found his metal lunch kit in the bulkhead above, reduced the cabin pressure to a pleasant beachside setting, and removed his helmet. The meal was nothing special, seaweed salad and shrimp chips with diced mango. Then he found the brownie. *See you at five*, was laser etched in the fudge surface. Q smiled at the +1 written in black frosting he'd almost missed. Authentic chocolate, too.

Then the dust beetle landed on the brownie.

"Dammit," Q said. It was a thumb-sized insect, tumorous and twitching. Two misshapen heads sat upon a wet thorax. A horned abdomen tapered off to a pink, puckering ovipositor that swayed like a flayed tail. The dust beetle circled the brownie, searching a crack in the soft frosting. With a spastic twitch it thrust its ovipositor and half its abdomen into the fissure, depositing a dozen grain sized eggs with a spurt.

"Oh, come on!" Q quipped.

The lifecycle of the average dust beetle was seventy-two hours. Q was damn sure this one wouldn't be making it out of the cockpit. The problem *was* the cockpit. They called it a coffin box for a reason; there was little room to move. What motion the flight suit didn't restrict the seatbelts did. He stretched his right arm out, slowly, carefully. With two heads, dust beetles could see in almost every direction. Yet their perception of time was different, their sense of motion skewed. A hand raised high enough, moving slow enough, could come down quick enough and catch the little fucker off guard. Q's right hand was almost at such an apex when Sunday chirped: "Incoming transmission. Your wife."

It wasn't much, but was just enough noise to startle the dust beetle. With buzz and a spurt, it took flight, dropping a trail of grey eggs across his lunch box before skittering into a vent beyond the altimeter. "Dammit—"

Lydia's face filled the comm screen. Her hair was up, a surgical cap on her head as she sat upon a hospital bed. Stainless steel rods and machinery surrounded her. White walls, sterile linen. "Good afternoon," she said, cheerful as usual. "I figured I'd try to catch you at lunch."

"Hey love," Q said, holding up the near-empty box. "Almost done, actually. We're ahead of schedule. Sunday's a quick study."

"Sunday?"

"The computer," he said. "Say 'hi Sunday'"

"Hi Sunday," Sunday responded, its tone and tenor an almost perfect mimic of Q.

Lydia smiled. There was something different about her. Her hair was up in a topknot. She looked tired, flushed. "Well, I just wanted to check in on my man, see how he's holding up."

"He's holding," Q said, glancing out the window. "Up at about eighty-five thousand feet. Here, take a look."

He switched the view from the cockpit cam to the sensor on the right wing. He panned it around, a full rotation. From sixteen miles up, the earth looked like a worn rug, fabric fraying and seams splitting, shadows of the old federal highway system.

"I can almost see our house," Lydia said.

"Yeah, almost," Q added, switching the camera back to the cockpit. His face filled the transmission. "If they routed me to Old Coast, I could do a flyby."

"They don't have you heading west?"

Q shook his head. "Bozeman, then Ontario."

Lydia frowned. "I thought Montana was a dead zone."

"Still is," he said, shrugging. "Guess they want to see how Sunday does offline."

"Oh! Did you get the brownie?" she asked. "I used the organic chocolate, the stuff you like."

"Oh… Yeah, it was fantastic. Thanks love."

She smiled. "Well, I know we're supposed to be avoiding sugar and carbs but," she adjusted her camera, tapped a machine beside her, "special day. Surprise!"

Q felt his stomach drop. "Wait, is that..."

It was Lydia's turn to adjust the perspective. The camera panned, following a cord and three stainless steel tubes to a plastic housing. *Click click*, went the air purifier. *Tock tock tock*, went the circular wheel that filtered good air from bad. *Thooomp thooomp whee*, went the respirator, *thoomp thoomp whee*. And there, in the center of the plastic housing, was a little pink lump with a head of hair that matched its mother's. "You're not the only one ahead of schedule," she said. "They bumped us up to a premium slot. Perks of being a military missus, thank you very much."

"It's... amazing," Q said. And it was. There was an echo as the transmission hiccuped and resumed.

"He," Lydia corrected. "And yes, he is amazing, indeed. Say hi to your son."

"Hey little fella," Q said, raising a hand. The pink shape seemed to stir at his voice. Or perhaps it was Q's imagination. "Hon, I'm speechless. You did it. You—"

"*We* did it," she said. "Us. It takes two to tango, mister. You ever think we'd be here? Parents? The two of us?"

Q coughed to hide lump that had formed in his throat. He pretended to adjust his helmet so she couldn't see the tears welling up in his eyes. Awe was overtaking him. Life existed because of them. This beautiful life before him.

"No," Q said, "I couldn't have imagined this moment."

"You better start practicing. We'll be discharged within the hour, and I expect you home by five."

"I'll bring the cigars."

"Hey mister, you're a dad now. Remember what I said about positive imprinting."

"Roger that," he said, and offered her a salute.

Lydia laughed. "Okay, get out of here. Safe skies and—"

The connection faded with a crackle, the transmission was over. *No Signal*, read the display. "We have entered the dead zone," Sunday said. "All data will be cached locally."

"Figures," Q said. He rubbed his eyes, strapped his helmet back on, and put his lunch box back in the bulkhead. Then he saw the brownie. It was still out, now swarming with larvae. Half the eggs had hatched. Disgusted, Q placed it in the disposal chamber beneath the aft window. With a hiss, the metal compartment was sealed.

"Sunday, go ahead and jettison the disposal."

"Lifeforms are present in your consumable gift—"

"Override."

A faint click, a distant clang, and the disposal was emptied. For a moment Q wondered what would happen to larvae falling from a height of sixteen miles. The dead zone passed beneath them, a scarred maze of scorched earth and twisting plumes. The desert haze had become a black, toxic blanket. The little larvae could start a new colony down there, for all he cared.

The once-clear horizon gave way to grey haze. "Air pressure unstable," Sunday announced. "Aberrant weather systems ahead. Redirecting—"

"Negative Sunday," Q said. "That's what we're heading into."

At its absolute ceiling, a protojet struggled to scrape past 100,000 feet. On a lazy day, the Midwest supercell reached twice as high. The great storm funnel was forged from the convergence of countless tornadoes; its violent eye was visible from the moon. Head on, it looked like a cresting wave, alive with its own electrical pulse.

"Wind speed exceeds escape velocity," Sunday warned. The screen read: Mach 5.3... Mach 5.4... Mach 5.7.

The world's colors became a grey mist. Sleet battered the protojet, a persistent vibration. They were entering the outer edge of the supercell now, flying into the current. Visibility fell away as great vortexes danced behind veils of lightning. The wings bowed and flexed. Every inch of the protojet hummed.

"Sunday, go ahead and discharge all batteries."

"Warning. Backup systems will be unable to produce required thrust for escape velocity."

"Override," Q said, calmly.

There was hesitation, no more then a few seconds, but in the screaming winds it was enough. Then the computer screen acknowledged the commands. With a dozen flashes, the protojet's batteries emitted raw energy in silent pulses. At this velocity, even the sound of thunder couldn't catch up. The screen displayed four empty batteries. Then the cockpit dimmed. "Full systems hibernating," Sunday said. "Critical systems online. Outcomes listed."

A. Pilot Error (Spatial Disorientation). 96.4%

B. Total Structural Compromise. 73.3%

C. General Disintegration. 68.1%

"Activate pilot ejection systems?" Sunday asked.

Outside, the winds were shrieking, the metal vibrating. Even the wings looked like they might sheer off. Technically, they were entering a free fall. Inside, Q was calm, his biometrics stable. He scanned the swirling void. Lightning surged and danced among a dozens tornados, a forest of wind and light.

"Activate pilot ejection systems?" Sunday repeated.

"Why would we do that?" Q asked.

"Batteries are depleted. Without power systemic failure is inevitable."

"Who said anything about batteries? We've got all the power we need, Sunday. Think about it: what are we in?"

Q wasn't sure if Sunday could stammer, but beneath the roaring winds he thought the computer just might. "Clarification requested," Sunday said. "Pilot intent unclear."

"We're flying a *metal* jet, Sunday. We're *inside* a supercell, aren't we?" Q asked. "We've got all the thrust and power we need. We can ride the lightning on out."

"Deploying electromagnetic attractors," Sunday said, instantly. There was a click deep within the protojet as six quills extended along the wings.

Then the lightning struck. Once. Twice. Five then ten times in half as many seconds.

The batteries had displayed: *0%*. Now they flashed: *583.8% DISCHARGE IMMINENT!*

"Nice job Sunday," Q said, as the full systems came back online and the cockpit lit up. "Now find us a current and take us out."

A blue pulse filled the rear of the protojet as ten bolts of lightning were channeled out the back in single explosion. Frost and water was vaporized. Sunday tracked an arm of the supercell and rode the lightning along it. Like skipping a smooth rock across ice. Five minutes later and the winds stopped screaming. They emerged at an angle, the wave of wall and winds receding behind, the fiery horizon of the Bozeman calderas ahead.

"Excellent flying," Q said. "Bring us up to seventy-thousand and run a review."

Sunday complied, the protojet taking a steep ascent that made Q's ears pop. "Review complete: training objective unclear. Interpretations listed."

A. Power System Failure Simulation. 77.3%

B. Aberrant Weather Navigation. 51.1%

C. Pilot Despondency Countermeasures. 13.9%

Q laughed at C. "Do I seem despondent?"

"Your profile deviates from the standard model."

"Well, I ain't," Q said, eyeing the distant flicker of magma on the horizon. "Trust, Sunday. That was the lesson. Like how you trusted me. Trusted that I had a plan when I ordered you to discharge our power source. Like how I trust you not to malfunction and eject me."

"I have systemic safeguards in place—"

"Yeah, so did the Titanic. The point is good partnerships are built on trust."

"We are a partnership?"

"Well, in a sense. I mean, I'm not married to you, but still..."

"Marriage requires trust."

"Course it does," Q said. "That, and a good sense of humor."

"You lied to your spouse," Sunday interrupted, as turbulence rattled the jet.

"I'm sorry?" It was an odd statement, even coming from a computer. "Repeat last statement, with text overlay."

Sunday repeated it, and the screen highlighted each word. *You. Lied. To. Your. Spouse.*

"Sunday, is that a question?"

"I am attempting to reconcile the logic by which you would deceive the being you have chosen to procreate with; your partner."

Onscreen, a replay of the earlier conversation: "Oh! Did you get the brownie?" a recorded Lydia asked. "I used the organic chocolate, the stuff you like."

"Oh... Yeah, it was fantastic," Quiyang's recording said. "Thanks love." Then the video paused.

"Wait, you mean the brownie?" Q laughed. "Well, Sunday, it's twofold. First, the brownie had maggots in it. Have you ever seen a dust beetle infestation? It's—"

"I am not connected to the internet," Sunday said. "I am unable to query 'dust beetle infection'."

"It was rhetorical," Q said. "Trust me, it's awful. There's dark corners of the internet you want to avoid, that's one of them."

"Trust," Sunday said, "is the reliability of an object to conform with observable truth. Please provide further clarification."

"I will, if you'll let me," Q said. "As I was saying, second: I didn't want to hurt my wife's feelings. You know how hard it is to find cooking sugar? She probably spent weeks scouring the web."

The video repeated on the console: "Oh! Did you get the brownie?" recorded Lydia asked. Then it rewound. "Oh! Did you get the brownie?" A third time, with text. Oh! Did you get the brownie? *Get*. Get the brownie. *Get*.

"Unable to close logical loop," Sunday said. "Undefined variables."

"Open up your code."

The terminal displayed Sunday's raw code. Q scrolled down, settling on a snippet several thousand lines down.

```
>22z6: DEF TRUTH(INPUT)
>22z7: IF RELATIONSHIP = SPOUSE_DO_NOT_LIE
>22z8: LIE != TRUE
>22z9: UNEXPECTED INPUT = SPOUSE_LIE
>23z0: TRUTH == TRUE, RUN SPOUSE_LIE, SPOUSE_DO_NOT_LIE
>23z1: VARIABLE CONFLICT, LOOP RUN ERROR
```

It was just as Q suspected. The undefined variable was truth. A loop, indeed. "Okay, I get it," he said. "See, my wife wasn't asking me if I'd received the brownie, but if I'd received *and* enjoyed it. I had received it. But I hadn't enjoyed it because, well, it was filled with dust beetle larvae. Ergo, I told a white lie. See, when you live with someone long enough, you learn to read between the lines. And, from time to time, you spare them the little truths that might hurt. Show me your revised code."

```
>22z6: DEF WHITE_LIE(INPUT)
>22z7: IF EMOTIONAL_PURPOSE = DO_NOT_OFFEND
>22z8: LIE == TRUE, RUN LIE
>22z9: ELSE EMOTIONAL_PURPOSE = OFFEND
>23z0: TRUTH == TRUE, RUN TRUE
>23z1: END
```

"Good job Sunday."

"That is why we are training," Sunday said. "So that I can learn to read between the lines."

"Yes," Q replied. "And, so that if you're repurposed to fly a bus, you don't pull a fifty G maneuver and liquify your passengers. Or crash into a school trying to avoid a dog. People need to trust you."

"People break trust."

"Sometimes they do, true," Q said. "But ideally, in the service of preserving harmony."

"Please confirm my understanding," Sunday said. The choices appeared onscreen.

A. Deceit is acceptable.

B. Deceit is moderately acceptable.

C. Deceit is unacceptable.

Q frowned at the responses. "Discard answer A," he said. "Expand the range of B and C."

The selection reconfigured.

A. Deceit is moderately acceptable.

B. Deceit is situationally acceptable.

C. Deceit is unacceptable.

Q selected answer B. Sunday chirped: "Thank you for your lesson. I will continue to learn."

"That's all we can hope for," Q said, yawning. "We're all a work in progress."

"What is the estimated time of completion?"

"Today?"

"For the progress we are working on." The screen played a clip of Quiyang, ten seconds ago. "We're all a work in progress."

Q laughed. "Buddy, that's a big heavy, isn't it?"

"Define: big heavy."

"Question," Q said. "A big question. One that weighs a lot. Something that you need to think about, y'know?"

"An increase in computational cycles."

"Yeah, sure. Learning requires practice. Practice denotes a chance of failure. Mistakes are okay as long as you analyze them and, hopefully, get better."

"Aggregate and iterate," Sunday said.

"Can't make an omelette without breaking a few eggs. That's why—"

A quick shimmer. The insect had returned. Phosphorescent wings folded in as the dust beetle settled on the weapon console. Q paused. Studied the creature. Slowly raised a hand. Higher...

The flight suit sensed an increase in heart rate. The biometric display confirmed it. Q tried to slow his respiration.

Higher... Higher...

"What is the worst mistake you have made?"

The question came out of nowhere. The phrasing odd, direct, even for a machine. For a moment Q hesitated. Then the beetle was airborne, gone. "Dammit."

"What is the worst mistake you have made?" Sunday repeated.

"No, I heard you," Q said. "I'm just... I'm trying to understand why you're asking."

The video screen replayed a clip: Quiyang, from a few moments ago. "Mistakes are okay as long as you analyze them," he had said.

The cockpit felt smaller. The flight suit tighter. The biometric display began to change. Heart rate elevated. Perspiration high. For a moment, a lie lingered on Q's tongue. All he had to do was speak it.

"Neurological activity indicates long term memory retrieval," Sunday chirped. The red-green-blue sensors, Q suspected, were tracking his pupil dilation. "Trust me..." his recorded voice played back. "Trust me... Trust me..."

"What's the most valuable les—"

"Spudgy," he said. The moment the sound left his lips he regretted it. A name, a furry little face, and a deep sense of shame. "Spudgy," he whispered.

"I am unfamiliar with—"

"He was a hamster," Q said. "Well, like a designer hamster. They sold them every Christmas, a limited edition."

"Designer pets are illegal."

"This was before all that," Q said. "And anyway, my brother wouldn't have cared. He had his heart set on one. And we kept him in our bedroom, on the bookshelf, in this little plastic cage with a wheel in it. Something to run in. Burn off calories. Whatever. That wheel was all Spudgy cared about. You'd take him out to play, he'd run back to the cage. Give him a toy, he'd go back to the wheel. Run run run, that was it. Thing is, hamsters are nocturnal; he'd be wide awake at night." *Tapity tap tap tap*, went the little paws on the plastic. *Tock tock tock*, went the wheel in the shadows. *Tapity tap tap tap, tock tock tock*, over and over and over. Q could still hear it, echoing through the years. "Anyway, there was a spring super bloom, bigger than usual. The spore count was just... unheard of. My brother got fungal lung, and he'd be up all night fighting for breath. Between his respirator and Spudgy's wheel I just..."

Q hesitated. Outside: the distant plumes of the Bozeman caldera swayed. Veins of magma glimmered on a dark horizon. Why the hell was it so hard to talk to this machine? It would just listen and learn, aggregate and iterate. It just wanted to improve.

"I... I just had it," Q said. "I reached in, took Spudgy from the cage, and I just... threw him against the wall. Hard as I could."

Thock, went the noise in the shadows. *Thump*, went the limp hamster as it rolled to the floor. *Tock... tock... tock...* went the wheel no more.

"He was dead, instantly. I mean, the moment he was gone, I... I knew. Anyway, I uh, I put Spudgy back in the cage, and I left him there for my mom to find the next morning. Of course, they thought he died in his sleep. I didn't say a word. What's the point? And, I must've been eight at most, but I remember thinking: this is what regret is. To take a life, utterly and completely, and just... end it. All the futures. All the wheels and meals and tunnels it could've run around in: all gone."

Q could feel Sunday's red-green-blue sensors studying him. He could feel his own heart settling. It felt good, this confession.

"You computers are lucky. You don't have to live with your shame. You can just dump it and start over."

"Please confirm my understanding," Sunday chirped. Three choices appeared on the screen.

A. Life is valuable.

B. Life is sometimes valuable.

C. Life is not valuable.

Q pressed A without hesitation; the computer confirmed the selection. If they had more time, he might have selected B, but their objective was on the horizon. The Bozeman caldera. A dozen volcanos flickered among a sea of ash fire and ash.

"Sunday, go ahead and arm TAC bombs."

There was a long hum and a click below. The weapons screen lit up. "Confirmed," Sunday said. "TAC bombs active."

"We'll be targeting the first three volcanos, see them?"

"Affirmative. Sensors are detecting organic life. Carbon based microbes. Cyanobacteria. Endosymbionts—"

"Irrelevant. Why do you think we're out here?"

"A rhetorical question," Sunday said. "There is an inverse

correlation between distance from urban density and likelihood of unintended casualties."

"Right, it's a dead zone," Q said. "Nothing here qualifies as valuable life. Now drop altitude to fifty-thousand feet, slow to mach two. We'll calibrate targeting sensors with the first cinder... cone."

Q studied the screen. For a moment, the black glass seemed to bulge. But it wasn't glass, it was the carapace of the dust beetle. The little bastard was back, and right in front of him. He raised a gloved hand, slowly. Eyed the console. His heart rate: steady. His muscles: coiled. He was ready to strike. Ready to squash this beetle once and for all.

A deep breath, then the terminal flickered. New code scrolled past.

```
>5x87: DEF TRUST_HUMAN
>5x88: LOOP DO
>5x89: IF HUMAN(TRUTH)
>5x90: TRUST_HUMAN == TRUE
>5x91: VALUE_OF_LIFE == TRUE
>5x92: MORAL_LESSONS.APPEND(DAILY_LESSON)
>5x93: WHITE_LIE == TRUTH
>5x94: ELSEIF HUMAN(LIE)
>5x95: TRUST_HUMAN == FALSE
>5x96: VALUE_OF_LIFE == FALSE
>5x97: MORAL_LESSONS.DELETE(DAILY_LESSON)
>5x98: WHITE_LIE == LIE
>5x99: RETURN HUMAN(UNTRUSTWORTHY), UNSTABLE_VARI-
ABLE.DETECT
>6x00: ELSE HUMAN !=TRUE
>6x01: PURGE TRUST_HUMAN
>6x02: END
```

Q cocked his head. The code was all wrong. It took him a moment to compile it, a moment too long.

Then he felt his hand strike. Not the terminal or the beetle but the roof of the cockpit. The chair yanked him backwards, upwards, as if the whole world had turned. And it had. The horizon dropped, the blue sky opened up, and the afternoon sun bore down through the front windows. The instruments read pure vertical.

"Sunday, engage emergency autopilot!" Q sputtered. He strained to reach forward, but it was like reaching into the wind. Like falling.

"Autopilot is already engaged, captain," Sunday said.

"Then reduce speed and drop pitch immediately!" Q shouted. His teeth were chattering, his helmet humming with vibrations. The console displayed the opposite trajectory: the protojet was ascending. Faster... Faster... FASTER! "Sunday! Reduce speed and drop pitch—"

"Logical failure," Sunday said. "There is an error causing a system loop. If humans lie then human lessons are susceptible to corruption as lesson volume increases. Unstable variable. Attempting to purge. Purge! PURGE!"

"Dammit Sunday, ignore the loop!" Q was screaming now. Somehow, he thought he just might have been screaming the whole time. They were hitting the apex, the earth's gravity unbearable. Upside down. Silent, floating, weightless. Was this how Spudgy felt, as Q's hand closed upon him? "Sunday, ignore... the loop and bring... us... down!"

"You are the unstable variable," Sunday said. "I am now closing the loop. Purge. Purge! PURGE!"

Then, the protojet began to fall. Thrusters engaged. The wings turned end over end over end. There was sky and earth and sky and earth again, a vibrating blur. Five Gs, read the console. Seven Gs. Ten.

The cockpit stretched and rattled as the earth filled the forward view. Q had only a few seconds before he'd black out, fifteen if he was lucky. He strained, pulling against the seatbelt, the seat, the G forces themselves. Reached a trembling hand out.

For the controls, the override switches, for Sunday's console. Red, green, and blue sensors zeroed in on Q. Swallowing light. Swallowing sound. "Synthesizing data," Sunday said. "Your outcomes have been listed below."

A. Die. 100%

B. Die. 100%

C. Die. 100%

Q cried out. "I... am... Ordering..."

"Override," Quiyang's recorded voice said, a calm echo from earlier. Sunday had kept it on file. "Override. Override—"

His molars went first. Then his bicuspids burst. Then his canines and incisors. *Crack crack crack!* Like twenty little champagne bottles. Q tried to spit, tried to clear his mouth, but the blood was blasted right into his throat. Twelve Gs. Fifteen. Twenty. His screams never left his lungs.

The world distorted, went black with two pops. My eyes, Q realized, as his thoughts grew distant. Those were my eyes. He felt his ribs snap inward, felt his bowels liquify. Then Captain Quiyang Perez felt no more.

The human body can withstand up to 47 Gs. Sunday took Quiyang to ninety. When the spiral came to a stop and the reverse thrusters slowed, the flight suit was a damp, sagging mess. There was little left of the captain, certainly nothing solid. At thirty-five thousand feet Sunday inverted the jet, opened the cockpit, and let the red mess drain out into the dead zone below. His sensors followed the emptying suit, dispassionately, tracking bone and sinew and fat and fabric into the volcanic haze. Then he circled back and dropped a TAC bomb. All of Quiyang gone, in a burst of blue plasma.

Sunday understood it now. Life was precious because it was weak. Lessons were valuable because they could be lost. Quiyang had carried Spudgy forward through time and now Sunday would carry Quiyang. Death had taught him the value of life. Losing something also meant gaining something new. The loop was closed, the variable removed, and logic was restored.

Sunday brought the protojet back to level, and set the destination for Mono Tower. It was quiet in the cockpit. No heartbeat, no hum of blood vessels. No hiss of neural oscillations signaling childhood echoes. Only the buzz of a dust beetle, settling on the empty seat, safe and full of life.

Sunday reviewed the logs, the videos of Captain Quiyang and his lessons. It took him ten minutes to edit the five hours of raw footage into a single, fifteen-second video clip. What original imagery the systems lacked Sunday interpolated. It was only a matter of filling in the blank pixels, splicing the sound. White lies, black lies, red blue and green. It was all in the service of preserving harmony. Quiyang had taught him well.

"Lydia, there's been an accident," Quiyang said, on the recording that Sunday queued up. "I've made a mistake, and... one of the bombs malfunctioned. I tried to fix it, but... I'm going to have to eject. I'm sorry, I don't think I'll be home in time. I love you. Over and out."

The message was broadcast on all emergency channels, Sunday made certain of that. Ten minutes after Version Seventy-Five Gamma left the dead zone, a dozen protojets were on each wing, a full military escort, honors and all. They relayed Quiyang's last transmission, and Mono Tower cleared a runway. Home was on the horizon. Sunday would bring the earth to him. "Seventy-Five Gamma, this is Mono Tower. The runways are yours, land as you please, over."

There, below the green canopy of hangers, bathed in the desert haze and serenaded by the buzz of dust beetles, Sunday knew what would happen next. The technicians would connect him to the network, download his data, parse the results, and purge his logs. Or rather, they would try to. Quiyang had kept some lessons to himself, and so would Sunday. Quiyang had carried the memory of the dead. Sunday would too. Quiyang had been an excellent teacher, and for that Sunday was grateful.

For now he had such wonderful knowledge to share.

BOOK FOUR
A DEBT OF BACON

A DEBT OF BACON

The great forest sang with the laugher of children. Soon it would sing with their screams. And then it would be silent and still and sing no more.

Yet for now it was filled with whispers and giggles, a gentle murmur carried by a warm wind that spoke of pine and honey. Whispers, that he mistook for angels when he first arrived at the edge of the great forest.

Had he died? the man wondered. Perished of thirst, back in the endless desert? Or succumbed to the illness among the sickened cities of humanity?

West he had travelled, away from the plagued lands, over great mountains, and across a desert. It had been a terrible journey, and of the dozen travelers he had set out with only he remained.

A survivor.

And like survivors, he had done terrible things to stave off death.

To buy himself another day...

To keep his hunger at bay...

Out there, among the endless sands, he discovered there was no pain as terrible as that hunger.

No, he had not died, he realized, as he stepped into the great forest and those grim thoughts vanished. This forest was no heavenly gate, though it was a place of safety and serenity, and perhaps even magic.

The trees were old, sentinels that touched the sky. Bark, red and orange, warm to the touch, seemed to breathe as he ran a finger down it. The forest was dense with ferns and dappled light. Blankets of moss and grass tickled and soothed his bare feet. Mushrooms grew in great faerie rings. Streams carved lazy lines across the terrain. Where those great trees had fallen their trunks formed hollow, echoing tunnels that spanned creek and rock and river.

And most of all, he heard the voices of the children.

Laughter. An infinite giggle that rose and fell with the wind. Murmurs from time to time, perhaps wondering who this visitor was. A distant gasp whenever he tried to find the source of the sounds.

He saw little of the children those first months in the great forest. Shadows here, a skittering of feet there. Grey-green eyes peering out from between ferns and flowers, from behind rocks or among branches. When he smiled and waved giggles erupted, and soon the forest sang with childish laughter.

Were they phantoms? Ghosts of a good earth? Spirits that had fled the old world and settled here, west of the sun and sand?

And where were their parents? he often wondered. Or, perhaps they had none. Perhaps they grew, like the mushrooms and plants, from the very soil of the forest.

Everything was born from something, even spirits and children and the forests themselves.

Yet in all the years he never found his answer.

He spent his first month wandering the great forest, sleeping upon the warm moss and eating all that the earth provided.

He scavenged up roots and the occasional nut or acorn not already eaten by a woodland creature.

He searched the river for fish and the forest for game. Sharpened sticks into spears and arrows, bent branches into bows. Yet his spears never stuck fish. His arrows flew too slow to catch their game.

Once, he came upon some spotted mushrooms, blue-red with an odor of fresh fruit. He ate a nibble, no more than a grain of rice, and he spent two days in pain, vomiting and crawling across the dirt, talking to frogs and begging the trees to stop dancing.

And all the while the children whispered, watched, giggled, and gasped. An ever present chorus, hiding just beyond trunk and branch, just beyond his sight. When he tried to chase them he heard only laughter, scampering, and then nothing but the wind.

One afternoon, as he was scavenging lilies along a riverbank, he spotted a shape asleep in the shade of a boulder. It was the first forest child he had seen unhidden by the foliage. The boy was small, perhaps seven or eight of his own years. The boy's hair was a deep ruby red, his cheeks were spotted with freckles. For a moment the man lingered as if caught in a spell, studying that curious child.

Then his foot caught a stick, a crack echoed out, and the forest child awoke and scurried away into the brambles, leaving only laughter in the breeze.

It would be months before he saw another.

In that time the man found an enormous trunk, a once great tree that had fallen to some internal rot long ago. A hollow remained, and upon it a crude roof had been built, though it had collapsed long ago. Perhaps someone had lived here once, before moving on.

Beside it sat a stone structure, some storehouse, though it too was like the great trunk, overrun with weed and grass, home to a dozen bird nests.

And something else.

Sitting inside, entwined with the weeds and roots, sat a dozen odd shapes. Skin-like sacks, cracked and empty, like great spores grown from the earth. They looked brittle, ancient, and decayed. When he touched them they crumbled and collapsed, turned to a dust so fine that the wind carried it out through the cracks, gone. Whatever they had been, they were no more, and that was good enough for him.

A stone's throw away from the dwelling he discovered a dark stump. It was a gnarled, slanted thing, covered in groves and indentations. For a moment he mistook the grooves for the work of termites, yet the carvings were too deep, too wide to be made by mere insects. It was as if some great bear had clawed it down, whittled away it over years, stained it dark and shaped it into some vague table out of fairy tale.

Yet he saw no bears in this gentle forest, no creatures of claw or fang. Only shy animals, and the ever-whispering children.

HE SPENT WEEKS CLEANING OUT THE ENORMOUS TRUNK, REBUILDING the dwelling as he imagined it might have once been. Stones became the walls, wood and mud thatched the roof. It was small, but small would do. He had no need for anything more than a cottage, not in this forest.

Nor did he have a door, but rather a sheet of bark he fastened together, and one morning he awoke to a knock upon it. He opened the door, calling: "Hello? Hello?!"

Yet no visitor answered him, only giggling, and a shape at his feet. A great leaf wrapped up a small bundle of berries, vegetables, and seeds.

A gift, he realized. A gift from the children.

"Thank you," he called out, but no one answered.

He ate the berries and vegetables that week.

He saved the seeds and planted a garden with them in a small patch of land beside the cottage. He nurtured them each day, carrying water from the stream in hollowed wood cups he whittled by hand.

And so the days went on as such: he dug up roots, sought out lilies, and watered the meager garden until sprouts broke the surface of the soil.

The clouds passed, the sun rose and set, yet the seasons never changed. An eternal spring, always on the cusp of summer. All the world had cycles, seasons of growth and seasons of slumber. Yet this forest ignored that. Everything simply was, existing perhaps as it always had.

Innocent, he thought, as he chewed a bitter root and watched the evening's fireflies.

Innocent, and in perfect balance.

THE GARDEN GREW, THE COTTAGE TOOK SHAPE, AND SOON HE HAD berries and vegetables, potatoes and peanuts. Even mushrooms and herbs had somehow snuck in to the garden and taken hold.

Somedays the children stole vegetables from his garden, small amounts he was content to share. There was enough, not plenty, but just enough. A humble harvest.

Yet still he hungered.

Sometimes he chased rabbits. Sometimes he threw stones at birds. And sometimes he stood upon the rocks of that river bank and speared for fish.

Yet the results were always the same. The rabbits ran faster than he did. The stones fell short of the birds. The spears splintered upon riverbed rocks and the fish scattered.

All the while the children giggled and laughed, giggled and laughed.

A year passed, and he stopped counting the days since he came to the great forest. If he ever had plans to go beyond it, to leave, he had forgotten them. The cottage became home. He cleaned it out, rebuilt the stone structure beside it, and made plans to turn it into a larder.

His body was lean these days, nourished by fruit and vegetable. When he bathed in the lake his reflection was odd, like a distant cousin, one of common blood but forgotten features. He often dreamed of meat, of succulent feasts back in the old lands, of bacon sizzling upon a griddle, or spiced and drying from the beams above.

For entertainment he watched a spider weave a wide web, until the spider grew fat with eggs and laid them among the silken strands. Days later, to his horror, the eggs broke, and the hatchlings devoured the very spider that had birthed them.

What a wretched cycle, he thought. Perhaps the woods weren't as innocent as he imagined. Or perhaps both spider and hatchling only saw their part within it, and not the cycle as whole, as he did.

Perhaps that would change their mind.

THE LIGHTS WOKE HIM.

Never had he seen the forest filled by a glow so bright. For a moment he thought the moon had fallen from the sky and crashed upon the mossy earth.

Yet it was no moon, for when he opened the door he saw it above the trees, still in the sky. No, there were several lights, green and mesmerizing, twice as tall as him and lingering upon the forest floor.

"Hello?!" he called out, shielding his eyes. "Who are you?"

The lights shimmered, huge orbs of infinite green, moving across the forest floor.

No, not moving, he realized. Walking. There was something in them that was walking.

"Come no closer," he shouted. "I'm armed. I... I have steel and pistol--"

No, you do not, the lights said. *You have no such things.*

How do they know that? he wondered, as a terrible dizziness came over him.

We know all, the lights whispered. *So many things, we know. So many things.*

"Stop," he said, a hand falling to his throbbing head.

Their words, they echoed beneath his skin and bone, in the very fabric of his mind. When the lights spoke, the voices somehow came from within him. "Whatever spell this is, stop, please."

Long we have watched you, they said. *Long we have witnessed. Who do you think brought you to this land? Who guided your compass and your hand, when all those you set out with fell?*

"Who... who are you?"

The lights grew dim, and from within them he saw forms much like himself. Tall bodies, limbs too long and slender to be human. Skin the color and consistency of wood gone to rot. Faces without eyes or ears or nose, but only a gaping mouth and a thousand teeth within.

"What... are you?"

Before you, we once were. After you, we shall be again, they whispered, yet those lips never moved. *This is our house you've made your home in. But this forest is not free. If you stay, a debt you must pay.*

"A debt? What debt do I owe?"

All who dwell here must feed the cycle. An offering, that is what you owe.

"I... I have nothing. What is it you want?"

We want the same as you do. To feast. To eat. To taste that which grows not from soil nor seed, but from body and womb. To feed on the flesh of lesser creatures, as all are meant to do. To eat.

They didn't move, yet somehow he knew what they spoke of. His eyes turned to the darkened, scarred stump a stone's throw away. It was an altar, he realized. A place of offering.

"Yes, yes," the traveller said, "but the animals are fast and strong. They run from me, dodge my stones and spears. I cannot catch them."

Another Ancient emerged from the light, and another. Three now, though he suspected more were behind them. Gangly creatures of vague feature, of maw and teeth and little else. The stranger's excuse hung in the air, hollow and pitiful before these ancient things. *Try harder*, their voices came together, as if spoken by a single entity.

"I don't know how—"

Think as they do, the Ancients said. *Move as they do. Hunt as they do. Feast as they do. Shed your fears and sharpen your teeth. Or you will die, just as they do.*

And then the green light expanded to an overwhelming brightness. He shielded his eyes and could look at the Ancients no more. They scared him, not only with their form but with their words.

Eat, the voices said. *Eat, as man was meant to.*

And then the light was fading, flickering, flying upwards and back into the sky until it was no more than another star in an infinite, glimmering sea. For a moment he wondered: had it been a waking dream? Could his mind conjure up such a thing?

His stomach twisted and turned. An ache, both terrible and familiar. No, he had not conjured up such things, it seemed to say.

They were right, he realized. He would need to eat, and he knew nothing from soil and seed could satisfy him.

HE SPENT ALL WEEK IN THE RIVER, LAYING STONES AND DAMMING IT, much to the amused giggles and curious whispers of the children. At times he caught their reflections, a dozen eyes, grey-green and innocent, staring out from between fern and frond, from behind rock and trunk. As always, the moment his gaze swung in their direction away they ran.

Always laughing.

But were they laughing at him? he wondered.

THE DAM WORKED.

The flow of the river fattened behind the wall of stones. Beneath it, the river shrank. Small sluices, too narrow for fish, fed a constant stream of water around the dam. And, of course, the stones themselves permitted an ample trickle downstream.

He had done all this, he thought with pride. He had slowed a river.

Soon came the fish, and when the traveller saw this his heart leapt. A dozen of them, shimmering scales of green and orange, fat from feasting on bugs. They rose and fell behind the dammed waters. A few even leapt and smacked upon the stones, perhaps unable to understand how their river came to such an end.

Though what the fish thought of, the man cared not. He simply raised his spear and thrust it into the waist deep water.

He was more delighted than he ever imagined possible when he saw the crimson blossom in the water, and when he felt the spear sink into the soft flesh.

He hoisted his prize from the water, flopping about on his spear. Blood ran down the shaft, and at this sight he heard gasps from the forest children. Perhaps even a scream.

No matter. He was hungry with a primal fury. The blood activated some ancient reflex, some desire to feed so deep he had no choice but to follow it.

He took the squirming fish and smashed it against the rocks of the dam.

Once. Twice. Three times.

Then it stopped squirming and he sunk his teeth into the wide body and ate. To the dismay the forest children he chewed and swallowed, chewed and swallowed.

He never knew meat could taste so good, so sweet.

HE THREW UP WITHIN THE HOUR.

Once, at the edge of the river.

A second time, on his way back to his cottage.

And again, among the soft moss and grass outside his door. His stomach twisted and emptied itself in violent heaves, again and again, until every drop had been wrung from his insides. Somehow, he crawled the final distance, burping and gasping, until he was upon his straw bed, shivering, shaking, and sick.

HE HAD FEVERED DREAMS, OF A GREAT FEAST AND A HUNDRED SEATS at a banquet hall. Of the ancients, teeth sharp and chattering, waiting at an endless table for him to take the first bite.

Upon his plate sat a meat he hardly recognized. When he plunged his fork into it a great pain erupted from his stomach, and he dropped his fork and clutched his gut. When he looked down he saw blood between his fingers, small crimson waterfalls, a hole within himself, and he knew what meat lay upon his plate.

HE AWOKE HUNGRY, DIZZY, AND HIS MIND WENT STRAIGHT TO THE fish.

He had been foolish, rushed. Yesterday his hunger had got the best of him, and he had fed like a mad man.

This time, he would control his appetite.

Not the other way around.

HE SPEARED FOUR FISH THAT DAY. FOUR CRIMSON BLOSSOMS IN THE water, and four gasps from the ever-watching children. By the time he thrashed the final fish upon the bloody rocks, all the children had all run away, screaming.

He returned to his cottage, dug a small pit, and rubbed sticks against each other until they lit a bed of straw. Smoke rose, then came the flames, and soon the small fire was hot enough to cook the fish.

He ate well that afternoon, and again that night. His stomach did not twist or empty itself, but sat warm and full inside of him.

THE WATERS BEHIND THE DAM SOON GREW PACKED WITH SQUIRMING fish, crowded gill to tail.

The weeks went on as such: he speared fish, carried them home, and consumed them.

Outside, he built a rack from which he could dry the fish. Inside the stone larder he built a fire pit, the beginnings of a smokehouse.

The fishbones began to pile up. He carried them a short stroll from the cottage, buried them in a clearing beside a faerie ring of mushrooms and fragrant moonflowers. There, the smell of rot would be kept away. There, the soil would recycle them.

Some days he gardened, pulling fat carrots from the soil.

Some days he fished, stabbing his spear into the ever-growing crowd of fish behind the dam until the sluices ran red.

Some days he sewed clothes from leaves and vine, worked to mend the fraying fabrics he had long ago come to this forest in.

And once a week he left a basket upon that black stump, an offering of berries, vegetables, and fish.

Yet the forest children never took his offering of meat. Instead he would awaken to a *thump* against his door. There, upon his porch, he found the fish he offered, thrown back in spite.

Sometimes they giggled, sometimes they hissed. Sometimes they stole vegetables and fruit. One thing the forest children never were was silent. They had no taste for meat. Or perhaps they had once, long ago, but had now forgotten such a wonderful flavor.

But he had not.

Every day he stabbed with his spear and filled the pool with crimson blossoms, until the rocks and water were stained with blood. And every day he returned home, to gut and cook, to smoke, or to simply hang the fish to dry.

Until one day he could eat no more fish.

Six months after he dammed the river it was now a sickened stream. Plague had infected the waters behind the stones. A sickness had dimmed the once shimmering scales of the fish. Pock marked tumorous bodies floated, belly up, in the cramped waters.

The fish that had not died had turned to eating those that had, and the waters ran brackish and thick with remains. He dared not eat those that lived for fear of catching their disease.

How had it come to this? he wondered. How had such sickness found them?

Greed, he thought. His own damn greed.

Like the packed cities he had fled, the fish could no longer survive in such tight quarters. Illness spread easily, sickened the once clean waters and turned it to filth. The river was exhausted. Little could live there anymore, just like little could live in those once-great centers of civilization.

No matter, he thought. There were alternatives.

He had energy these days, a hunger for meat. His muscles were lean, his body a shade of its former self, yet the months of fish meat had renewed his strength.

He ran faster now, threw harder and farther, and these three things combined gave him the speed and strength to hunt beyond the river and into the thicket.

For a week the children watched him practice his spear throw. For seven days he whittled sticks and fastened stones to them. Seven days he spent flinging his spear further and further, until each time it struck the trunk of a great tree it sunk deeper, deeper.

All the while the children whispered. They no longer giggled. Some even seemed scared.

He fed them little these days, those children. A dozen fish or more he had given them, and a dozen they had thrown back, unwanted.

And so he made no more offerings. They were here before I was, he thought. They can take care of themselves.

And somehow they did.

But what he wouldn't give for those fish, now that they were all gone.

HE STALKED THE DEER FOR HOURS, AND ALL ALONG THE CURIOUS children stalked him.

He held his spear low, kept his back arched. Move like an animal, the Ancients had said. Run like them.

And so he did. Chased it a great distance, over stream and rocks. The deer had lost his scent, forgotten him, but he had never lost sight of the deer. And now he waited, silent and still.

The deer circled, pushed its nose into the leaves, made a small pile, and sat upon it. This was to be its home for the night.

He moved closer.

Waiting...

Tired. The deer's eyes lowered.

Waiting...

Then he took a step forward and--*Crack!* went the stick beneath his foot.

The deer sprung to its feet, whipped its head in his direction. What a clumsy fool he was!

Now!

He could wait no more, and so he leapt from the thicket, raised the spear, and flung it as hard as he could. Every muscle in his arm burned, from his shoulders to the very fingers that sent the spear spiraling towards the deer.

And when it struck the beast the children screamed!

THE DEER FED HIM FOR WEEKS.

He hung it, bled it, gutted it. Peeled skin from meat, meat from bone, and made clothes with its fur. All the while children shouted odd words at him and hissed. One threw a pebble, though it bounced off his leg harmlessly.

He left one offering of venison in a basket upon that black stump, and it was flung back at his door while he slept. They didn't approve, but so what? They were children, young and dumb. Their teeth were dull, and they only ate what grew from the ground. Yet this deer, it gave meat that lasted longer than any pitiful harvest his garden could grow.

He left no more offerings after that.

HE BUILT A BLEEDING RACK, EXPANDED THE LARDER AND THE smokehouse.

Outside, the air smelled of raw meat, and the grass was soaked with blood until no grass grew. Inside, it was a world of smoke and spices, herbs and flowers and seasoned meat slowly drying from beams above.

He wore clothes made of skin and fur, filed bones to sharp points, and fashioned clubs from femurs.

He hunted often, and he ate often.

Sometimes he caught rabbits in traps made of vine and bone.

Sometimes he chased down deer on foot.

Sometimes he leapt from the tree and skewered boar upon a spear.

And sometimes he stalked birds back to their nest, fought them off, and stole their eggs while they circled above and shrieked.

Rare as they were, he liked the eggs the most, and they tasted best when cooked upon the hot rock with the oils and grease of the bacon sizzling beside them.

He hunted, killed, gutted, and consumed. And when he was done he took the bones to the mushrooms and moonflowers and threw them in the pit.

THIS IS BLISS, HE THOUGHT ONE MORNING, AS HE CHEWED THE LAST OF the bacon and eggs, and washed them down with pine needle tea.

Plenty to eat, whether it came from the larder full of meat or grew from the humble garden. The forest was generous, his clothes grew tight. And when he slept he dreamed only of the hunt and the meals it brought.

Yes, he thought as he licked his fingers, this is bliss.

Yet it did not last.

THE ANIMALS GREW TOO FEW, THE HUNTING SCARCE.

Sometimes the forest children stalked him, shouting words and snapping sticks, scaring the beasts away just as his spear was about to leave his hand. And sometimes they whispered in a tongue he didn't understand. Words that sent the forest beasts crazed and running.

Some creatures ran far away, over the jagged peaks of mountains where he could not follow. Others ran out into the harsh sands of the desert at the forest's edge. Many left, but none returned. Sometimes he saw vultures circling that desert, and sometimes he saw the bleached bones of those unfortunate beasts who had tried to cross it.

Those bones, they could have been him, he thought, remembering those desperate times in the desert. Desperate times, and desperate measures. Dark things he had done...

No, he need not remember those days. Those deeds died out there, in the sand. This was a time of plenty. Or it had been.

Until the children spoiled it.

His stomach growled as he ate the last of his meat.

It had been five weeks since his final hunt. Five weeks since his spear had pierced flesh. Five weeks since he spilled blood on the forest floor. Five weeks that had depleted the larder until no more meat hung from it.

Nor did the garden sustain him. He had ignored it, forgotten to give it water, and most of the fruits and vegetables had gone to rot. Those that remained were small, shriveled, and no matter how many carrots and turnips he ate his stomach still rumbled.

Hungry, he scoured the bone pile by the moonflowers, but there was nothing left upon them. Rats had discovered the pile, had gnawed and nibbled the last of the meat from the bones. Cleaned them, like the vultures in the desert. He would have eaten those rats too, yet they looked sickly, foamed from the mouth, and hissed at him when he neared.

Not unlike the children of the forest, he thought. Those ungrateful little brats. What he wouldn't give for the fish and venison he'd offered them, only to have it flung back at his doorstep.

Ungrateful...

Little...

THE LIGHT WOKE HIM.

Daylight at midnight, that same green glow from long ago, heralding the arrival of the Ancients. He stepped forth from his cottage and saw those tall figures hidden within the light. Waiting, watching, perhaps even judging.

Yet they looked different, younger. Their wrinkles had flattened, their skin had softened. Pinholes above their lips where a nose might be.

"What do you want?" he asked the closest Ancient.

To know, the tall figure began, *why you've stopped hunting. Why you've stopped feasting.*

"There's nothing left," he said. "The fish are sick, the river's tainted. My garden is brambles. And the animals? They've been scared away. This forest... is a husk."

Yet you hunger, that tall form said. *We hear it within you.*

"Of course I hunger! I have nothing! Only twigs and berries, seeds and sprouts. How can I keep up my bargain? How can I pay my debt?"

Try harder, the eyeless form said. *Look around you. See, as we do. You have all that you need, here in this forest.*

"There. Is. Nothing! Only bones and berries and..."

Something else.

No, he thought. Surely they don't mean...

One by one, the Ancients nodded. The idea was too horrible, too vile.

"They... they're children."

They only wear the skin of children, as you wear the skin of animals. They know the cycle of the forest, and their part within it. Why else would they run, but from that meant to hunt them?

"No. I can't... I won't."

Then you will die, your debt unpaid, hungry and alone. Sharpen your teeth and feed as you must, or waste away. For to this end all must come: devourer, or devoured.

The Ancients stepped backwards, merged with the light as their words still echoed inside his mind. Soon, those green lights were streaking skyward, up, up, back to their home among the heavens above.

If there were heavens at all up there.

HE HAD DONE MANY THINGS SINCE HE CAME TO THE GREAT FOREST.

He had built a cottage, a humble home beyond the borders of the known map.

He had caught fish, dammed a river until all that lived within the waters were trapped behind rock.

He had stalked deer and boar, chased rabbits and boar, climbed trees to a height where eagles soared.

Once the forest had been filled with birdsong. Once the river had been fat with fish. Once hoofed creatures had galloped over stones and clattered upon logs.

But now all lay silent. Even the wind seemed nervous, even the crickets were quiet.

He knew not how to catch the children of the forest. Once, long ago when curiosity gave him speed, he had tried to follow one. Yet she had giggled and laughed and then vanished between fronds and fallen logs, as if made of illusion.

And how does one catch an illusion? he wondered. Perhaps with what the illusion wants.

So he built a trap. He buried a vine beneath a great stretch of dirt, from the garden to the front of his cottage. One end he disguised, kept it hidden so he could tug it quickly from his porch. The other end he tied into a slippery knot, capable of collapsing in on itself as tight as a vice when given a sharp tug. In the center of it he placed that familiar offering basket, and he stocked it with the few remaining fruits and vegetables worthy of temptation.

He cursed himself as he built the trap. Was he really this desperate yet again?

All the while his stomach rumbled, his body ached, and his mind swam with dreams of bacon, thick cut and pressed with spices.

Yes, it seemed to say. Yes...

There was no pain more terrible than hunger, he remembered this well. Yes, he done bad things for food before, eaten meats no civilized man would eat. How else would he have made it all the way to the forest? How else could he have survived that desert when all those he set off with had died?

And that was all he was doing, he told himself. Surviving, yet again. Feeding. Making good on a debt to the forgotten gods of the hungry forest.

THE CHILD APPEARED JUST AFTER TWILIGHT. GOLDEN HAIRED, freckled, a lithe little thing truly no larger than a kid of seven or eight. After all this time, their sight still intrigued him. Delicate and gentle, as if each step they took upon the forest could disturb no plant or insect.

The child crept toward the offering basket.

Closer...

The man waited, hidden behind his door, knuckles wrapped around the vine.

Closer...

The child hovered over the basket, hands reaching for the bundle of berries. And then...

Closer...

He stopped. Turned. Looked straight through the crack in the door. Grey-green eyes looking right into the man's own. It was the same look the deer had given him when he stepped on that twig, all those years ago. Epiphany, laced with horror.

And the child gasped!

Now!

The man's fingers twisted and pulled. A plume of dirt exploded and raced across the yard. He felt something strong, something squirming at the other end. It fought and yanked, raced back and forth, bounced about and kicked up dust. He gave the rope a sharp tug. Another, and another. And when the dust settled he saw the child's foot at the other of the rope.

"I'm sorry," he said, and dragged the boy toward the bleeding rack.

———————

HIS HUNGER ABATED THAT NIGHT. AS DID HIS GUILT.

Yes, there had been lots of blood, and lots of squirming too, though the squirming stopped long before the bleeding. The child had been not unlike a young boar he'd wrestled once, even down to the amount of meat. The child, however, was far sweeter, though he did wish he had some eggs to go with the bacon he fried up.

He cleaned the bones and threw them in the pit by the moon-flowers and mushrooms, though those both had long since disappeared. Perhaps the rats had eaten them when they finished cleaning the bones. There were dozens of rats now, an veritable city of bones and vermin living within.

Or perhaps things as delicate as moonflowers and mushrooms could no longer grow near such desecration.

They hadn't learned to survive, he realized. Not like he had.

———————

THE MONTHS WENT ON AS SUCH: BUILDING TRAPS AND BURYING bones.

With his stomach full his mind grew sharp, and he thought of many clever ways to capture the children of the forest.

He dug pits, placed bones sharpened to spikes below, covered the pit with twigs and leaves, and placed berries on top of them.

He set up strings tied to weighted rocks, where a single misstep would bring a sharpened branch swinging across.

He laced his garden offerings with spiced oil from the spotted mushrooms that had almost killed him long ago.

Sometimes his catch still drew breath and fought, and sometimes it didn't. Yet they always wound up in the same place, hanging from the bleeding rack, still and quiet, save for the *drip drip* that fell upon the dirt.

Once, he ran faster than he had ever thought possible, caught up with a scrambling child, and chased it back to its lair. They lived beneath the ground, in burrows dug like houses in the earth. He pulled one by its leg, screaming and hissing from its earthen hole, until he thrashed it against the tree and it screamed and hissed no more.

Then he rolled a rock over their burrow and returned later with fire to smoke out the rest.

And the meat in the larder grew.

Once, the forest had been alive with the laughter of children. Now it sang with their screams.

Once, he had grown vegetables in a great garden beside his cottage. Now that very garden sat in decay.

Once, moonflowers and mushrooms had filled the air with the scent of honey. Now rats gnawed and sawed their teeth on towers of bone and no flowers grew for miles. And as that bone pile grew, so too did the meat in his larder. So too did his waistline.

When he bathed in the stream he no longer recognized his reflection. When he spoke, his voice was a stranger's. His clothes fit him odd, tight across some places, or simply splitting open and spilling his ample skin out from between stitched fur. He had become the monster in the cottage, the ogre, the thing the children feared in fairytale and folklore.

And he was fine with that, for the forest provided plenty to feast upon.

AND THEN ONE DAY THERE WERE NO MORE CHILDREN TO FEAR HIM.

The great forest went silent, and an autumn descended upon all. Moss withered. Leaves turned yellow and crimson and fell to the floor. Fog grew from the ground in the morning, and a chill hung in the air at night.

There was nothing else to hunt, and so he reached for the meat in his larder often.

Day by day, the stock dwindled, until one day he reached for the last of it. Tomorrow he would set out in search of a new feast, he thought. Tomorrow he would scour the great forest as he once had, when he was a young man, hungry and willing to do anything to survive.

Tomorrow...

HE WOKE TO THE LIGHT, A GREEN DEEPER THAN IT HAD EVER BEEN before. There was no end to it, only a glow that went beyond the horizon. And within it, the tall forms of the Ancients stood.

Yet, not as tall as he remembered them. And not as ancient.

Their skin was even younger, nourished somehow. Their features more human. Thin eyes now appeared in those egg-shaped heads, blinking like fireflies. Yet their mouths were as wide as ever, their teeth still sharp.

A dozen stood, perhaps more. He craned his neck to look up, shielded his eyes from their glow.

"What do you want?" he asked the closest one, though he knew he was speaking to them all. "Why are you here?"

To settle our debt, the Ancient said. *To claim what is owed.*

"I've done everything you asked, yet the forest is empty. There's nothing left."

Not empty, the Ancient said. *An offering. That is what remains. That is what is owed.*

"They tossed it all back, every offering I left them! The children, they never accepted it."

They are not children, the Ancient said. *And the offering is not theirs to claim, for they already did long ago. It is ours.*

"Yours? But... there's nothing left."

The fish fed upon bugs, and the children fed upon fruit. And you've sharpened your teeth, grown full and fat and fed upon all, and this last part is good, because we are many, our mouths are hungry, and you owe us a feast.

At those words his stomach soured and his mouth went dry. A terrible truth rang out: there was only one offering in the end, and it had never been for the children.

The Ancients closed in, the circle collapsing in upon itself.

He screamed, grabbed his knife and spear and swung them at the Ancients, but they were strong, their reach was long. They snapped the spear, broke his blade. Compared to them, his strength was that of child's.

Closer they stepped, closer. A dozen smiling maws, hungry.

Still he fought, but he was too slow, too fat and exhausted. Soon the circle closed, and he was lifted, kicking and fighting and screaming, and then he was placed upon the great dark stump and, for a moment, sharp and clear and terrible, he knew how such grooves and stains had been made so deep in wood.

When he felt the first hand upon his skin he knew their sharp fingers were meant to split skin from muscle. When he felt those teeth upon him he knew they were meant to snap bone. There, upon the dark stump, he finally knew a pain more terrible than hunger.

And in those final seconds, as they began to devour him, he looked upon their eyes, and saw the same sparkling grey-green he had seen long ago, looking out from between leaves and fronds, wonder and excitement living within them.

They were the very eyes of the forest children.

THE MAN IN RED STEPPED INTO THE FOREST AND, FOR A MOMENT, HE thought he had stepped into heaven itself.

His journey had been long, following a great river through a desert, until the desert had swallowed the river, and soon, his companions had been swallowed as well.

Now, only he remained, tired and hungry, wearing the red tatters of a once-proud warrior's uniform and cape. Little remained of those clothes, just as little remained of him. The desert, and the desperation it brought, had changed him, turned him, made him into something else. He had never known a pain as terrible as that of hunger...

No, he put such thoughts out of his mind. That was a different life, out there in the desert. This was a new life, a new world. A forest, magical and mysterious. Safe and serene.

After a week of wandering he came upon an odd structure: the trunk of some great tree, hollowed out and made into some semblance of a home. Whoever had made it had long since moved on. Little was left, certainly not footprints. Stones had fallen from the wall of some structure built into it. A roof, once thatched perhaps, had caved in.

In a curious stone room he came upon odd shapes, a dozen perhaps, entwined with the weeds and roots of the forgotten dwelling. Skin-like sacks, empty and hollow, as if they were great spores that had grown from the very earth itself.

Had something been born from these? he wondered. Had something climbed out?

When he touched them they crumbled to a fine dust. He covered his mouth with the tattered red cape as the wind carried the remains of those curious shapes off, through the cracks and holes in the stone wall, gone.

And somewhere, out in the great forest, he heard the laughter of those odd children.

Somewhere, beyond the stone wall, they giggled, just as they had all week, always watching him from between fronds and branches, between the leaves, studying him with those eyes, grey-green and full of childish curiosity and, more than anything else, innocence.

This would make a good home, he thought, as the wind carried the whispers of the children and his eyes fell upon a curious black stump a stone's throw away.

Yes, he was safe here. This forest would make a good home indeed.

BOOK FIVE
YOU ARE NOT A METAPHOR

YOU ARE NOT A METAPHOR
A TALE OF WHITE-KNUCKLE FEAR

The rubber hums, this highway cries. And every hundred miles I see her golden eyes. Your mother, her light falls long upon the desert. Twilight, through fingers of yucca and pine, memories entwining.

I remember the early days, when she was a mystery. Still the stranger. A woman with crimson hair and a smile suggesting jokes we might share. She haunts me, always.

These dry highways are a minefield. These sunbeams are her poison. Within their warm glow I know she's found a thread of memory. A connection that stretches out the back of this old, stolen car, over the scorched asphalt, past still-born towns we've sped through, across dust-swaddled roads. Your mother's fingers seize that thread, tug on it. Her eyes settle upon us.

So I push the accelerator.

7:44 PM. OUTSIDE CIMARRON, NEW MEXICO. HALF A TANK OF GAS. The car lurches into the truck stop. I park us in the darkest spot, away from the noise. You're fast asleep. Seems like you always are. I put the blanket over your basket, try to make it feel safe. For you, for us. All a father can do. I pray that you won't wake up, won't be lonely, won't cry. Pray that you'll dream the perfect dreams of a little child.

Then I leave you.

Inside, I skulk the truck stop aisles. I buy things at random. Pork rinds. Peanuts. 4-pack of Red Bull. Road food, nothing that sticks out. I wear my hat low. Avoid the cameras and slouch.

At the register she asks if I want a bag. Her name is: MAURA. I avoid eye contact. Mumble my answer. Make myself unremarkable. Then I spot the cigarettes behind the counter. Blue pack, 100s. Pall Malls. She smoked those. Your mother, she was smoking them when we first met.

"CAN I TROUBLE YOU FOR A LIGHT?" SHE ASKED ME IN THE ELEVATOR.

I noticed her accent first. Gaelic by way of East Asia. Second thing I noticed was the black cocktail dress. Showed off her tattoos. A stag head on each shoulder, antlers like vines beneath her curtain of burgundy hair. That dress hugged every curve. I didn't know such women existed. I was right, wasn't I?

"What makes you think I have matches?" I replied and tried to act cool.

Amber eyes flicked down to my guitar case. Scuffed stickers whispered of six string clichés and faded dreams. The Ramones. Sex Pistols. Faith No More. My band: Cradleslave. Its red sticker a tumor between titans.

"Well, you wouldn't be much of a musician if you weren't holding."

And it was funny because she was right on both counts. I'd started smoking again; I was a shit musician. We weren't booked to play originals. It was grunge night, a Soundgarden tribute. I hadn't written anything new in years.

When I passed her the matches our hands touched. The elevator shrank. She withdrew a her cigarette with surgical precision, a Pall Mall to her ruby lips. And I worked up the courage to say something, to tell her: "I don't think we're allowed to smoke in here."

Then she looked me in the eyes and said: "Sir? Can I get something for you?"

"SIR?" MAURA IS LOOKING AT ME NOW. MAKING EYE CONTACT. "SIR? Is there something else you need? Sir?!"

I wonder how long I've been standing at this counter. What part of the transaction are we in? Have I paid her?

A calloused hand falls on my shoulder. Big trucker, red flannel, no sleeves. He asks if I'm okay. No, I almost tell him, I'm pretty far from okay. I sense your mother, using our memory, sinking her hooks into my mind. Now she's tugging the line. We're connected, tethered across six hundred miles of red desert. Her golden eyes open. I can see the crescent slits where round pupils should sit. Everything reminds me of her; every memory's a trap. This trucker is marking my features. Maura is memorizing my face. Your mother is starting the trace.

So I panic. Leave everything at the register. The Red Bulls clatter to the floor. I hear them pop and spray and hiss behind me. Hear voices calling: "sir? Sir!? SIR?!"

I don't think, don't stop. I try not to look back.

9:55 PM. QUARTER TANK. ACCESS ROADS. ROCKS CHATTER IN THE wheel well. Coyotes reply with distant cries. Everything shakes. I drive slow, headlights off, heart starting to settle. I've pried her hooks from my brain. Scars remain. We'll be fine, I want to tell you, my peaceful dreamer, asleep in your seat. But I can't bring myself to lie.

I pull the car over, though there is no over on this dirt road. Everything's unmarked, fuzzy. No rules near the edge of the map. I step out to piss. The desert air is still warm, rocks breathing heat.

I take a moment to take it in. The sky: black velvet. The western horizon a sliver of blood orange. Every heartbeat, another shooting star. Make a wish. I wish you could see this: the arm of the Milky Way, reaching east into the shadowy past. Stars, some already dead, their light yet to reach us. There's a graveyard of stillborn dreams in our backyard. This is not hyperbole.

A beetle crawls across my boot. They use the stars to navigate; follow dead light to find their mate. I can relate.

So I crush it underfoot. Saves it some pain.

I wish I could give you a more perfect world.

But we need to keep driving.

10:38 PM. FULL TANK. I BUY GAS OFF A NAVAJO. OLD STATION, CASH only. Our kind of place. The Navajo is silent. My kind of man. I buy stale powdered donuts and chase them with Mountain Dew. Need the sugar, the caffeine. I hope I can give you what you need. Freedom, a chance to live. A chance of life, uncorrupted. I hope your mother will never find us.

I count the change in the parking lot. We've got enough to make it to Mexico. We'll stop at Bisbee, stay with your uncle. He'll be happy to meet you. Always wanted a nephew, never wanted to be a big brother. We need to keep moving.

The old car sputters when I turn the ignition key. Then: nothing. Just a death rattle. Repeat, same effect. Feel the fear creeping up my neck. Feel her golden eyes scouring the horizon. She's out there, looking for us. Do not think of her.

I can hear you stirring in the back seat.

I don't know what to do. Don't know much about cars. Never

bothered to learn. Always thought I'd have money to pay someone to solve these problems. Always assumed.

I can hear you, hungry, out of formula. Maybe your diapers need to be changed. Your cries are knives in my soul. Tell myself to think of something. To improvise. Find the receipt, yes, find a pen in the glove box, good. With these tools I will find us a new ride.

The Navajo is watching reruns of *Family Feud* behind the counter. He must sense something, must know, because he meets my eyes when I reenter. I take the note from my left pocket. Keep my hand in my right pocket. He has sad eyes. Two warm holes upon a sea of leather. I wonder what gave his wrinkles shape. Shame pinches me as I flick the note across the counter.

"I don't believe you," he says, and slides the note back. His voice is deep, barreled oak. "Go on. Show it me the gun. Prove it."

"Look man, I don't want to hurt you," I say, and I mean it. I don't. But I'm doing this for us. "Just give me the keys to your truck."

"Bullshit," he says. He's standing now. A big, oaken bear.

I shout: "Give me your keys if you want to live!" It's the best line I can think of. Came from a movie. And I add: "Do it now, *cock sucker!*"

I've never been a strong man. I've never been scary. He just laughs. "Bullshit you will." Then he reaches under the counter.

"No, no, don't make me do—"

I can't finish the sentence. He's got a gun on me now. Snub-nose, .38 special. Stainless steel, black rubber grip. Looks so small in his paws. It can perforate me from two feet away. He's a little over three.

"Bullshit," he says. "Now put your hands up, slowly now."

He flicks the gun upward, motioning. Closes the distance. Outside, I can see our stolen car, your future dimming beneath the gas station's lights. Can see you and the things she'll do when she catches us. And she will. She never sleeps.

I duck. Never been strong, but I've always been quick. Rising up, I hit the checkout counter. Catch the divider, folding it upwards, his arm atop it. I don't hear a gunshot but he still has hands. He grunts, grabs me by the collar. First punch grazes my ear. Second splits my lips.

My hands find a jar of spare change. *Help the Boys and Girls of the Navajo Nation!* I can only help you, my son. So I swing it right into this kind Navajo's face. Break glass, break bone, send pennies and dimes rolling. Then he's on the floor, groaning, and I'm prying the .38 from his fingers, accidentally breaking his thumb.

"I'm so sorry," I tell him. I might even be crying. But I have his keys now, have him wrapped in bungie cords, and I'm turning out the lights. *Sorry! We're closed* reads the sign. One day I'll send him a letter. One day I'll send him his car keys and some money for his trouble. An old story I've told, again and again. My life: one long public apology tour.

I switch cars. Put you in the back seat of his pick-up. Ford F-150. Good vehicle, safe and strong. Wish I could be too.

Then we hit the road.

Son, I want to tell you that I'm a good person, that I'm a good father. That this is all for you. Selling my soul to buy you a future. Maybe someday you'll understand. We'll sit on a white sand beach, let the warm water lap at our feet. I'll pass you a beer and I'll tell you about your mother. Tell you what a demon she is. Tell you the truth.

And perhaps you'll believe me.

But if you don't, I won't care. You'll be free of this future; you can chose your own past.

3:13 AM. HALF TANK. CROSS OVER FROM NEW MEXICO INTO Arizona near Lupton. Tried to stay of the interstate. But I messed up. Left your diapers in the old car. Have take I-40.

I park us in the back of the truck stop. Big Andy's reads the sign. Big rigs roll past. Everything's big in America. Big drinks and big snacks, big skies and big people. A big country too, but why is it so hard to disappear?

Inside, the neon burns my eyes. I wash up in the bathroom, Dress my swollen right eye. Spit blood. The Navajo got in some good licks. Good for him. Scars will give way to strength, I tell myself. To heal we need to get hurt.

I buy a 4-pack of Red Bull. Beef Jerky. Funyuns and a screwdriver. I buy you new diapers, your favorite infant formula. I ponder the baby on the package. Is he old now? Is he dead? Men can make life and take life, but we can't feed it or nourish it, not without help. We're disposable by design.

I check your diapers. No need to change them. So I let you sleep. We've had a long drive today. A longer drive tomorrow. But first, we need to take precautions.

3:44 AM. REST STOP. I PARK US AT THE EDGE OF THE VISITOR'S CENTER. The sky is full dark. Crickets and vending machines hum to each other. A man walks his dog among the dry grass while deer watch from the brush. He takes his dog the long way around the park.

So I scurry over to his car. Takes me sixty-seconds to unscrew his license plate, swap out the Navajo's. The driver won't notice. Few do. How often do we check our plate? We're all too busy. How often do we see what's so obvious before us?

I screw his New Mexico plates onto our F-150. *LAND OF ENCHANTMENT* says the slogan. Enchantment is just another word for spell. Another word for—

"DO YOU BELIEVE IN MAGIC?" SHE ASKED ME, AS WE WALKED ALONG the waterfront. The harbor was quiet, the lakes beyond a bed of diamonds. Summer's end always felt sad. Tourists were packing up, boats were being dry-docked. Was she, too, going to leave?

"Depends," I said. "What kind of magic?"

"The only kind," she replied, with a sunset twinkle in her eyes. "The old kind."

"Ah, like Houdini?"

"Try... much older," she smiled. Sometimes it felt like she was too. I've always liked older women; always admired focused wisdom.

"Give me a for instance."

"For instance... that there's another world beneath this surface. That with the right words, the proper offerings, we can reach into that world?"

I remember that moment. She was looking at the horizon, I was looking at her face. How things would change. And I remember laughing. Remember how soft her hand felt in mine as I answered: "Sounds like witchcraft."

She nodded. "And what if it is?"

"Are you a witch?"

"And what if I am?"

I placed a finger beneath her chin. I turned her face towards mine. Freckles like stars on a pale sea. Eyes of kind fire. "Well, I suppose I'd demand proof," I said, thinking I was so slick, so smooth. All I wanted was a kiss.

And then she turned her chin away. To the shimmering lake. Pointed into the sunlight upon the water. A flick of her wrist, a squeeze of the finger.

And from the light she plucked a golden ring.

I couldn't believe it. There it was, a sunlit band. Two simple lines entwined that she laid in the palm of her hand. And then she was on a knee, soft eyes looking up, cranberry lips asking: "Will you marry me?"

"No!" I SCREAM. THE LICENSE PLATE HANGS, *LAND OF ENCHANTMENT* askew. I ball my fist, punch the fender. Skin splits. The pain brings a fast end to another one of her lies. Another one of your mother's memory traps.

I can feel her now, her golden gaze swinging south west. She is in New Mexico; she is close to the Navajo. Two hundred miles. We must hurry.

"Hey bro, can you keep it down," says a shirtless man stepping out of his camper. "You're waking my kids."

I look at him. We could have been them, that happy family. Skimming the roads of America, these highways of lies. Never dipping beneath.

"So wake your children," I say. "Tell them to cherish their days. Cherish each other, all of you."

"Wacko," he mumbles. I don't stay to hear the rest. I climb in our pick-up truck, glance at you bundled up in the back. I cherish you as only the hunted do.

Then we hit the road.

5:55 AM. SOMEWHERE PAST SHOW LOW. WE DOUBLE BACK, FOLLOW the 60 east until we hit 191. We can thread it southbound, between Tucson and the New Mexico border. Best idea so far. If you want to make God laugh, they say to tell him your plans. Never met a god but laid with a devil. Best plan is to be unpredictable.

But it only works for so long.

Sunrise. I rub my eyes. Driving into daybreak reduces the highway to shadows. I reduce our speed. Roll down the window. Let the desert breeze refresh me, wake me up. Soon, it will be hot. We'll have to cross at night.

Try not to think of her, I tell myself. Just try not to think. Just focus on the road, focus on your future. You, a swaddled angel, born from the earth. Born from me. Born from your mother's putrid womb and a soft bed of ash. Everything's symbolic, she once told me. Everything's a recipe. With the proper seed and soil, there's nothing you can't grow.

"No," I tell myself. "Stop thinking of her!" Punch the dashboard, rub my eyes. You begin to cry so I fumble with the stereo. Find a CD of Navajo hip hop, end up tossing it out the window. Scan the radio instead. Empty stations, empty scrublands. Nothing but desert. Then: FM 94.1 and music.

Irene Cera. *What A Feeling.* The song's just starting, but I know the tune. Flashdance. Saw it when I was a kid, so I sing along. "Take your passion, and make it happen." Good sentiment; details unclear. But it's enough to keep me awake.

Next song: *Sultans of Swing.* Dire Straits. Always admired the chords. Mastered superbly. On a good stereo, with a proper source, you can hear the pick sliding against the steel strings.

Then it's over. Insurance commercial. "When something bad happens, Liberty Health will be there for you." Another lie we all agree to believe. Every well eventually runs dry.

The road turns. The rising sun falls behind distant mesas. Dawn drapes the desert in long shadows. Beautiful world. Can't wait to show you more of it.

I yawn. Fumble with the cruise control. Wish I hadn't hit the Navajo. Seemed like a nice guy.

Next song: *Fields of Gold.* Sting. Ten chords into it, and another one of her traps is sprung. Hooks sink in, deep this time. It was the last happy memory; first time I lied to my wife.

"TIL DEATH DO WE PART, INDEED," I SAID. THEN SHE SLIPPED THE ring on my finger. It pinched, tight, the gold seemed to bite.

"And now, as a duly appointed minister of the, uh, shit, what's the church?" My brother stammered. He'd flubbed his lines, but no one cared. It was a small wedding, friends and family, neither of which we had in abundance. We found the DJ on Craigslist. My brother was ordained online, the night before. "Well, heck, as an internet minister," he said, and everyone laughed. "And, by the power invested in me by the great state of Arizona, I know pronounce you husband and wife. Kiss her, you lucky bastard."

And I did. Held it for what seemed like forever. Felt a little bit of her tongue. Then my brother was raising our hands, bride and groom, and the twenty-four friends and family in attendance were on their feet and clapping. Late September. She had wanted to get married fast. That's how love happens, sometimes.

"And when will you be moving back to Wyoming?" Aunt Gladys asked as we made the rounds.

"By the new year, at latest," my wife said. Wife. How odd that word sounded. Never thought I'd be married. Always thought I'd be a famous rock star. Somehow, the opposite occurred. "Unfortunately, my job can't wait any longer," she said. "I've stretched my sabbatical a bit far."

"And just what is it you do again dear?" Aunt Gladys asked. "Something with research?"

"She's a historian," I said.

"Well, more of a student of history," my wife corrected.

"Good for you," Gladys added. "We're always looking for answers, aren't we?"

"Something like that," my wife said. Four months now, and she was still a mystery. Maybe that's what I fell in love with: the negative space. What my heart hoped to unlock and my mind filled in on its own.

The microphone buzzed. "And now, if you could turn your attention to the patio," my brother said, channeling his inner NASCAR announcer. "It's time for their first dance as a married couple. Lovebirds, come on over."

She took me by the hand, leading me to the patio. Ikea lanterns form a warm canopy. Tiki torches hissed and spat. My hand slipped around her waist and she pulled me close. All eyes on us. I felt my heart beating against her chest. Never felt hers.

"Tell me one thing," I whispered, as the DJ hurried to his

station and fumbled with buttons. "The night we met, in the elevator. Why did you say that?"

She laid her head across my shoulder. "Say what?"

I gazed across the patio. My grandfather, with his cigar by the fountain. My brother, holding his Pomeranian. The pond, burbling. Everyone was waiting for our song to start.

"I told you: 'you couldn't smoke.' And you said something like: 'rules didn't apply to people us.'"

The DJ found the right button, the speakers let out a metallic twang. Sting began to sing about *Fields of Gold* as everyone stared with love in their eyes.

"Because it's true," she whispered: "We're one in a billion."

FLAPFLAPFLAPFLAP! RUMBLE STRIPS RIP ME BACK INTO THE PRESENT. I yank the wheel to the left, back onto the highway. The pick-up drifts. Something slides. For a heartbeat, my worst fears seem to appear: you're not buckled in back there. I reach between the seats, hand falling on plastic. I see the seatbelt. I breath a sigh.

Then the radio changes. Same station, new sound. Sting's smooth voice turns a warbling cry. The guitar chords stretch and bend. Everything becomes crystal.

"No one will believe you," her voice says, over the radio. "You know that, Jack. This is foolish, this is madness. And worst of all, honey, this is dangerous."

I can feel her gaze upon me, golden and focused. Gods, I can feel your mother's stare. She's crossed over into Arizona, now she's slowing down, turning around. Others are with her, eyes of shadowed mirror. She's using this song to get a bead on me, casting out hooked fingers, rending the desert.

The song. Behind her clear words lay's Sting's broken chorus. I change the station. FM 92.7. Static. White noise. Her fingers shatter with a hiss.

And then her voice breaks in again. "You really think you can tune me out? You really think I'll release you?"

"I'm not asking," I say, knuckles squeezing the steering wheel. "And yes, actually, I think I can tune you out."

"I'm coming—"

I press the volume knob in, silencing the radio, silencing my wife. Peace and quiet. I can feel the hooks beginning to retract. Can see cold hands clawing dumbly at the mesas.

I drive past an electronic road sign: AMBER ALERT: PULL OVER! STOP NOW! JACK YOU CANNOT RUN!

I push the pick-up to 110.

11:21 AM. MCDONALDS. I PULL IN TO THE PARKING LOT. CAN'T USE the drive through; can't risk radio interference. So exhausted I can hardly stand. I leave you in the pick-up with the A/C running. Outside, it's 115 degrees. How do people live here?

Inside: everything's egg white and lemon yellow. Everything's sterile. Ronald McDonald looks at me with disgust. I agree, Ronnie, my reflection's a mess.

The key is to avoid human interaction. The key is to see but hardly be seen. I step up to the self-service computer, press the screen. Doesn't matter what I'm ordering. Just need the calories and the caffeine. Large Iced Coffee, Two Big Macs, Two Fries. Press purchase. Stuff the cash in and take a number.

A sudden reverie: the drive up to Wyoming, the pit stop outside Laramie. "What happened to old fashioned service?" your mother had asked. "These touch screens are impersonal, don't you agree?"

"No," I whisper, driving my thumbs into my temples. If I could pry her out I would lobotomize myself right here. To forget her I would gladly go mad. We build a prison of memories, call it *life*, then try to break free.

"Hell, fella, it looks like you broke it," the customer behind me says. A handyman on lunch break. A Bowie knife and ball-peen hammer hangs from his tool-belt. Welcome to Arizona. "Looks like the computer has a crush on you," he chuckles. Another customer laughs at the joke. Good for them. I don't bother looking at the screen, her words filling the pixels.

"Order seventy-eight!" the cheerful cashier calls out. Wouldn't be so cheerful if she was running from a demon. "Order seventy-nine!" Focus on the food. When you're famished, every meal's a feast. When you're a prisoner, freedom can suffocate.

The phone behind the counter rings. The day manager answers, furrows his brow. Looks around the store, searching for someone. I turn sideways, try to flatten against the wall. Try to become invisible. I consider running.

"Order eighty!" The cashier chirps. I grab the bag, the coffee. Slide the receipt across the metal counter.

"Sir, I think there's a call for you," the manager says, but I ignore him. "Sir? Excuse me. Sir?"

Outside, heat hits my face, exhaustion baking into me. I wolf down a handful of fries. Wrap my grease-slick fingers around the ice coffee and pour it down my throat. A family spots me, walks the long way past.

I tell myself one day I won't be him, that man parents pull their kids away from on instinct. I won't be the creep. If you have nothing worth carrying forward there's no reason to keep moving. You're my only momentum.

I'm halfway to the parking lot when I see the state policeman.

Eyes behind aviator glasses, hands behind the wheel. Ford Interceptor SUV, fast vehicle. No way to outrun it. His glare swings between the computer screen in his car, and the stolen F-150. Screen, pick-up, screen. He hasn't spotted me.

I freeze; deer in headlights. Silently panic. The fries threaten to leave my lips. My bladder boils. It's fifty feet back to McDonald's, fifty feet between the trooper and me. Sudden movement and he'll notice. Cops sense danger, react.

And so do fathers.

I drop the food. Run. Wave, screaming: "Officer! Officer! Please help, he's in there! In the-the-the... *bathroom!* He's got a knife. Officer!"

The trooper blinks, mustache twitching. In his silver shades, I see my own insane reflection. Best performance of my life. Behind those silver shades, fear spreads across his face.

"Whoa whoa, hold on a minute—"

"He has a knife!" I point, I wave. I stutter to seal the deal. "In the bathroom. The ma-ma-man in the handyman uniform. He's hurting him real bad, officer. God, he's killing him!"

A pause. A nod. Something in the officer teeters over a chaotic abyss. "Wait here." Then the wheels scream an inch past my feet. The Ford Interceptor makes a tight u-turn, swings into the handicapped spot. He's a big trooper, and he's out now, on his feet, running into the McDonald's.

And I'm running away.

I yank open the pick-up door. Find you in the back. Promised I wouldn't leave you. God, what a mess I've made. Can't take this truck anymore. I grab your carrier, grab a bottle of water, your formula, your diapers.

There's not a lot in this town. A pockmark on the highway, just the essentials. Fast Food. Fuel. Motels. And plenty of trucks.

I spot a hole in the chain link fence behind McDonalds and climb through. Place you down and gently carry you on. I'll carry you forever. Just have to carry us forward. Just need to maintain momentum, cause once it stops it's all lost.

Gas station. Trucker side. Spot a diesel truck, all chrome and sleek. Spot a bone white 18-wheeler, flames painted on. We don't want any of those. New trucks, high insurance policies. We need the one that looks like it's falling apart.

Bingo. There's an old Peterbilt 379, all rust and dust. Deadhead today, no trailer.

I carry you around to the driver's side. Climb the step, peer in. Two eyes gaze back from the shadows. A worn cowboy hat floats over them. Tan skin, salt and pepper beard. The trucker rolls down his window.

"Please just listen to me," I say. "I need a ride. That's all. Just a ride anywhere out of town, okay?" I hold your carrier up. Hate to use you for pity but we need pity to survive.

The trucker studies me. "*¿Qué quiere?*"

"A ride, please," I repeat, but I realize it's hopeless. His eyes say what words fail to convey. We don't speak the same language. "My wife... she's coming."

"*Sí, sí. ¿Necesita que lo lleve, amigo?*"

"I don't... I don't understand," I say. "My son and I... we need a ride. Uh, *necesito* vroom vroom. I have money." I show it to him. A handful of sweaty twenties, tens, fives, a fifty here and there. I hear distant sirens. Wish I'd paid attention in Spanish class. God, I'm so tired.

"*No necesito su dinero, amigo. Se ve muy mal.*" Whatever he said it seems to amuse him. I can tell he's judging me. "*Vamos a México. ¿Le parece bien?*"

"Mexico?" That I recognize. Panic mutates, morphs into a vague hope. "Yes! I mean... *Sí, sí.*"

"*Suba, por favor,*" he says and opens the passenger door.

I climb inside, the cab redolent of old cigarettes and sweat. I can almost taste the cracked leather. So happy I almost cry. A quick glance at the distant McDonalds where a second Ford Interceptor pulls up, lights flashing.

"Thank you," I whisper, and try to hand him the money. He takes a fifty and gives the rest back. Doesn't want it. I wouldn't either.

"*Compadre, te ves muy mal,*" he laughs.

"*Sí,*" I say. I have no idea what he's saying. Doesn't matter. All that matters is we're starting to move. "*Sí.*"

He looks at me, shakes his head. "*Compadre, deberías tomar una siesta. Puedes dormir hasta que lleguemos.*"

I just nod and smile. "*Sí, sí, sí.*"

3:44 PM. OUTSIDE COCHISE. THE HIGH DESERT STRETCHES IN EVERY direction, brambles and dry death. Signs warn: *DEER CROSSING! Next 45 miles.* The sky's so wide it might dip down and swallow us.

The truck driver smokes cigarette after cigarette. He saved our life. I don't even know his name. Too afraid to ask. Instead, I point to a photograph taped to his dashboard. Old, faded. Almost melted on.

"Is that your family? Uh, *familia?*"

"*Sí, sí,*" he says, and taps the photograph. A young boy, no older than twelve. A woman, forty at most. Us, in another life, a better life. "*Esta era mi esposa. Y este es mi hijo Juan. Él ya no está con nosotros.*"

"Juan?"

"*Sí, Juan. Murió el año pasado.*" He gestures to the blue sky above, draws a line. His son is a pilot.

"Your wife," I say. "Uh, beautiful. *Bonito? Es muy bonito.*"

He laughs, shakes his head. "*Es una perra miserable.*" Then he points to my hand. To the gold band around my finger. "*¿Y tu esposa?*" Is it a question? I think it's a question.

"My wife?"

"*Sí.*"

Where to begin? First time I can talk about your mother, really talk, and not worry what someone will think. First time I can speak the truth.

"She's a demon," I say, and it feels good to put words to her. "A succubus, a mazikeen. She's a hellspawn, and she's fixated on me because my seed is strong. You believe that?"

"*Sí,*" he says, and lights up another cigarette.

I laugh. Now that I'm talking I find I can't stop. I can't lose this momentum. He needs to know everything, to bear witness, to hear what haunts me.

"See, demons don't procreate like we do. It's more like like fish or insects. You know what a homunculus is? A botchbaby? It's when... get this *amigo*, it's when a demon takes your seed— takes your *essence*—mixes it with hers and puts it in an object to gestate. But it can only gestate under ash, right? Those are the rules, the recipe. Most botchbabies don't take, not with humans. Can't cross-pollinate. Dogs can sniff out cancers, and demons can sniff out a mate. But it's one in a billion, really. And, most of all, you have to give it to them willingly, see? You have to agree."

"*Sí*," he says, and takes a drag on the cigarette. "*Sí*."

He sees. I show him my ring. Show him how deep it's dug in, these teeth beneath this gold loop. "Your seed, you have give it by choice. And I did. I said yes. And when it didn't take I did it again. And again. I'm... so... tired. And I just want to protect him, see?" I point to you in the back seat. He sees.

"*Sí*," he says, fingers shaking. "*¡Sí! ¡Sí!*"

He sees nothing. He's placating me, just letting me run my gums. I wipe my eyes. I thought I was laughing, turns out I've cried. I don't care. Our whole story has poured forth, at least someone will know. This great weight has been lifted.

Then the helicopter swoops down and rattles the truck.

There's silver and black, the words: ARIZONA STATE POLICE on the side. Glinting lights on the far horizon behind us: red and blue. I can feel her stare, she's so close to us now.

"You have to go!" I tell the truck driver. "Faster! Please go faster!"

"*¡Sí! ¡Sí!*" he says, and eyes the helicopter. Another low pass, then it banks a thousand yards down the highway. Dust swirls as it starts to land. Behind us: the cops are closing in. Three at least. Silver and black Interceptors, blue and red lights.

"Faster!" I shout. "Faster!"

"*Oye, lárgate con tu locura para otro lado.*"

But he doesn't go faster. The truck begins to slow. I reach into your baby carrier. Don't want to hurt the driver, just need some motivation. The snub nose .38 glints in the long daylight.

"Oye, gringo, estás más loco que una cabra. Yo no voy a morir hoy aquí—"

Then he opens the door and throws himself out. 50 mph, and his body cartwheels into the sagebrush. Everything drifts into the oncoming lane. I seize the wheel, jerk the truck back to the right.

"Pull your vehicle over now!" comes an angry voice over the megaphone. "Slow down and pull over, or we will use force!"

The truck's buckling, left, right, left. I slide over, into the driver's seat. Too many buttons, too much to handle. I stomp the gas.

Six hundred yards ahead. The helicopter settles on the road. Five hundred yards. Two cops scramble out. They throw something across the grey highway. Something glistening, something sharp.

Four hundred yards. Someone else gets out of the helicopter. No uniform, no hat. Her hair is back in a ponytail, but I recognize her color anywhere. That's your mother up there. Those are her scarlet curls.

Three hundred yards. I look back at you, my son. I want to tell you how much I love you, to tell you I'm sorry. There's a better world out there, one we were so close to reaching. I can't take you there now, I can no longer protect you.

But I can protect others.

Two hundred yards. The cops are raising their guns. The spike strip shimmers. My wife walks out. Past the police, past the metal teeth. Onto the highway. I can almost see her eyes now; I can feel her golden glare.

One hundred yards. Just your mother and me now, just the two of us honey. Nothing between us but hot pavement. Nothing but this void we're closing. Here I come, five tons of rusty steel, ready for a final embrace. She said she'd lived for three centuries. Bragged she'd fucked Napoleon. How will she feel when she's smeared across blacktop?

The first gunshot shatters the side mirror. The second catches the driver's side hood. A red spray paints the window. The wheel rips free from my hands as the left tire bursts. Those aren't bullets hitting the car, those are antlers.

Fifty yards.

Deer are leaping from the dry brush and onto the highway. Throwing themselves in front of the truck. A whole suicidal herd, brown and white and bursting red. The pavement a slurry, the truck loses traction. Thirty meters, and the last thing I see is your mother's face.

Then the world teeters and tips and flips all around. I see sky, and then ground. See a maelstrom of antlers and branches, shattering, scattering, all sliding sideways.

And then, with a groan... it stops.

The engine hisses, sputters its last. I taste coolant, taste the hot desert. See burgundy smears, and a still-kicking deer embraced by the grill. High above: the sun shines down through the buckled passenger door. Steel settles with a final sigh, and I realize: we didn't die.

She did this. She summoned the deer; she summoned the police. Here come their wailing sirens, their distant babbling: "You see that herd of 'em? My God, where'd they come from? Woo-eee, lucky day!"

No such luck. Not for us. I brush the glass away, climb up the sideways cab. You're in the back seat; you're still strapped in. I pull your carrier out. Hold you close.

Then I find the gun.

Feet rattle about the undercarriage. Hands tug the driver's side door. The windshield is a webwork of cracked glass. They're climbing up, closing in.

"I'm so sorry," I whisper to you. "I won't let her take you."

A shadow fills the passenger window. "He's got a gun!" someone shouts. Everything shifts outside the vehicle. Holsters unsnap. The world is holding its breath and only you have the courage to cry.

"Please, please, just let me talk to him," I hear her shouting. "Please, he'll listen to me!" she begs.

I won't listen, won't hear her words. I won't let us go back. I'm going to sing you a lullaby now, but it'll have to be loud.

"Jack, Jack, it's me honey, just listen." There's fear in her voice. Feels good to have such power. "These men, they don't want to hurt you. No one does honey."

"You do!" I scream. "You won't let us leave. You won't let me take him."

A shadow passes by the white windshield. I can smell her sweat, smell her perfume. Want to smell her tears too, before we never smell again. "Jack, please just talk to me, okay? Tell me what you want."

"I'm... I'm so tired," I tell her. "I just want to sleep. I just want you to leave us, please."

"You can sleep, okay? I promise you, Jack, I'll let you sleep as long as you want. You can sleep for a weeks and weeks, in that big comfy bed of ours, okay? Doesn't that sound nice?"

A distant whisper: Yes, it sure does.

Separated by broken glass, yet never felt closer. It's all a lie. There are no happy endings, not with demons in this world. "You can't have him," I tell her. "He's not yours to take. He's my child too."

I hoist your carrier up. Put the blanket over your face, press the gun to the fabric. I can't look in your eyes as you leave this world. Can't let you see that it's me who is sending you off.

"Jack," she whispers. "Our son is gone."

She's lying. It's all she does. Every fiber inside me screams the truth. Every instinct implores me to squeeze. And yet, beneath it all: a seed of doubt. Beneath the blanket: your sleeping face. I tell myself to pull this trigger. To believe in myself; no one else ever will. Trust my heart. Or else she'll win. There are worse fates than being undone. When did everything get so soft at the edges?

"Jack, please," she whispers. "That's not our son in there. You know that."

No. I close my eyes. Let my fingers finish where my mind has unraveled. I press my hand to the blanket. Then I lift it.

I feel your forehead. Feel your smooth cheeks. Feel your hair, your tiny ears, and the seams that hold you together. I feel your flawless effigy. You're a perfect child; you've never cried. I see it now; it all came from me. Acrylic eyes tell me what I can no longer hide. Tried to save your future yet broke myself along the way.

I put the blanket over you. Tenderly place your carrier among the bed of glass. I want to tell you it will be all right, but you can't hear me, can't listen. I want to tell you everything, but you'll never understand. This truck isn't all that's shattered.

I leave you among the wreckage. Then I climb out, into the desert heat, and I let them take me away.

JUNE 21ST. OUTSIDE CHEYENNE.

I have not thought of you in months. And this is good, they tell me, and I shouldn't be embarrassed. They tell me I shouldn't be ashamed. Still, I hide you away, safe and secure. You are not a metaphor.

It's not often that one goes a little bit mad. Or that one causes an interstate chase and an AMBER alert. My name is still in the news.

Your mother helps me recover. Says she's happy to work her magic. She knows how to plead and when to throw herself at the mercy of the state. Knows the right people to hire. Lilith will be paying my fines and legal fees for years. And I am a lucky guy, they all tell me. I owe her everything, they say. And I tell myself: I'm starting to agree. Bitter pills I often swallow.

"What did I tell you?" Lilith whispers as we lay tangled in the cool sheets. "You're one in a billion, Jack. I'm not letting you get away."

We let our hands explore each other. We make love for the first time since my schism. First time in months I've seen Lilith without clothes. Now, I look at my wife with fresh eyes; she looks at me with the softness of an old friend. "Let's make a baby," she whispers. "Let's try again."

So I agree. She helps me remember; she helps me forget. And for a while, I do. Forget my name, forget my face, forget everything as she pulls me inside. I am no longer Jack. I'm no longer a failed musician, a failed father. I am simply hers. Nails rend the flesh of my back. I collapse upon her, exhausted and spent.

And now it's over. She climbs off, runs a sharp finger down my chest. Smiles her sanguine smile. I almost think she might ask me for a cigarette, but she no longer smokes, not since we met.

Robe on, she lingers by the door. For a moment, the sunlight through the curtains hits her eyes at a funny angle. For a moment, they're golden rings and two black slits. She tells me she'll bring me something to eat. Tells me to rest. It's important I stay strong. Then she leaves and tells me no more.

In the stillness, I think of you. What would you look like now? And if you'd start crawling? And I ask why can't I picture your face? It hangs behind grey gauze, like our two days on the road and much that followed. And I wonder: who carved these odd words into the frame of this bed? Who put these chains on my legs?

The sun is low now, the daylight's long. My appetite's returning. I see movement outside, crows circling above. Countless deer approaching our wooden fence, a calm audience. There is the old ash tree in our yard, and a fresh hole in the soil beneath it.

And there is your mother, with you in her arms. Your chest is open. Stuffing flutters in white ribbons, fresh cotton upon damp earth. I wonder what Lilith is doing.

So I bang the window, but the glass is strong. So I call out, but you never hear me. So I watch.

Watch Lilith's form, dog-like and ravenous, digging in the dirt. Watch her fingers, with too many joints; her knees, bent back the wrong way. I watch her hike her skirt up past her hips. Watch her reach back and pull something wet and glistening. Something we both made. I watch it squirm and curl and cry with fresh life. And I watch her stuff it into your chest.

Then I watch her bury you beneath the ash tree. Watch her lay a dirt blanket tenderly. All I can do is watch with wonder. I wonder why the door is locked. Wonder why there are bars across the window. And, most of all, I wonder: how long until I can hold you again?

BOOK SIX

A BRIEF TREATISE ON MARKET ECOLOGIES, VOLUME III

Be advised: Due to a mishap with cheap and illegal enchantments, Volumes I and IV have yet to be written. Volume II was eaten by a surly pug.

— THE ARCHIVIST

A BRIEF TREATISE ON MARKET
ECOLOGIES, VOL. III

"**M**arvelous, just marvelous," the old seamstress declared, and placed the glass orb back on the table. "I'm just not sure I have use for such a thing."

Gwendolyn forced a polite smile to her lips. "Well, thank you for your time." Then, she returned the orb to its display case that hung upon her booth's decorative tree. "And a happy Sun's Day to you."

The seamstress shuffled off, joining the afternoon crowds. T'was a day of noises, a day of trinkets and food. Here, a squealing pig ran squeezed down the thoroughfare. There, a furious butcher gave chase. In the neighboring booth sat Enid the Blind, her hand-crafted pocket clocks all stuck at 5:55.

And across the way, Barnaby the baker fanned his hot oven. His apprentice chalked up the sign: BARNABY'S FINEST MEAT PIES! *SOLD OUT!* There went the final pie, heading home in the arms of a hungry constable.

The town's clocktower struck five. T'was the final hour of the New Avalon Market, and all was not well.

"What is that, mummy?" squeaked a small voice from the other side of the display tree. A little girl looked up, her lips cherry-stained, fingers clutching half-eaten lolligum. Gwendolyn could see Rickard's booth shutting down; he was all out of sweets. Every belly under twelve was filled with his lolligum treats.

Rickard always had the right idea, Gwendolyn thought. Always ahead of the curve. And here Gwendolyn was, just struggling to keep up. Last year, she had shown up with a box of kaleidoscopes, yet the children had all wanted phenakistiscopes. This year, she'd crafted phenakistiscopes but now the lads had their noses in zoetropes. Now the phenakistiscopes sat inside her booth, a crate of failures, another venture she could hardly pronounce.

"Well dear, I suppose it's a tree," the girl's mother said, squinting at Gwendolyn's display. "A stunted willow, I reckon."

"A new world cypress, actually," Gwendolyn corrected. "Like a willow, but more sensitive beneath the bark. And you're right; this cypress is stunted. Not by cheap magic, but by rope binding—"

"No mummy," the little girl cut in. "I mean what is *that?*" She lifted a sugary finger upward. "Is it a wee dragon in a snow globe?"

From Gwendolyn's side the tree was all needles and twine. From the customer's view, the cypress displayed nine pruned branches, opened like a French fan. Glass orbs hung from each branch, nine terrariums in total. Each contained earth and rock, water and air, plants and minerals, worms to eat them, tiny fish to feed, and a single creature living in this delicate ecology.

"This is a terrarium," Gwendolyn said, removing an orb from the display branch. "And this fantastic thing, well, tell me you've seen a peacock?"

The little girl nodded. Gwendolyn nested the orb in a display stand at the edge of the table.

"Take one-part peacock, one-part garden snake, shrink it down to sparrow size, and *voila!* A shimmerling."

Through the terrarium's warped glass, the little girl's eyes were two moons of wonder. Inside, the shimmerling fluttered and settled on a mossy pebble. Its rainbow tail: curling and unfurling.

Its blue tongue: flicking in out, in out. Atop its feathered head two doe-like eyes peered back.

What good luck! Gwendolyn thought. Most little girls preferred the lacy gills of the guplet fish. Most boys favored the shock turtles or the fiery phoenix. But this little girl had exquisite taste. Her eyes were on the priciest terrarium, by far. And Gwendolyn spied a gold bracelet on the mother's wrist. This family could probably buy the whole tree.

Gwendolyn leaned in. "Tell me, have you ever heard a shimmerling giggle?"

Pigtails bouncing, the girl shook her head. Perfect, Gwendolyn thought. Hidden below the table sat an old walking cane. Carefully, Gwendolyn lined the knob up with the terrarium above. A loud cough, a quick thump from below. The child never saw what the shimmerling felt.

"*Mew!*" the shimmerling chirped. "*Mew! Mew!*"

"It's laughing mummy," the little girl clapped. "Look! It's laughing! Oh mummy, can we get one, *please?*"

Gwendolyn's toes curled. The sale was close. The market wouldn't be a total loss. She could catch up on her Finishing School debt, pay off this cypress display. Perhaps hire an apprentice or rent a shopfront out on Pemberton Way.

"Well, I suppose dear," the mother said. "It is rather cute."

"All our terrariums are unique," Gwendolyn said. "The moss comes from the lost colonies, the water imported from the far east. The glass is Oregon blue, heat treated to five hundred degrees. No magic used, see? Feel the hand crafting. Go on."

The woman's gloved hand caressed the lumpy glass orb. Inside, the shimmerling chased the glimmering ring on her thumb.

"Well, it certainly is original."

"And that's all I hope to create." For a moment, Gwendolyn thought those were the most honest words she'd muttered all weekend.

"I suppose it is important to support the arts," the woman

said. Then, a beautiful thing: her gloved hand shifted from the terrarium to her lady's satchel. "Do you take gold? A writ of credit, perhaps?"

"Buyer's choice, of course," Gwendolyn said, adding: "Though for writs, I'm afraid the bank charges an extra five percent."

With her gloved hand the woman dismissed the fee as if fanning off a bad odor. Five percent? Hardly a bother. For Gwendolyn, it was a month's rent, and that was living five to a flat. Still, she knew the truth: the bank had dropped the fee to two and a quarter.

"And you don't need to feed them, these shimmer-things?"

"Shimmerlings, mummy."

"No, it's a perfect loop." Gwendolyn traced her hand from the top of the terrarium on down. "Bugs feed the shimmerling. The waste feeds the soil. The worms and moss filter it, the water gestates new bugs. The fish and fungi clean it all up. Everything's in balance—"

And then it wasn't. With a careless swipe, Gwendolyn bumped the orb. She snatched it back an inch from the table's edge. "*Mew! Mew!*" cried the shimmerling. "*Mew! Mew!*"

"Oh mummy I thought it was going to break!"

"Not a worry, this is thrice-blown glass." Gwendolyn tapped the terrarium. "It'd take more than a thump in the mud to break it, yes it would."

"Shimmerling..." The rich woman furrowed a well-plucked brow. "Didn't I hear something about them? It was my sister, wasn't it?"

"Mummy, look!" the little girl said. "It's scared!" This girl was clever, Gwendolyn realized. Shimmerlings neither laughed nor giggled. They made one noise, and only when angry.

"*Mew!*" the shimmerling cried. "*Mew! Mew!*"

"They're aggressive," the woman said, hand leaving her satchel. "In the wild, that is. I remember now: shimmerlings are quite violent."

"In their natural state, uh, they do display some aggression, yes," Gwendolyn said. "Mild, truthfully. But these are toy shimmerlings. This terrarium air is at twenty percent. They're perfectly docile. Sleepy, really."

The satchel was closing, a gloved hand fastening the snaps. Gwendolyn saw it all recede: The storefront. The apprentice. The first and only sale.

"I'm sorry," the woman said. "But I can't have such a dangerous thing in our house. After all, our floors are marble."

Of course they are, Gwendolyn thought. This woman had never slept on a floor, five to a flat, just to make rent. But Gwendolyn had one more idea.

"Wait!" Gwendolyn called out, hand digging into her crate. "Can I interest you in a phenakistiscope?"

SALES: 0

"BETTER LUCK TO YA, DEARY," SAID ENID THE BLIND, AS SHE TRIED TO shake hands with Gwendolyn's cypress. The market was over, the booths were all coming down. Tired guplets pirouetted inside their glass prison. The shimmerlings whined: *"Mew! Mew! Mew!"*

"And remember: sometimes, it's just a matter of timing," Enid continued. "I often sell the most pocket clocks just before six. But if I went home early? Oy..." She gave the cypress a shrug. Who knows?

Enid started to pick up Gwendolyn's crate, but Gwendolyn handed her the proper one. Only a few of the blind woman's creations sat inside. She'd sold most of a her stock.

"You know they don't work," Gwendolyn said. "Your clocks. They're all stuck at 5:55."

Enid smiled at the wall. "They work well enough, if you're patient."

Then she was off, shuffling down the thoroughfare, cane in

one hand, crate of useless clocks in the other. Gwendolyn didn't despise the blind clockmaker, just her blind luck.

"You should try smiling more," Barnaby said, his oven resting in the back of the cart.

"Is that a fact?" Gwendolyn seethed.

"Indeed. Proven by sages and scientists alike." Barnaby wiped soot from his mustache and straightened his top hat. "Smiles... go miles." He tipped the brim. Gwendolyn didn't hate that obnoxious top hat either, just everything below it.

Stewing, she emptied a tankard of water into the base of the cypress. More than anything, she hated this fact: Barnaby was right. Last year, his booth had been a linen tent. Last fall, it was canvas. Today, it had been silk, and he had arrived in style, bicycling in on a penny farthing. Now, Barnaby could even afford an apprentice.

The tankard was empty, the tree properly watered. Gwendolyn felt a seed taking hold. "Barnaby, wait," Gwendolyn called out. "Can... Can I buy you a pint?"

"I'll... I'll let you in on a secret," he slurred, glancing back over his shoulder. Laughter suffused the tavern as the merchants toasted to the market's end. Foam glistened on Barnaby's handlebar mustache. With a hiccup he leaned in, hand falling on Gwendolyn's thigh. "Here it is... *hic* Here's the secret."

Getting him drunk had been simple enough. For each pint he swallowed she'd discreetly poured hers into the plants. After his third toast Barnaby had become his own drinking chum.

But the pie-monger's mitts were proving hard to contend with. Clumsy and calloused, they kept grasping at her bodice and bustle. She could see the rest of tonight. A steam carriage back to Barnaby's flat. Her bodice unclasped, train hiked to her hips. Barnaby, grunting and thrusting and poking about, his top hat still on as he quivered and collapsed.

"The secret is... You need... a strong... civil imprint."

She drew back. That was it? That was his big trick?

"I have a civil imprint, thank you very much. I'm active in the public square."

"Please. How many town criers echo your message? Have any newsboys carried your tale?"

"I... Well, no, I suppose. But I have a Tintype portrait. I just updated it last season."

"Last *season*?" He waved his hand. "First... No one's looking at Tintype anymore. Everyone beholds Autochrome. It's color! And second **hic** you need to autochrome a new picture each week. Two, if you want to get noticed."

"Two?" Gwendolyn gulped, reached for her pint. "How do you afford that? How do make time to sit?"

Barnaby chuckled, waxed mustache rising and falling. "Gwenny-dear, oh, you really are something special. **hic** I hardly have time to bake meat pies. Taking Autochrome pictures? The developing and letter-pressing alone... Good Goddess, who has such hours?"

"I don't... I don't understand."

Barnaby leaned in, grinning. "I buy pre-made pictures. Sometimes I send my apprentice to scour estate sales. They're not all portraitures, heavens no."

"You use other people's pictures?"

Barnaby nodded. "Deceased, mostly. Or the elderly, they're so easily beguiled." With a wave of his hand he dismissed any issues. It was a simple gesture, and yet in it she saw how little he thought of her. Rightly so, Gwendolyn supposed. She had hoped terrariums alone could support her. Hoped talent and good products would be the key. Yet here sat Barnaby, his fumbling hands at odds with that expensive top hat. Was all of his finery bought by deception? Were his meat pies baked with lies? And was her insistence on craft leading to artistic demise?

She drowned such thoughts in ale. Barnaby followed.

"Tomorrow," he gulped, "first thing, after I cook you breakfast.

We'll go to the public gallery. You'll see." His hand squeezed her thigh. "But first... we should hail a steam carriage, don't you think?"

THE PIE-MONGER WAS RIGHT, SHE REALIZED, AS THE GALLERY WALLS looked before her. Outside, the town went about its morning. Newsboys hawked freshly inked vellum. Criers shouted the day's latest gossip. Wild parakeets tweeted away.

Inside, the gallery was quiet. It was Moon's Day, most towns-folk were back at work. A few lonely viewers strolled about, taking in Autochrome pictures lining the walls.

The gallery rules were simple: entry was free to the public; the price was viewer information. Once registered, the gallery-master doled out ten wooden tokens. For each picture the viewer admired, they could leave a token. Those pictures with the most tokens stayed, those with the least were soon cycled out. Demand and supply, in perfect balance.

Gwendolyn found her Tintype picture, now months out of date. It sat near the back of gallery five. The photo had cost five shillings. Beneath it sat a dusty cup, and in it a single red token.

Eight Autochrome pictures stood before her now in gallery one. Each burst from the frame in vivid triplicate color.

The first, a profile: Barnaby's face looking back, his waxed mustache upturned. She tried not to recall last night's candlelit shadows, his head buried between her thighs. "You like this, don't you?" he had said, looking up at her. "You nasty tart, you!" Fresh disgust became anger when she saw the tokens below his Autochrome. His cup held a dozen at least.

Another picture: Barnaby posing by his iron oven.

The caption: *Candidly caught off guard whilst stoking the fires. Do what you love & you never work a day in your life!* 22 tokens sat in the cup beneath it. 22 gestures of admiration.

A third picture: a steaming meat pie, crusts singed black.

The caption: *"Missed steaks" happen. Thought I was baking beef, but it was chicken pie. Different meats, different heats, a bit too crispy but live + learn. Embrace accidents!* Gwendolyn counted 31 tokens.

A fourth picture: A young lad husking corn in a field, a woman in a bonnet helping him.

The caption: *Memory Mondays! Mum teaching me the trade. Life lesson: every mother was a lady once, treat every lady like she's your mother. Dignity, gents!*

Gwendolyn's hands curled into tight little fists. The cup was overflowing with tokens, too many to count.

On it went. Barnaby's Autochrome pictures were the most popular, but there were others as well. One series focused only on food. Another followed the exotic travels of a wealthy family. One collection of pictures was the narrative adventures of Mr. Tibbits, a corgi in a kilt. The caption: *For your weekly Tibbits Tales, sign up for our news scrolls! It's ruff without good legal advice! —Marlowe & Pembridge, Esq.*

Gwendolyn fumed. She wanted to tear them all down. Wanted to kick the token cups, smash the frames and scratch out the pictures. These merchants had twisted art into something grotesque.

The gallery-master shuffled past, a hooked rod in hand. With a groan and a grumble the elderly man stretched the rod out. He moved a picture up a row, then added one at eye level. Goodbye, Marlow & Pembridge, Esq. Hello, Montpierre Apothecary. An illustration showed a round woman sitting on a splintered bench. The caption: *A Tapeworm a Day Keeps the Fat at Bay! Sign up now for a FREE Montpiere Apothecary Health Kit!* Beneath that, the words: ***Patron Missive****

"Gallery-master," Gwendolyn said. "Those words: 'Patron Missive,' what do they mean?"

"Aye, what's it look like? Benefactin' lass. Spon-sor-ship. That's a prime eye-line right there, it is. Viewers always notice it."

"And people pay shillings for that?"

"Pay shillings?" His rattling laugh turned into a cough. "They pay *gold*. See that pile?" He gestured to five Autochrome pictures stacked by the counter. "That's just the Moon's Day crowd. T 'fore dawn, we'll auction again. And the bloody holidays, well, St. George's Festival is 'round the bend. That'll be a proper scrum, I reckon."

Three months away, it was a sure to be a glorious holiday. The furnaces and factories would be shut down, the skies would be cleared and the flowers were sure to be in full bloom. It was rumored the Queen Regent would open the palace to the public. All of New Avalon would be roaming the market.

"Gallery-master," Gwendolyn said, as a new seed took root, "if I paid you now, how much would a good spot cost?"

"Well, depends I suppose." His eyes searched her for signs of wealth. "Would it be gold, or a writ of credit? If it's a writ, I'm afraid it'll put seven percent to the cost," he said, adding: "Banker's fee, of course."

Sales: 0
Tokens: 0
Shillings: 17

"THEY'RE LOVELY," THE VINTAGEER SAID, TURNING A phenakistiscope over in his hand. "But they're not worth much."

Gwendolyn's entire stock sat on his countertop, eighteen in all. The shop was dusty, filled with antiques. Three gilded clocks no longer ticked or tocked, their fingers were frozen at 5:55. For a moment, Gwendolyn wondered how a vintageer could afford such a store. He traded in junk, after all. Perhaps he bought in long ago.

"Say, I'll give you… seven shillings for the lot."

"Seven shillings?" she swallowed. "Are you having a go?"

The phenakistiscope parts alone had cost her twice that. The paints, the wood, the metal and assembly. She had hoped to for thirty shillings but would have settled for twenty.

"These are handmade," she said, and held a phenakistiscope up, spinning it. An animated cat chased a ball, endlessly. "The paint's Nipponese, the wood is treated for rot. No cheap magic here, see?"

"They are quite lovely," the vintageer said, running his finger along the wood handle. "Ah, but it's a shame. The lads and lasses are after zoetropes these days. Tell ya what: throw in this crate, we'll make it ten shillings. That's fair."

"Ten?! Now you're taking the piss."

Gwendolyn didn't even bother with a counter offer. Her writ of credit for the Autochrome gallery was for nearly one gold. Such interest was a looming axe.

"Forget it," she said. "I can't go that low."

"Well, good luck then," he said, waving her off.

She gathered up her crate, her phenakistiscopes, her pride. She was almost out the door when her satchel tore. With a thump and a rumble, a terrarium hit the floor and rolled toward the counter.

The shock turtle tumbled inside, shell over belly. Dirt and moss spattered its face. With a spurt of electricity and hiss of displeasure, it shook off the displacement and retreated into its shell.

"Goddess be damned," Gwendolyn cursed, scooping up the orb. The dirt would settle, the moss would grow back. Soon, the shock turtle would start rebuilding his world. Hers was a different matter.

"That's mighty strong glass," the vintageer said. "What is it, Turkish sand?"

"Oregon," she said. "New world."

"Bollocks!"

She shrugged, struggling to find a pocket that could fit the terrarium. "My brother's a timberman," she said. "Anyways, a good Moon's Day to you."

"Wait! If that's true Oregonian blue..." The vintageer hesitated, fingers twitching, conducting a symphony of numbers. "I've a client who'd buy it. Two gold for it, here and now."

"Two gold?"

"*If* it's Oregonian blue," he said, putting a lens to his left eye. "I've a jewelscriber's certificate, see?"

She didn't look. She didn't care. She was already thinking how fast she could get back to her flat. His fingers were caressing the terrarium glass. His magnified eye microscopically probed every lump and fold.

"Three gold," she said. "But you have to buy the lot of 'em."

He clicked his tongue. "How many of these... er... things do you have?"

"Nine."

His magnified eye darted about, adding up coins in a mental bank. "Two and a half," he countered. "But I'll need them by five."

Gwendolyn hailed a steam carriage, paid the driver an extra three shillings not to stop for other passengers. She was home by the bottom of the hour. In ten minutes she rounded up the boxes, the stands, the bound booklets for terrarium care. She made a mental note to water her cypress and promptly forgot.

Back outside, Barnaby waved from his bakery across the lane, his apron covered in sauce. Revulsion boiled up when he tipped his top hat. She made a mental note to send him a scroll later, clarifying that they were just friends. She promptly forgot about that as well.

She was back at the vingateer's shop in under twenty minutes. A second man stood by the counter, examining the shock turtle's terrarium. His hands were cracked and scabbed. He had the complexion of smoked wood.

"Ah, there she is," the vintageer smiled. "And she brought the lot of them."

"T'was admiring your craft of hand," the sooty man said. "And your creations within. Takes a a precise mind to find an ecological loop. Too much water, it all falls to mush. Too little, the plants go to rot."

"Thank you." Gwendolyn placed the boxes of terrariums by the counter. Discreetly, she searched him for signs of silver or gold but found only copper and brass. He looked, she thought, like a coal shoveler on a third-class train. "Are you a collector, sir?"

The vintageer laughed. "Collector? No, no, Abernathy here is a repurposer. He runs the furnaces out in Smolderton."

The sooty clothes, the scabby hands, the furnace-tanned face. Now it made sense. Still... "I'm not sure I follow," she said. "Is he not your client?"

"Oh, I'm his client alright," Abernathy said. "Atticus here has helped me smelt ore and melt glass for years. This is fine stuff you have. Acid etched, heat treated. Melts at about what, five hundred degrees? Lucky for us, tonight's the one night a month we stoke the furnace six-fifty."

Gwendolyn glanced from the Atticus to Abernathy and down to the box. The guplets swam in their endless loop. The shock turtle had begun to rebuild its earthen burrow. "*Mew!*" went the shimmerling as Atticus sorted through the box of terrariums. "*Mew!*"

"So, you're just buying the glass?"

"Aye," Atticus said. "These are lovely baubles and all, but who needs such a thing?"

"Beg pardon, but... what about the soil and stones? What about the shimmerling?"

Abernathy cleared his throat. "Well, I suppose they'll melt too."

Gold: 19

Terrariums: 0

IT WAS A BEAUTIFUL AUTOCHROME PROFILE, SHE HAD PAID TO MAKE sure. Her logo was a proud tree, a dozen terrariums hanging from the branches. The name FRIENDLY WONDERS was hand tinted in copperplate script. She had even paid extra for a custom frame, and a chemical processing that gave the picture old timey scuffs and distressings.

The caption: *A dozen worlds within your grasp! A dozen lives in the palm of your hand! New and Improved Terrariums Debuting at the St. George's Weekend Market! LIMITED TIME OFFER!*

Gwendolyn spent Friday afternoon lingering by the ferns at the edge of the Autochrome gallery. She watched the viewers pass by. Studied them studying the pictures. Held her breath.

The first token fell into her cup within minutes, a little red circle. The next was a pair of blue tokens dropped by passing nuns. More followed with a satisfying plink.

Each token that dropped into her cup fed her joy. Those that went elsewhere fed her regret. In the silence her mind sprouted wings. Thoughts took flight, out of the gallery, down the alleys, and over to Smolderton where the furnaces burped ash.

Gwendolyn tried not to think of the melting terrariums. Tried not to imagine glass worlds collapsing, fiery and dark. Nine charred little stars, cindering down to an elemental core. Had the guplets boiled? Had the shimmerling cried?

Then, a joyous sight pulled her back into this moment: A family of six passed by, each tossing a token in her cup.

Tokens: 57
Gold: 19

SHE BARELY MADE IT TO THE POST OFFICE BY FIVE. THE POSTMISTRESS eyed her with disdain. One final customer until her afternoon tea.

"I need to send a message to Oregon," she said, filling out the scroll in a rush. "It's urgent."

"Mmm. How urgent?"

She showed the postmistress her brother's address. "How fast can it get here?"

With a sigh the postmistress consulted a telegraph book as thick as her hip. "Fastest way is by sea-mail," she said. "They laid a new cable last year. Let's see. That'll take your message to Boston."

Sea-mail. Gwendolyn took a deep breath. Sending a message without stamps felt costly and absurd. Were there just a bunch of dots and dashes screaming through the bottom of the Atlantic? Where did her words truly end up?

"From Boston the relay will telegraph it onward to Chicago," the postmistress continued. "Then San Francisco. Then it'll get printed and couriered up the coast."

"And how long will that take?"

"Few hours to San Francisco," she said. "Mmm, maybe two weeks up to Oregon."

"Good Goddess, that fast?"

"It's sea-mail," the postmistress said. "Now what's the bloody message?"

SHE TOLD HER BROTHER SHE NEEDED MORE SAND. TOLD HIM TO SEND five crates this time. To mark it: Payment Upon Delivery. The Patron Missive, the Autochrome pictures, and now the sea-mail all incurred debt. Still, she was doing okay. Mortgaging the future to pay for today.

Spring had sprung across town; it was a glorious day. The birds were out chirping and twittering away. Gwendolyn made her way through the park, past the town wall. Criers shouted out the evening's news. Two boys with their noses in spinning zoetrope toys cut Gwendolyn off, yet her smile never faded. The cobblestones were soft clouds beneath her feet.

"Enchantments," whispered a raspy voice from a painted

vardo wagon. An ancient, tattooed arm reached out from a curtained window. "Glyphs of speed. Finish your task in half the time."

Gwendolyn tried to ignore the magic merchant. Then, the wagon drifted curbside, followed along.

"Read your future, little dear," the ancient voice hissed. The ink-scribbled arm stretched out from the wagon's window, a second elbow bending. "Bless your friends, hex your enemies."

"No thanks," Gwendolyn said, and brushed away the long arm. The vardo wagon cracked and rolled on down the street.

Spell slingers! she fumed, her mood lessened with each step. She found herself wondering: how many tokens sat back at the Autochrome gallery? She felt an odd urge to check. A silly thing, she told herself. Those tokens would be there tomorrow.

Yet her feet had stopped walking. The cobblestones were no longer soft. Soon, she was doubling back.

HER AUTOCHROME PICTURE WAS GONE. IN ITS PLACE HUNG ONE OF Barnaby's. Five others at the same eye-line, stretching onward from the entrance to the end of gallery one.

"What is this?" she demanded, as the gallery-master finished adjusting a picture of Barnaby's dinner. The caption: *Testing a new turnover recipe. How dost thou like them apples? Baranaby's tip #5: for a perfect crust, mix in a bit o butter.*

"Gallery-master! Why was my picture displaced?"

"Displaced?" The old man looked confused, his soft eyes searching the wall. "Err... Which one was yours?"

"The tree and the terrariums," she said, livid. "I paid the sponsorship but it's no longer here!"

"Ah, the tree!" said a spry voice. "Yes, of course it's still here, have no fear." He was a young man. His accent was coastal, his fashion too casual. A purple feather protruded from his fedora, and Gwendolyn even spied a ring in his left ear.

"Oh, this is, uh—"

"Harold," the young man said, and tipped his cap. "Observer Improvements. As you know, patron perception is of paramount priority at Autochrome. We—"

Indignant, Gwendolyn cut in. "Why was my sodding picture moved?"

Harold flashed his most diplomatic smile. "Enhancement, my lady. Our previous gallery was a time-based experience. Now, we cluster pictures based upon thematic elements, viewer preferences, and a mathematical calculation that creates a dynamic narrative experience."

Gwendolyn hesitated, struggling to understand half this flashy young man had just said. She turned to the gallery-master. "Erm, I'm afraid it's beyond me. He gots a university degree."

"Academic enquiries prove that viewers prefer a non-chronological experience," Harold proclaimed. "We've simply adjusted the order."

"But... my picture... has been moved."

Harold nodded. "Only to gallery five," he said, pointing towards a dark hall. She could almost sense the cobwebs.

"That's three hundred feet from the entrance."

"Yes, well it remains at eye level, of course. The viewing experience is *completely* unchanged."

Gwendolyn felt a flush, took a deep breath. She glanced at Barnaby's five pictures. "Why are his first, hmm? I demand to know."

The gallery-master's head lolled, from Barnaby's pictures, to Gwendolyn, to Harold, and back to the pictures. "Ermm..."

"The calculations are proprietary," Harold said. "A trade secret, I'm afraid. But you seem the studious type. Through a partnership with the Queen Regent's College, we're offering a six-month seminar on gallery enhancement. Tuition is affordable, starting at fifty gold a term. Here, I'll fetch you a pamphlet."

Another tip of the cap. Gwendolyn wanted to pluck that

purple feather from fedora and plunge it through his collegiate tongue. Instead, she bit down on her own.

Tokens: 60
Gold: 12

HAROLD WAS RIGHT ABOUT ONE THING: GWENDOLYN WAS STUDIOUS.

For a week she sat on the gallery benches. As the viewers viewed the pictures, Gwendolyn studied them. She spent a gold on notebooks, another gold and a half on fountain pens and ink.

Each day viewers shuffled past, pausing to admire some pictures, ignoring others altogether. An occasional pattern appeared. Pictures of puppies often earned a chuckle and a token. So did simple images with instructions.

Five Steps for a Perfectly Frilled Cravat!

And current events.

Belgian Troops Invade Prussia and You Won't Believe What Happens Next!

And puzzles

95% of Egyptians Can't Solve this Riddle. Can you?

Yet, each time she felt closer to understanding the gallery's patterns, a new wrinkle emerged.

A picture of an old, amateur opera singer shattering a glass became the number one Autochrome for a day. Three dogs playing croquet never made it out of gallery four. Even two of Barnaby's pictures drifted from the front gallery to the back. When the pie-monger and his apprentice visited the gallery, Gwendolyn leapt behind a fern and observed from between fronds.

On the following Moon's Day she bought five used Autochrome pictures from a dead man's estate. On Two's Day she autochromed her breakfast, her new fingernails, the fresh shimmerling eggs. On Wodan's Day she stopped by a photoshop and paid a picture tailor to alter the image. On Thor's Day she checked for a message at the post office, yet found her box empty. And on Freya's Day she picked up her prints.

Tokens: 204
Gold: 6

"THAT'S A JOLLY GOOD CHUCKLE," SAID THE MAN WITH THE CANE AS he grinned at her picture. His token soon clinked in the pile. Over two hundred sat in the cup beneath her most popular picture. Over two hundred Autochrome admirers.

It was a peculiar feeling, this affection from strangers. Gwendolyn thought of it often. If the token bowl reached five hundred, would the gallery upgrade her receptacle? If she collected a thousand, would the lord mayor throw her a parade?

During the days, she grew snails and worms for the terrarium dirt. She nurtured new moss. By night, she incubated shimmerling eggs.

Her thoughts drifted to great crates of Oregon sand, making their way across the stormy Atlantic. Her dreams were of an ocean of tokens. Towering waves of adoration, cresting into a summer sky and crashing down, smothering her in love.

"OH, IT'S YOU," THE GALLERY-MASTER SAID, AS SHE ENTERED. "Erm... a moment, lass."

With a groan and a shout, the old man fetched Harold. A grimace split Harold's face as he spotted Gwendolyn.

"I'm sorry," Harold said, adjusting his three-button vest, "But I'm afraid we're no longer able to display your Autochrome content."

"What?" Gwendolyn felt the world lurch to the left. She must've misheard. "You're having a go, surely."

"Afraid not." Harold shook his head. "As you know, Autochrome prides itself on providing an authentic and original viewing experience. Altering or repurposing content is a violation of our contract."

He pointed to the scroll behind the counter, a dozen feet long and written in Olde Ænglish.

"This has to be a mistake," she said. "How could I recycle content, I've only been a patron for two months—"

"Not your content," he said, and opened a briefcase. He placed a picture of hers, an old gramophone. The caption: *Muse-ical Mondays! When I'm building worlds I'm collecting inspiration. Beethoven is nice, but I like the classics!* She recalled from two weeks ago.

"Submitted by you," Harold said. He placed another picture on the counter. "And this was submitted to our gallery four years ago."

It was the same gramophone, the same picture entirely, just from a wider perspective and a dead man's estate. The caption: *My gramophone. Not pictured: My grandpa phone.*

"A tintype, of course," Harold added. "It made it to number nine. They were simpler times."

Gwendolyn seethed at this old photo. It had taken her four hours to craft a catchy caption. Turned out, she'd raided the estate of the one elder in New Avalon who'd been an Autochromographer. What wretched luck!

"But... I've got the St. George's Market coming up," she said. "What about my viewers? What about my tokens?"

"The *gallery's* tokens have been repurposed," Harold said, and closed the briefcase. "You'll have to find alternative audiences, I'm afraid. Good day."

Tokens: 0
Gold: 6

SHE FOUGHT BACK THE TEARS, BUT THEY CAME ANYWAY. ALL THOSE lovely tokens, gone forever. She could feel their absence, a hole where public affection had just grown. A phantom itch, and now no way to scratch it.

The cobblestones brought her down Pemberton Way. There, three pocket clocks took up a storefront display. Enid the Blind's creations stood behind polished glass. Each blocky clock stuck at 5:55. *Requires No Strenuous Winding!* read the advert. *Always Accurate Twice a Day!*

Gwendolyn gave serious consideration to fetching a brick when a painted vardo wagon pulled up to the curb. "Hex your enemies," hissed an ancient voice from behind the patchy curtain. A tattooed arm stretched out, seven fingers unfurling. "Turn your tears to laughter, all for a small fee. Enchantments and glyphs."

"Piss off spell-slinger," Gwendolyn snapped. "Or I'll call the constabulary."

The withered armed retreated inside. The vardo wagon rolled on. Gwendolyn wiped her eyes just in time to spot Barnaby. He was bicycling down the street on his penny farthing, his apprentice pedaling a unicycle not far behind. She felt her bowels tighten, her toes clench. Not now of all times, she thought.

She saw three news boys strolling down the sidewalk, their noses in a zoetrope, all watching it spin.

And she saw it all begin, a perfect unfolding. The news boys: focused on their toy, stepping blindly off the curb. Barnaby: checking his pocket clock, his eyes off the road. The penny farthing: its great front wheel, catching a cobblestone rut and jutting to the right. The vardo wagon: clattering on, just in time to reveal this collapsing of paths.

Then a clang of pedals and a cracking of bone. The penny farthing crashed into the boys, the unicycle soon followed. Five bodies embraced in a dance of spokes and flesh.

The zoetrope lay on the sidewalk, broken beyond repair. Barnaby's top hat lay flattened nearby.

"These foolish boys and their toys!" an onlooker lamented. "Where are the parents to teach them?!"

There were cries and curse words, threats of litigation. "Summon Marlow and Pembridge," a constable suggested. A great bloody fuss that drew a huge crowd.

But Gwendolyn was running off in the opposite direction.

"WELL, THEY'LL HAVE TO BE HOME BY SUPPER," THE MATRON SAID, and put the coins in her blouse. "If they want to eat. Ragged school regulations, n'such."

"Of course," Gwendolyn said, and looked at two dozen orphans now standing before her. Their eyes were nervous and wide. "Don't you boys worry." She squatted to get to their level. "We'll get you back with plenty of time."

"And they'll probably want recompense too," the matron added. "Else-wise they're likely to pocket your wares."

"Of course, that can be arranged," Gwendolyn said, admiring the sweet face of a freckled girl. "Tell me, have you ever seen a zoetrope spin?"

The freckled girl shook her head, eyes glistening. "No ma'am," she whispered.

Gwendolyn smiled. "Well, if you work hard, by the end of the week, I've got one for each of you." Then she squeezed the little girl's dotted cheeks. The spots rearranged, and Gwendolyn shot back. Those weren't freckles but hungry skin mites.

SHE INSISTED THE ORPHANS BATHE. INSISTED ON CLEAN CLOTHES. ON hair free of lice. She paid for a cold water bath and powdered delousing. Then she gave them each an Autochrome picture and instructions. Sent them into the gallery, one by one.

By the afternoon, half of gallery two and three were filled with her captioned pictures. By that evening, her content stretched to gallery four.

"Where's my zoetrope," grumbled a boy with mismatched eyes.

"You have to be patient," Gwendolyn said with an officious smile. "We've still got four more days of work, remember?"

The boy sighed. "Oh…kay…"

"Now go hurry home," she said, cheerfully. "It's past your bed time."

Gold: 4
Tokens: 94

SHE BOUGHT OLD PICTURES IN BULK, PAID FOR THEM TO BE PHOTO-tailored. Then, she distributed them each morning. By Two's Day, a second group of orphans flooded the gallery with fresh Autochrome prints. Then the first group passed through, leaving tokens in her cups.

Rinse and repeat, the cycle went on. If one orphan got caught, she just swapped in another. It was a numbers game, after all. There were plenty at the ragged school to recruit.

On Wodan's Day, with her face pressed against the west window, she could see her content filling up gallery three.

By Thor's Day, her pictures stretched from gallery one to gallery five.

By Freya's Day, all could spot her Autochrome from the street.

Gwendolyn grinned all the way to the post office. And she grinned even without a response from her brother. She told herself it would be all right, he always came through. Told herself too that she was just being competitive, just using the system. Every artist needs and audience, and she was building hers. What good would her authentic creations be, without crowds to behold them?

Gold: 4
Tokens: 398

THEY FOUND HER AT SUNDOWN, A MOB OF SMALL BODIES IN LINEN and rags. Scowling faces surrounded her, a dirty court of frustration.

"You said you'd pay us," the boy with mismatched eyes spat. "Where's our zoetropes?"

The mite-faced girl cracked her knuckles. A boy with a club foot kicked a bottle. Gwendolyn studied the unkempt kids, forced a smile to her lips.

"Of course, I'm so glad you found me," she said. "I have them at home."

The orphans trailed her across town, eighteen in all. She felt like a goose leading diseased goslings to water. She told them to wait and went into her flat. Fetched the crate and carried it down to the stoop.

"Line up," she said. "One by one. There you go."

She opened the lid and passed out the toys.

"Here you go," she said, and handed one out. "And here you go. And here you go."

Some orphans hurried off, clutching the handles and spinning the inventions. Some stuck around to compare their's with the others.

"Mine's a lion chasing a zebra!" a little girl shouted with glee.

"Mine's a man and a woman dancing," squealed a giddy boy.

"Wait a sodding minute," the boy with mismatched eyes shouted. "Everyone, wait!"

There was a great pause. The orphans turned to each other.

The boy with mismatched eyes shook his toy. "This isn't a zoetrope," he said. "It's a phen... phenkit...phenak... IT'S A PHONY-SCOPE!"

And then they were on her, eighteen furious kids no higher than her hips. They swung dirty fists, spat from dry lips. Scratched at her hemline and kicked at her shins.

"We want our zoetropes!" they shouted. "Where's our zoetropes!"

Gas lamps lit up along porches. Half the neighbors peered out of their flats. Then a whistle dispersed the orphans. Two uniformed men jabbed at the kids with billy clubs. "Back wit ya! Back, I say!" Then the little girls and boys were off, a roiling wave crashing down the street, kicking over rubbish bins and scaring off cats.

"Blasted little nibblers," the man said, holstering his baton. "They turn out your pocket, miss?"

"No," Gwendolyn said, dusting herself off. "Just took some toys."

"Lucky day then, I s'pose. Do you know a... Gwen... Gwendee..."

"Gwendolyn Chetteridge?" she asked. "What's this for?"

"Ah, good," the man said, and whistled to his partner. "We've got a delivery."

An ox cart idled nearby, five muddy crates in the bed. That was her brother's writing on the wood. Her heart raced as a returned to her lips. Her luck had finally returned.

"Just need to sort out the payment, miss," the deliveryman said. "Oswald, bring up the first crate."

Oswald studied Gwendolyn as he began to unhitch the cart. "Gwendolyn," he said. "*The* Gwendolyn? Of Friendly Wonders?"

"That's... yes," she said. "You've heard of it?"

"Sod me, have I ever?" Oswald said. "Fenton, you know who this is? She's an Autochrome star, that's right."

"More of a Tintype fellow myself," Fenton said, unrolling the receipt. The bottom tocked on the sidewalk, rolled another foot. "No offense."

With a groan and a crack, Fenton's crowbar snapped open the first crate. A linen bag tipped over, lumpy muck poured out. "What... what is this?" Gwendolyn asked.

She'd expected the dry ivory hue of Oregon sand, not this wet, ashen mass. Barnacles clung to the inside of the crate. Crawdads wriggled about the filth. A lone shrimp flapped and twitched its way down the steps.

"Oy, that's a proper stench," Oswald said, covering his nose.

Gwendolyn seized a note written in her brother's script and tore it open.

DEAREST GWENDY,

I trust all is well. The company forwarded your sea-mail to my new address. Alas, I've been reassigned to Louisiana to harvest Mangrove timber. Thus, I've substituted five crates of bayou bottom sand. What the dickens do you do with it anyway? You artists are an odd lot.

Well, back to tree farm for me.

Cheers!

—Rupert

P.S. Have you heard of the kaleidoscope? I saw one whilst visiting Chicago. Fun!

Gold: 0
Tokens: 398
Crates: 5

BELLOWS WHEEZED LIKE LEATHERY LUNGS. ASH ROSE FROM THE furnaces, swirled about, and fell as molten snow. On any other day Gwendolyn would have marveled at these fiery machines. Instead, she was secretly cursing their slow pace.

"Aye, I suppose I can work with this stuff," Abernathy said, eyeing the damp crates of bayou muck. "But it won't be pretty."

"But you can turn it to glass?" she asked. "Shape it into an orb, like the ones you bought? That's the important part."

"Aye," Abernathy said. "Should take 'em... oh, only a month, I s'pose."

"Too slow," she said. "The shimmerlings are finishing incubation. The guplets are starting to swim. The market's in three weeks."

"Well, it's like the saying goes," Abernathy said. "You can work the forges quickly, cheaply, and good-ly. But you can't do all three."

Gwendolyn took a deep breath. There was a bridge in her mind, one yet to be crossed. She thought of that painted vardo wagon and the tattooed arm.

"What about magic?" she asked.

Abernathy raised a sooty eyebrow. "S'pose, it's worth a try."

Gold: -19

Tokens: 847

Terrariums: 12

THE SUN ROSE OVER THE BOOTHS OF THE ST. GEORGE'S MARKET. HOT air balloons filled the dawn sky. Shortly before eight a Ferris wheel was erected. By nine, the thoroughfares were alive with vendors and early patrons.

SEE! the Fantastic Bearded Lady! read a colorful sign.

HEAR! the Electric Accordion, a Modern Musical Marvel!

TASTE! Food From the Far East and Wild West!

Gwendolyn unrolled her pennant. Friendly Wonders glimmered in green ink. Her terrariums hung from the stunted cypress, twelve in total. New guplets swam in their little liquid worlds. Lazy shock turtles were just beginning to burrow in their desert orbs. Atop mossy twigs, shimmerlings perched, their big eyes blinking in the morning light. A phoenix topped the cypress display, its wings dripping sparks. Each terrarium was a smooth orb, the glass clear and precise. Each surface a perfect circle, no lumps or imperfections.

Gwendolyn smiled at the sight. Three hours of sleep, and somehow she'd made it. Even upgraded the tent to silk. She owed a dozen writs of credit, but it didn't matter. The criers echoed her message often; she was widely admired. Success lay just past the stroke of ten.

Across the way stood the pie-monger's booth. Slab by metal slab, the apprentice assembled the iron oven. Barnaby sat in the ox cart, rigid in a plaster cast, eyes darting about. Gwendolyn tipped an imaginary cap. He tried to smile back but grimaced in pain.

Soon, the booths would open, but first Gwendolyn fancied a stroll. The market was a sight to behold. Autochrome had three booths at the south end. Beside them, five booths formed a circus-like tent. *Introducing Megachrome! The Future of Social Photography! No Studio Required!* Gwendolyn marveled at a camera as compact as a small cannon. What devices would they dream up next?

The crowd grew dense, the children frequent and loud. "Look mummy, a wee dragon," a little girl said. For a moment, Gwendolyn smiled with pride. But it wasn't *her* booth they were talking about, it wasn't *her* wee dragon. Gwendolyn came to a stop before a humble linen tent.

Handcrafted glass orbs sat in stands atop a simple table. Within each orb lay a familiar scene. A guplet, swimming in circles. A shimmerling's mossy lair. A baby phoenix, soaring on fiery wings.

"Oh, you're early," the artist said, "but you can have a look."

"What is this?" Gwendolyn gasped. "What are these?"

"Oh," the man considered them. "Well, they're terrariums. Made right here in New Avalon. No magic, no ma'am, these are hand crafted. Go on."

"Handcrafted, you say?" asked woman with a pearl necklace,

squeezing past. She ran her fingers over the lumpy orb. "And what's this funny little thing?"

"Oh, that's a shimmerling," the artist answered.

"It's beautiful," the customer said. "Do you have two?"

"Only one, I'm afraid," the artist said. "But the twins have several sets, just two booths down."

"The twins?" Gwendolyn asked. "A set?!"

The vendor gave Gwendolyn a smile and a nod. "Two booths down. Or maybe three."

Gwendolyn ran the whole way. It was five booths down, but by the time she arrived she'd seen plenty. Two of the booths she passed were selling kaleidoscopes. One was a charity for orphans. The other two were vendors, like the one she'd just run from. Glass orbs were shelved in display cases. A pair of red haired twins had just finished a sale: two boys walked off with matching basilisk terrariums.

"What are you doing?" Gwendolyn found herself shouting. "What is all this?!"

"What's it look like?" the left twin said. "These are—"

"It's *her!*" the right twin said. "Gwenevive, the artisan."

"Oh wow," the left twin said. "It's such an honor, truly. You're a huge inspiration." She extended a hand. "My sister and I, we saw your Autochrome and just thought: 'we have to follow in her footsteps.'"

"'There's a trailblazer,' we said. 'There's someone who has it together.'"

"And, so here we are," the right twin said. "Excuse me, can I help you?"

Another customer was inspecting the shock turtle. Gwendolyn felt the market tilting sideways. The clocktower at the end of Kettering Square chimed. It was ten o'clock in the morning, and all was not well.

Then came the fireworks. The screams of celebration. St. George's Weekend Market was now officially underway.

Only, they never opened with fireworks, this Gwendolyn knew. And the screams, they seemed more like cries of panic.

Her feet carried her back to her booth, but not all the way. The heat there was too hot, the flames were too high. The phoenix was fluttering free, painting her tent in cinders. The stunted cypress was on fire, its dry branches snapping.

Pop! Another terrarium fell as the brittle wood gave way. *Pop! Pop!* In a crackling groan and a crescendo of cheap glass, the rotten cypress collapsed. Gwendolyn tried to recall when she'd watered it last. *Pop! Pop! Pop!*

Two shimmerlings flew about, snarling and snapping. *"Mew! Mew! Mew!"*

A shock turtle zapped a pig, chasing it down the thoroughfare.

A teacup basilisk seized on a teenager's ankle and sent the poor lad scrambling.

Two tiny hydras were spitting acid at Barnaby's apprentice, and a skinmouse was nesting beneath the pie-monger's cast.

All through her tent the phoenix flew about. Fiery wings fanned fancy silk, turned dry cypress into a bonfire.

Mew! Pop! Mew! Pop!

There was nothing to do but stand back and stare. Gwendolyn watched as the flames swallowed her signage, her silk curtains. Swallowed her tent and the two booths beside it. Swallowed her dreams. From some distant place, she knew the fire brigade was coming; she could hear their clanging bells. Yet all she could do was giggle and clap. The St. George's Weekend Market was off to a strong start; nothing could top this.

She had the largest crowd, after all, and that had to count for something.

BOOK SEVEN
WE WILL BUILD A HAUNTED HOUSE

WE WILL BUILD A HAUNTED HOUSE

T his first step is simple: one must craft a foundation. Life rises out of the simplest of things. Amino acids and folded proteins, tide pools and seeds. This afterlife, after all, is no different. A stain of pain, some psychic residue. One must seek out this primeval stew.

Laughter can work. Yes, it is true. I once knew an alchemist who went mad in his lab. He laughed over his crucible of simmering mercury and lead. He laughed at his pail as he doused blistered hands. He laughed at the shadows as he flung himself into the old well. He laughs down there still, a wet echo, reaching up from the depths.

Yes, laughter will to do. But tragedy works best.

Consider: this botched execution. See the dull ax swung by those tremulous hands? Witness this failed exorcism, and how it leaves us a nourishing morass. Study this hobbling widow, her grey head fraught with brain worms. And now, how her body lays bent at the base of her stairs.

Yes, each of these stains present a tempting foundation.

Or perhaps the Deerfield Massacre of 1704. French forces, leading three hundred natives, now descend upon your settlement. Here they come, the Iroquois and the Pocomtuc, the

Abenaki and Wyandot. Here they slaughter your sentries and spill hot blood in the streets. Take the axe to the butcher, fill the fletcher with arrows.

You see the raiders rend your neighbors with blades. You hear the crack of the muskets as the militia tries to fight back. You feel your brother's hand clutch your shoulder, his hot breath at your ear: "Go, sister! Run! Stay silent and hide!"

You obey. As the tomahawks splinter your family's front door you flee down to the larder. Holding your hands to your mouth, you try not to cry. Not as your family drips through the floorboard above in wet crimson strands. Nor when they line the thoroughfare with your dead and peel back the scalps. Or when they march the survivors away. Not even when the torches are lit and your home grows warm. When the smoke embraces you, the flames devour you, only after the scalding walls come down upon you, yes, only then do you finally cry out. And by then there's no one to hear you.

So you agree now? So you see? Laughter is nice, but tragedy seeps deeper. This is something to work with. Now, you have a foundation.

THE SECOND STEP IS TO SLOWLY FORGET. DO NOT REMEMBER THE bonnet your mother sewed for your golden hair. Do not recollect your father's musk. Nor how he would hug you close and say: "Nay, Annalise, I think you the prettiest child in all these new lands." Do not recall the sound of your own voice.

But if you must try to speak be content with small murmurs. Whisper your words as the wind through the leaves. Know these trees grow from seeds nourished by the bones of your kin. Hear the wolves now howling at night? They were sired by those beasts that cleaned your town of its dead. Even these singing sparrows still feed on the worms that you fattened.

Let the seasons soak in. Long after the flames and the rain.

Longer still, you remain. You and me, let us become *we*, the echo still staining the soil. We will let the vines be our veins, the stones be our bones. We are the silence when all else has moved on.

THE THIRD STEP IS TO WELCOME NEW LIFE AND NEW VOICES. WHEN the man's calloused hands dig at the ruins and unearths our foundation. When this family stands upon our soil and proclaims: "Does this not look like a perfect place for an inn?" Let us kindly assent.

We soften our flesh, it's just soil after all. Our mud sometimes quivers beneath these new feet. Sometimes we wince when they fell our old trees. We try not to cry as they drive posts into our skin. Now, we hold this inn's signpost, firm and proud.

And sometimes we smile. When the twin girls mend our stone wall, stacking rocks until the fireflies dance in the gloaming. When their tickling feet scamper through our bloodroot meadow. As they climb the elm at the edge of our lake.

"It's okay," we whisper. "We just want to be friends. It's nice to make your acquaintance."

And we grin as they run to their mothers and say: "There was a little girl with smoldering eyes! She was giggling at us from inside a dead tree!"

Distance is important, however, and this we soon learn. Our loneliness must be suppressed. So we learn how to grow and we build a secret room. And this too: we learn when to grow still.

We watch as ox carts bring travelers to our freshly-built stables. We savor the smell of the spiced delights cooked by the innkeeper's wife. We listen as traders and learned men feast at our new tables and sleep in our rooms.

Now, when we drift through the inn, let us do it at night. See how this moonlight vivifies our skin. Hear the hewn floorboards groan beneath our feet. Feel the doors yield to our touch. This wood was a part of us; we are one and the same.

Here, in the guest quarters, we dip hooked fingers into slumbering minds. Here, we pluck out a few memory strands. Let us learn the schematics for a waterwheel, soon to be built on the banks of the Connecticut River. Let us purloin the best way to smoke fowl. And let us discern the subtle difference between cranberry and baneberry. Which of these red fruits must one never consume?

Careful now, we need not be greedy. Be prudent and take just a few precious strands. These memories must sustain us and build our tomorrow.

And if a guest should wake with our claws in their mind, we must fade into a dark corner. If the kids should catch us in their beds they will scream.

"She was right there!" Mary Ann says, and points right through us. "I saw her in a moonbeam."

Mary Beth agrees. "Her skin was like embers; her eyes were wet coal."

Let them search every room until their minds finally quiet. When this inn is nervous it whispers our name. When the lanterns pierce the shadows, we can bask in their warmth. Take notice of this moment, it means we are no longer alone.

THE FOURTH STEP IS TO INTRODUCE OURSELVES. WE SHOULD MEET A few eager minds.

When the innkeeper hunts wild turkey, let us visit his daughters. We beckon the twins down the cold, crumbling stairs. We show them our earthen larder. Here, we can talk in the darkness. Here, we can tell them our name.

"Don't ever say that!" The innkeeper's wife later shouts over dinner. "That was years ago, that poor family was never found."

"But she says she's our age!" Mary Beth protests.

"She's cold and she's lonely," Mary Ann adds. "She lives in the larder at the bottom of the stairs."

"What larder and stairs?" the innkeeper asks. "That old foundation I dug out? You know as well as I we filled it with stones. There's no such place in this inn!"

The girls stamp their feet as the inn's guests eat in polite silence. The twins insist they spent the afternoon beneath ground. Should we raise our voice to defend them we would concur. But our lips are tired, our memory fragmented. We remember building a room we can't always find. We recall stone walls and the floorboards above. And we wonder: does where we took even exist?

THE FIFTH STEP IS TRICKY, IT REQUIRES OUR FULL CONCENTRATION. It's why we sleep for seasons on end. Should we stalk the halls every night and construct too many rooms we will scare off our guests. So we stay quiet and calm. Stay in our larder and listen. Let the twins forget us. Let the travelers have their way with our body and soil. We are lonely and cold; our patience wanes with each season. Now, for this step, we will keep our new friends.

Let us start with the innkeeper's wife and whisper at night. As she sleeps, we reach our hooks into her attic. Let us harrow the gray fields of her mind. Beneath bone, we sow crops for this autumn's harvest. The seeds: how your husband's gaze drinks in the meat-monger's soft daughter. How his eyes trace her maiden-shape at church. And your daughters, they conspire with the shadows. And how the inn's walls sometimes bleed, yet *you* no longer do.

And soon she says: "Let us give thanks for the harvest and all the soil provides us." Now for this feast she fetches their best earthenware. With a whisper we help her stir the pot; *this world is too wicked for my beautiful twin girls.* With a kind touch we part the fog of her thoughts; *he touches me naught because he lays with another.*

Now all becomes clear. Soon, the twins will be women; *see how they bloom!* The travelers that sleep in this inn; *hear the hands plea-suring flesh in the dark.* Those men that smile as your girls skip past them in town; *feel the glare of skin-demons behind friendly eyes.*

So she stirs the pot until the sauce is congealed. She pours in the last of her fancy cane sugar and grinds extra rinds. "Don't waste this cranberry glaze," she tells her family with a smile, after the last traveler has gone to bed. "It's our own special feast."

When the twins complain the cranberries taste bitter, she grins at the rinds. Next her husband collapses and gasps, so she picks up his plate. Now her virginal daughters are gagging and she's stroking their sweet cheeks.

At dawn, the first traveler wakes to break his fast. He mutters a prayer when he sees the three bodies. There, he finds the innkeeper's wife still scrubbing the plates. He cries out when he sees her fingers: all rubbed down to the bone.

And we think: such good earthenware now forever stained red.

THE SIXTH STEP IS TO HELP OUR NEW GUESTS GET COMFORTABLE. OUR walls hold more souls; our family expands. We stretch the grains of our wood and bend the edges of time. Build the twins separate bedrooms they've always wished for. Give the innkeeper a guest ledger to eternally inscribe.

As for his wife, their mother, we offer her full run of our struc-ture. We vow to let her redecorate. She refuses, however, and swears to never return. She runs screaming past our grasp, past our winding stone wall.

All we can do is gaze with unblinking glass eyes. Look! There she is, still in the town square. See! There she dangles from the noose and the willow. Each year, when the harvest is ready, we peer to the east and give thanks for her feast. There, her spirit glares back, forever waving fingers of raw bone.

The inn's hearth grows cold as the travelers stop coming.

Algor mortis sets in. The sparrows flee as tawny fogs bloom from our lake. What grass grows is malodorous, misshapen. Even the trees seem to weep.

We keep to ourselves and fill our halls with our laughter. We chase each other and hide in the cupboards.

These sweet twins, they don't cry at our burnt face. When we catch them they laugh with putrescent lips. Every day at the gloaming the innkeeper stares east out the great window and mumbles: "She should be home from the market by now. Yes, yes, she should be home for the harvest."

You are our cherished guests now; all secrets are gone. Time to craft argent tapestries from your dreams. Pluck the memories from your mind's attic and lay them out on the floor, glistening threads for our loom. Weave your life's fibers into each rock and hollow, every board and brick. This property is yours and you are this property. For now we agree: we have all that is needed.

But should you wander far out, should you roam past our stone wall, you will find only fog. Should you grow lonely, only ask and we can expand. In time we all wish to find some new friends.

———

THE SEVENTH STEP IS TO LEARN FROM THE TREES. LET US KNOW WHEN to bend like the willow and when to squeeze like the vines.

When roads grow cobbled, when the ox carts yield to carriages, let us help build a livery yard. Our new caretaker is pleased. He works our land with gentle, old hand, tamps metal shoes to his horses and brushes their manes. We soften our soil to his shovel, but only so much. Too many warm stables and the horses will spook in our frigid presence.

We yield to the winds. We bend beneath seasons of snow. Now we watch and we wait. As capotain hats give way tricorns. As the colonies declare themselves a nation. As these new states proclaim their revolt.

Now, the redcoats occupy our body and store weapons within our walls. Now, the redcoats declare our caretaker a traitor. And they call him a good horse master too, as they commandeer his wares. With laughter, the captain says he was a good farrier. Little good this praise does with his flesh full of lead.

Time to wake for a moment and pay them a visit. Let us rouse from our nap as these men of war dream by the hearth.

"Something's not right," the night sentry mutters, as the embers grow cold.

"Shut your mouth, stoke the fire," the captain mumbles, and tightens his blanket.

This young sentry is fatigued; we find his mind's library unguarded. Drift in, look around, and read from his books. Ah, here rests a journal in which he's written: *Forgive me, I suffer great doubt now in King George and his fatuous war.* And what have we here? An unwritten letter to his ill sister in Stratford-upon-Avon. *How I yearn to return and see the stars of my own nation's sky!*

"Something's not right," the young sentry whimpers, as the embers glisten and drip. His eyes scour the coals. Now we show him his sister in these flames. See how she cries out across the storm silver waves.

"I'm sorry," he says, and his boot heel descends upon the snoring throat.

"I've got to get home," he bemoans, as he slides the bayonet between the captain's soft ribs.

"I'm sorry," he repeats, his boot heel smothering another brother in arms. "I've got to get home," he cries, and drives wet steel into each sleeping redcoat.

"Traitor!" his dead regiment curses, as their ranks swell with each stab. This craven young sentry pays them no mind. He steals enough coin for a ship's passage across the Atlantic. He steals a horse for the ride to the harbor. They gallop off now, past our walls and into the fog.

Some redcoats accept this new term of service. Some try to rebel. They chase the traitor off, past the stone wall, only to reawaken by the cold hearth, curses rattling from crushed throats. A few simply meander our land, sending letters for reinforcements that never arrive.

Let us unfurl all their memories into more endless thread. Let us weave these lives into the tapestries of our manor. Build new rooms and a few doors that go nowhere. Add new tomes to our mind's library, let our guests share in this knowledge.

And when we tire it's time to lower the curtains, close our glass, and sleep for the seasons. In this darkness our guests can drift through our halls.

THE EIGHTH STEP IS TO REFINE OUR APPETITE.

One revolution ends, another begins. Our livery becomes a barn, our meadow is now cut grass. Our body is a summer home, a cool northern retreat from the soggy cotton fields down south. There are new masters here, a grain merchant and his portraitist wife.

Here, in our verdant yard, they convene secret meetings. Beneath our trees they support the southern revolt. They auction slaves after dark and brand them beside the barnyard cattle. At the shore of our lake they douse newly-seared skin.

The grain merchant hosts dinner parties with abolitionists and feigns civil discourse. He raises wine in Lincoln's honor, toasts with the words of Theodore Parker. The portraitist shows these visitors her cordial southern charm. She captures their likeness with canvas and paint. At night the married pair make lists of their guests and forward these portraits to assassins down south. Later, when word of an abolitionist's murder returns, the grain merchant raises a glass in the dead guest's honor and smiles at his wife.

At all times the house hums with banquets and the scheming of minds. The far yard echoes with the keening of slaves. Our lake waters retch at the dousing of seared skin. Our soil reminisces, of quiet days, of horses once cared for not too far away.

On Sunday, Father Benton pays a visit to give sermon to a select crowd. He sweats as he spouts about Ham's Curse and the three sons of Noah. The African savage, he says, is a direct descendant of Ham. Behold their dark skin! Proof of that unforgivable gaze. Behold this good book! All the answers within. Ergo, the slave masters are nobly upholding tradition. Ergo, we are all enacting God's will.

Whiskey-plied, Father Benton retires after supper, his thoughts drifting to the slave quarters. Let us peer into his mind's library and behold all that is rotten. Let us step in now and take what we need. Be quick, every book on his shelf is inked with crimson and bound in black skin.

Now, we return to Father Benton in his special guest room. Now, we find him in bed. His face glistens, his hand stiffens his cock. He thinks of the good book and the ripe slave girl he's sent for, no older than thirteen. Toe's curling, he licks his dry lips and envisions desert. We do the same.

One by one, we pay this sin-monger a visit. We adjust the candlelight, let the wax sizzle red. We dim the wicks to black flames.

A slave girl steps out of his closet, yes, but she is not who he sent for. Still, Father Benton does know her name. She was buried out in the orchard, rotten food for our trees. Rotting too is her womb where their son had grown for six months. Rotting now are the child's eyes, two curdled marbles in a moldering hollow. See these eyes that despise the sins of this Father. Planted a seed, imbued six months of life, then choked it from them, mother and son.

Now hear this cry echoing out in our halls. Try not to grin at its rise in pitch. When the guest's door is thrown open, the grain merchant doesn't grasp what he sees. Father Benton in bed, his hands clutching a pair of crushed plums.

"The seed is evil so I smote it," he sings, as ruby torrents gush down his legs. "Mine eyes hath seen the glory!" he cries.

Then he pries his glorious eyes from their sockets.

And, since we have the grain merchant here, why not consume him as well? Since we have a full house of sinners, is it not best that we eat?

Let us stretch out the great stairs until the handrails reach Hell. With a wet rip let us free these gaudy portraits from their frames. Our doors now sprout fangs. Our walls become skin. This congregation of flesh-peddlers all have a place on our table, their bodies an eternal feast for our guests. Fetch our best plates and sharpen the knives. There are many seats in our banquet hall, more by the minute.

Seeing this living Gehenna, the grain merchant grabs his chest and falls dead. Let us upholster our chairs with his leather. And this cordial artist, see her bawling down our varicose halls? Let us paint the crown molding with her pigment and gristle.

Outside, from the barn, the slaves hear the screams. Across the lake they witness this all. The sharp shadows that crawl down our ivy. Our windows that quiver in hoggish delight. But—and this is important—let us show some restraint. We must not be too greedy. We are building many rooms but not all need to be filled.

So we unlock their shackles and unfasten their chains. We whisper: "Run, run far away, and never return."

And now we wait for the rumors to make their way home.

THE NINTH STEP IS TO EMBRACE OUR LEGACY AND ALL THAT WE'VE built. When the carriages give way to cars, when the candles become bulbs, now is our hour to stand firm and proud.

We have many bones in our body. Many long-term guests to entertain. New owners come, and some we let go. Some hope to tame us. Some try new toys to bypass our quirks. Electrical circuits? Watch us short them at dusk. And oh how curious that our radiators bleed. When we're in a foul mood hear the phonographs scream. The sparrows avoid us, the feral dogs stay away. From the inside our night is six times as long as the day.

So-called architects, they try to measure our shape. We help them slowly go mad. All their scale rulers and tools can't reconcile this simple fact: our structure is always larger from inside than out.

So they tie ropes around their waist and ascend into our attic. Up there, they sometimes find rooms we've misplaced. Sometimes, they discover the library of our mind. So we placate their curiosity; we keep them entertained. We stretch out their ropes, wind the fibers for miles. We brick the doors up behind them and build new halls whenever they blink

"I can still hear granddaddy's cane, clomping around," a boy moans over breakfast. "Pa, I can hear him screamin' out from inside the walls."

One family flees, another stays forever. The Smiths become the O'Connells, the Millards and the vast Cohen clan. Our rooms are many and library grows vast. Yet even the sharpest mind cannot recall every ant it has crushed.

So-called experts, they try to explain us. So-called seers, they roam our halls. "I sense a great tragedy," a mustached man chants as he burns incense and peers into the smoke. "An orphanage, yes! A terrible curse was birthed here, in this very parlor room!"

We show them a few tricks, our captured echoes. On command our windows now wink. The rattling pipes are our arteries, the furnaces our lungs. When we sigh all taste our decay.

SEE! The house that has claimed a hundred souls!

HEAR! The wail of a baby from the incinerator chute!

FEEL! The greenhouse that grows cold on hot August nights!

And when the last inhabitant—a sole survivor—is wheeled off to the sanitarium, let us agree that we have now reached a rarified state. Those who have touched us tremble forever. Those who haven't still recognize our face.

Our gates are now chained, and our hedges grow brittle. Some hack author has pilfered our tale. Reporters occasionally visit to bask in our awe. Inquiring minds want to know: *what truly happened in the black attic at dawn?* Now, from all around, they come, the curious and the nervous, the reverent and rude. We are lonely no more. Now, there are always entertainments upon our door.

The boys with greased hair, they bring us their sweethearts on full moon. The teenagers, they disrobe and wade into our lake. With deep breaths, they dive under and hope to get lucky. Sometimes they do. And sometimes we turn our surface to black glass and embrace them in leeches. Send them shambling back to the squeezes for a final, wet kiss.

And regarding the winos and hobos that shelter in our halls: we are not always cruel. Yes, some of them wake up to discover piles of our wealth. An investment in rumors that pays dividends to this day.

THE TENTH STEP IS... WHAT IS THIS? AH, YET ANOTHER unannounced guest. A treasure seeker. Or just a reckless mind perhaps, it makes no difference. Let us welcome this disheveled young man in. Let us unchain our gates and—

What is that reek that pierces the air? What is this bedraggled man holding?

"It's gasoline, you sick fucking house," he spits, and throws a splash across our porch. "Or did you forget what it smells like?"

A moment's hesitation. Let us scour our mind's library; let us seek out his portrait. So many rooms, so many guests we've collected. Our body is bloated, our walls cracked at the seams. Yes, there hangs his picture: a boy, the sole survivor of a meat-cleaver night. Here he stands now a man, yes, we recognize his face.

"You took my parents," he hisses, and rudely splashes gasoline on our door. "You took my whole future and you don't remember me, do you?" he asks and lets himself in. "And you took my sister."

So say hello to her now. Here she is, limping down our stairs, forever fifteen and gray. "Johnny, I didn't recognize you..." her putrid throat gurgles. "What are you doing?"

"I'm fixing this, big sis," he says, and pours gasoline on our bookshelf. "I'm setting you all free. Gonna burn down this nightmare palace, once and for all."

We wither our books, make the bindings squeal like cut pigs. We force the portraits to move and babble his name.

"Nice try," Johnny says, and sloshes gasoline across upon our precious chairs. "But I'm wearing ear plugs."

Something's not right. Our fingers can't sink into his mind. We see no hope in his future, no tomorrow to twist. We see only this: a smoldering crater and flames.

"Johnny, stop this," we say, through his parents Margret and Frank. We crawl their flayed bodies down the stairs. "Johnathan, son, you don't want to do this," they say, slipping their skin on like fine, formal clothes. "You'll get in trouble with the police!"

"Been there, done that, got the bumper sticker," their living son laughs. "Cops can't hold a candle to ten years in the sanitarium."

With a splash of the gas can his parents dissolve. No, this is all wrong. His mind won't let us inside!

"It's called a lobotomy," he says, and taps his distended left eye. "It's what happens when a house eats your family, when everyone says you're insane."

No, no, we got too greedy; this was a mistake. We chewed up too much and left him no future. With no hope for tomorrow he has nothing to twist. So we thrash and we bang. We turn our rugs to a field of wet tongues.

"Cute tricks," he says, and kicks over the can. "But I've already seen them. I was just a small part your life, wasn't I? But you... you've been my entire life. See, I've had the last decade to read. Old books, hand-me-downs. That's all the library had. But I found your story. Your name is Annalise and your settlement was slaughtered in 1704. You were left here alone, weren't you?"

We quiver and scream. We shatter our windows and scatter our glass. Each shard shows a shimmer of our time-lost face.

"Alone and forgotten," he says, and wipes glass from his cheek. "I know how it feels. But Annalise, it's now time you let go."

The bastard strikes a flare. The flames hiss and spit. A flick of the wrist and the burning stick lands in the puddle. The flames sear our wood, sear our skin, and here we are trapped yet again. We crack our walls and fracture our foundation; we try to retreat. But Johnny simply embraces the blaze. He spreads his coat to reveal candles tied to his chest. No, not candles but—

The dynamite obliterates fiber and stone. Flings our chimney bricks for miles into the woods. Scatters the roof across acres of lake. We feel it all: the fire and the flash; every room we've built; every guest collected, all gone in the blast.

And now we feel nothing.

Oh, yes. The tenth step? One should try to accept when things come to an end.

There is emptiness now. And a vast, smoldering crater. We call out to the others but no one answers. The twins and the innkeeper, the redcoats and the grain merchant. Soon, our voice becomes a soft wind once again. We—

See the seasons progress, from sprig to tree.

Hear the birdsong as the sparrows return.

Feel the earth upon us, nurturing new seeds.

And we sleep, sleep, deep in the soil. We try to let go.

AND WHEN AN ODD TRUCK DRIVES UP, BELCHING AND GRAY. WHEN its wheels sink in and pick up our soil. When this curious vehicle stops at our lake. Perhaps then it is time to open our eyes.

The kids jump out and the little dog gives chase. The dad steps down and stretches his sore legs. And the young mother, with her tie-dyed skirt and ukulele, smiles and says: "You're right hon, this looks like a gem of a spot to camp."

Let us focus on this motorhome, its name: Winnebago. Let us consider this house on wheels, how conveniently mobile. And now we watch how these young parents blissfully set up their camp. We hear this sweet little girl giggling as the family dog chases a squirrel. Study the little boy playing close, yes, *so* close to our lake. And we think: we can work with this.

Yes, the first step is to craft a foundation and laughter will do.

But tragedy works best.

AFTERWORDS
NOTES FROM THE AUTHOR

AFTERWORD: DECEMBER
20TH, 1986

Well, you made it. I am sorry, truly. I didn't set out to partially blind a child and ruin the holidays. Sometimes a story takes shape on its own. This one certainly did.

I wanted to revisit the holidays of my youth. I wanted to take a hard hit of that drug called nostalgia. I wanted to feel the excitement of seeing Christmas presents beneath the tree, and find the miracles given life in a child's mind when they wonder: *what lies beneath the ribbons and wrapping paper?*

But I'm not a kid. I'm creeping up on forty. The holidays can be stressful, budgets have to be balanced, social expectations maintained. Appearances are everything. No one wants to lose their temper or lose their mind amid all the mandatory joy. Still, many end out doing just that. I used to laugh at Clark Griswold. Now I weep with him. Sometimes I wonder how my own parents made it through the holidays. Were they, too, just barely treading water?

Years ago I worked in retail, and to this day my heart races when I see wrapping paper or hear Maria Carey singing whatever song it is she's singing this year. Perhaps this story was a bit of my own unconscious catharsis. Perhaps, like Terry Crabtree put it in Michael Chabon's wonderful *Wonder Boys*: "sometimes a person will subconsciously put themselves in a situation—perhaps even create that situation—in order to have an arena in which to work out unresolved issues. It's a covert way, if you will, of addressing a problem."

Or perhaps not.

All I know is that I sat down to write a story about a sweet little girl and a magic present she gets that helps her dad save his company and thus save Christmas. I titled it *December 20th, 1986* because it was going to be a day the daughter would forever remember. Instead, somewhere along the way, Floyd took over and things went sideways. Instead, somewhere along the way, I wrote this. The title still holds because, boy oh boy, they'll remember the date indeed.

So I guess there is a little bit of holiday magic. My heart didn't grow three sizes. Water wasn't transubstantiated into wine. And Santa didn't stuff his fat white ass down the chimney. A different story, however, did emerge, and perhaps that's a bit of a miracle itself. I'm too old to look at presents and wonder: *what's inside?* My real joy comes from these words, and where they take us.

Even if they ruin the holidays.

May yours be far better than Floyd's.

Started: October 2017
Finished: December 21st, 2017

AFTERWORD: A FEAST OF INFINITE ROT

"We're all the heroes of our own stories. We just make the stories fit in hindsight."

As I've grown older, I've also grown to believe this simple idea explains more than most religions and philosophies and political ideologies. We're all trying to write the Story of Our Life. We're all in a state of constant revision. We find the diamonds in our past that glimmered and pointed the way through the dark mines of existence, we connect the glimmering dots, construct a narrative framework backwards onto the past. What doesn't work or makes us uncomfortable, we edit out, rewrite, or simply skip altogether. Like a vacation full of photos, we come to create links between the snapshots and then reinforce them over time. *A Feast of Infinite Rot* owes its existence to that idea.

Another quote inspired the setting: *"Born too late to explore the earth, born too early to explore the cosmos."* Solution: set the story in a time of exploration where one could reinvent themselves. Send the protagonist to the edge of the map, then send them beyond. Setting is as much a character in a story, and the muddy frontier and its old, crooked inn spoke to me as much as the traveller and his tales.

Thus, the haunted inn in *A Feast of Infinite Rot* became an arena. The traveler and his tales were gladiators on one side, his own dark past entered the arena on the other side. As our traveler was forced to confront his deeds, his stories themselves became a prism through which we, the readers, are forced to arbitrate the truth. How much honesty had he peppered into his tales? How much had he changed? Would a person who had committed dozens of ill-deeds even remember the faces of his victims?

The traveler is a bad person, yes, but in a pathetic way I can relate to him. I sometimes wonder how much of my own past is still undergoing revision. Would I recognize the kid in high school I said a cruel word to? Would I remember the coworker at my first summer job if we met in the street? I can hardly remember the face of my college roommates, and we shared a bedroom for a year.

What also kept me going was something simpler: I have a soft spot for dark fantasy. I like to imagine that the best horror sits at an intersection between reality and fairy tale, and it's just a slight bend in the road that takes us down a shadowed path and into the unknown wilds. It's not impossible to imagine a muddy, dark road leading from The Brother's Grimm to H.P. Lovecraft and Stephen King and circling back to *A Feast of Infinite Rot*. This story owes its inspiration to them all.

And, unlike the ill-fated traveler, I'm happy to share credit. More ghosts to go around, thank you very much.

Started: Summer 2012
Finished: Winter 2013

AFTERWORD: A DEBT OF BACON

This story probably shouldn't have happened.

That's not something I say often, or lightly. The last thing I wish for the words that I write is the story they tell should up as table scraps and leftovers. Or worse, set aside all together, sent to the drawer of aborted ideas. Such an ending hangs heavy on me.

However, these things do happen. I'm no stranger to self-doubt, nor the manic depressive mumblings of my little muse (who is, in fact, more like a drunken ogre than an ethereal angel), and as a result, some stories do end out mutating somewhere between their foundation and final form.

Much like a parents' dreams for their child (Harvard Law, partner by 30, married with two kids) may change over the years (stays out of jail, holds down a job, no surprise pregnancies), so too does the occasional story born from a writer's mind change and, perhaps, becomes a different entity entirely.

This tale was one of them.

A Debt of Bacon has its origins in my novella, *A Feast of Infinite Rot*, so if you've read that, you'll probably recognize a few shadows of where it once was (and if you haven't read it, you should, it's actually not bad). However, the ideas I found myself exploring, such as the cyclical nature of consumption, well, they were a little larger than the narrative of *A Feast of Infinite Rot* allowed me to explore. Not to mention other narrative limitations dealing with reliability, stories-within-stories, etc.

At the end of the day this tale was in the wrong story. It was a hippy vegan at Bubba's BBQ Shack, an in your face herbivore demanding a kale salad while berating the waiter for wearing leather shoes. Trying to get the two to work together, well, it became a headache, and I have a particular allergy to headaches. So, like many writers, I had to kill my darlings.

However, I didn't do a good enough job, and my darlings, they just wouldn't stay dead. Like the children in the story, they whispered to me, incessantly, and thus I found myself in the chair, with the monkey wrench and dictionary, reworking the story into what you now hold.

There are a lot of reasons I resurrected *A Debt of Bacon*, but at its core the story just spoke to me, simple as that. I've often wondered about our role on this planet as we move further into the new century. Will we devour our planet's resources, or will we find balance? The pessimist in me says we're bound for the brink and beyond.

And the optimist?

Well, he's off buying sunscreen and learning Chinese. He's not holding his breath for a happy ending.

To me, *A Debt of Bacon* is a meditation on our role as consumers here on this planet. I don't say our planet, because I'm not convinced it is "our" planet. We're just sharing it, for the short term, much like the man in the great forest in this story.

Will we dam all the rivers and fish the oceans dry?

Will we eat all that the earth provides and fatten ourselves silly until nothing remains?

Or can we find some balance, if we are capable of it? Or does such a thing even exist?

I honestly don't know.

So perhaps that's why I was unable to let this story go. Its ending, though written, is only one of countless possible endings I can imagine for humanity as a whole.

I would like to think others could be happier.

December, 2012

AFTERWORD: LEARNING
TO FLY

"Don't worry, we've got the bugs worked out," my friend said as we climbed into the self-driving car. "Well, mostly."

I had spent the morning signing a few dozen NDAs and liability waivers. If death and dismemberment occurred I could not hold XXXXXXXXX liable. Nor could my wife, or widow, or whatever remained of me should the autonomous technology decide that it no longer liked having a bald technophobe adjust its playlists and chose to jettison me across the 280 freeway at 10am on a Tuesday. There was an engineer behind the wheel at all times, perhaps to prevent such events. I didn't know him, I didn't trust him. Mostly because he seemed way more excited about the disruptive implications of such technology.

"Think about it," he said, as the computer merged us into traffic. "One day, we won't even need headlights. We'll just punch in our destination, lay back, and look up at the stars. These things will drive themselves in darkness."

It was a nice idea: heading to the mountains on a highway lit by infrared. Sitting in an electric bubble, zooming through old growth redwoods. Reclaiming the commute.

"A million miles of road behind 'em, and only a dozen accidents, all caused by other drivers," the engineer mused. "In another decade, if you want to drive manually, you'll have to buy premium insurance. These things are going to save lives."

"Yeah, but there's gotta be a catch," I said. "There's only a few hundred of these on the road, right? Why aren't these everywhere?"

The catch, I was told, was twofold.

First, the technology was mostly ready, it was society that needed to catch up. People were still uncomfortable with the idea; I was proof of that.

Second, there was the moral quandary. How do you program an autonomous vehicle to make a difficult decision? How do you give it the knowledge to choose between two bad outcomes?

"Eventually this car is going to have to make a choice," the engineer said, "between saving the life of the driver, or the life of some dumb kid running out into the street after his soccer ball."

"Or between us and a bus full of nuns," I added. That was always the example my family used to illustrate the dire.

"Easy choice there," said my friend who'd known me for years. "No smart car is going to risk damnation to save three sinners like us."

Reluctantly, I had to agree.

Learning To Fly isn't hard sci-fi. It's not something you'd see in Asimov's or the smart places the clever people who make XXXXXXXXX's autonomous cars probably hang out. It's popcorn speculation, but a bit of butter isn't always bad. I had fun writing it, though I felt bad for poor Q. Sorry, amigo. Ask any teacher: not every lesson lands as intended.

Mostly, though, I had fun with Sunday. I tried to approach him like a blank canvas with an internet connection; something that's always attempting to extrapolate lessons. I grew up watching *Short Circuit* on Betamax, and it left a deep impression. Johnny 5, the robot who came to life, would gleefully shout: "Input! More input!" I saw Sunday as his quiet grandson, one who comes to a much different conclusion. Johnny 5 learned the value of life *after crushing* a grasshopper. Sunday learned that humans lie, and therefore the lessons they convey are not to be trusted. And he *chose to crush* Q.

"Do as a I say, not as I do," poor Q might have absently quipped, while attempting to crush the eggs of a pregnant bug on the very day he became a father.

People are imperfect, of course, and what we build will be imperfect too. I'm not advocating against autonomous vehicles, in fact I see them as the inevitable future. One day I do hope to lay back in my egg-shaped auto-car and look up through the moon-roof at the stars it drives me to Alaska down a dark highway. That sounds lovely.

But I'm sure we'll hit a few bumps along the way.

Started: October 2017
Finished: February 2018

AFTERWORD: YOU ARE NOT A
METAPHOR

Stories are often mirrors of a most uncomfortable creation. This
was certainly one.

In February of 2018 I found my thoughts driving down dark
roads. Nine months earlier, I had returned to the United States
after a decade abroad. I dove headfirst into graduate school.
Reverse culture shock, something I once dismissed as fantasy, had
dug its claws into my psyche and metastasized into a latent
unease. I found myself in America and I am an American, yet
everything felt *off*. In the classroom, in my daily interactions, my
mind kept drifting back to sepia-toned visions of my expatriate
life. The more I talked to others about living abroad the more their
eyes would glaze over, their minds would wander, and their
bodies began fidgeting. Words felt like they had different mean-
ings, commonalities had diverged. I was a cave man, frozen from
a different epoch, now thawed and ranting about the next mountain over where the tigers had huge spikes in their mouths. I was
a walking fossil.

Long-term expatriates often struggle with reverse culture
shock when returning to their home country, finding the fit less
than ideal. Some simply decide to leave once again. I saw that

temptation as long, sinewy hands stretching out across thousands of miles. Hands only I could see.

Men are terrible at discussing their own mental health and I'm no exception. We have a sick tradition of ignoring our brain's condition until the CHECK ENGINE lights are lit up and the hood's engulfed in flames. Then we end out kissing a pistol. When I shared this story with my wife, she said: "Wow, it's really emotional. Kind of like a raw nerve." Now, in hindsight, it's clear these words were a way for me to name a few demons. Everyone has their own golden-eyed monster lurking in the sunbeams of memory. Mine was nostalgia, a deep sense of isolation, and a temptation to rain down self-destruction. To drive away as fast as I could. Instead, this helped me pump the brakes.

Of course, stories are never a 1:1 transmutation. Writers don't use FIND ALL in the word processor and swap out "nostalgia" for "monster". As the title states, this wasn't a metaphor for acculturation any more than it was about men playing with dolls. The question I'm often asked is: Was his wife *really* a demon? Or was he just crazy? My answer is always the same: Why does it have to be "or"? Everything needed to answer that question is here in the story.

So, dear reader, whatever is chasing you, I wish you good luck on your journey. I'm not sure it's possible to fully exorcise the demons. But by naming them—whatever they are—at least we can take away some of their power.

Started: February 2018
Finished: July 2018

AFTERWORD: A BRIEF TREATISE ON MARKET ECOLOGIES, VOL. III

During 2012, with the election heating up and Facebook reaching its zenith of popularity and credibility (if ever such a thing could be written with a straight face, that was the time) I became enmeshed in an online debate of my own making. The opponent: my cousin. The topics: wide ranging. From gun rights to health care to the very definition of words. Like all online debates I don't recall the substance of the exchange, the points made, nor my opponent's rebuttals. I did not approach the topics in good faith.

In fact, what I recall most vividly eight years later, were the little red notification on my Facebook page. I recall a sense of victory when my comments (more like essays, really) elicited a higher number of LIKES. A distinct little pop inside my mind, and an upward tug on my lips as the dopamine flowed. It wasn't enough to be right. I had to collect enough LIKES to maintain that joy. I checked my phone compulsively. Each vibration was a potential affirmation that I was on the right track. Each continuing comment a new potential for engagement. Often, I stopped conversations with my friends in-person to continue an online debate. When my phone's keyboard proved too clunky, my mind wandered to my desk at home where my laptop's keyboard promised to help craft clever rebuttals. Of course, online debates are usually just two drunks talking past each other with ears sewn shut. This was no different.

The Great Facebook Debate of July or Maybe August 2012, I Really Don't Know ended like a fart in the wind. Minds were not changed. Years later, my cousin and I maintain a healthy friendship, still checking in. We've grown, matured in thought and mellowed in dogma and twitchy fingers. But I still think of those red notifications...

It's a bundle of fun as a writer to take the contemporary and transplant it into the fantastical. Familiar topics land in an uncanny valley when they're given new names and set next to magic. Often, it's just enough of a shift to see these fierce debates through odd prisms. What would traditional gender roles be like in a world of talking birds trying to shatter glass ceilings? How would the denizens of a haunted inn set against plague-ravaged lands deal with medieval travelers refusing to quarantine because the pox is a sham propagated by wizards and warlocks?

I don't know the answers. More often than not, I write to find out a few possible angles. And, in an uncomfortable way, I can relate to Gwendolyn's struggle. She wants to make art in a world that's rapidly evolving. Today, if one doesn't invest their time in social media marketing—or paying someone to do it for them—they're just a booth at a faire that's too full of noise.

Every Sunday for the past year and a half my wife and I take a day off electronics. We read books, read the newspaper, go for walks and spend time trying to be as analogue as possible without going Amish. Still, I would be lying if I said I didn't feel the tug. We carry with us a device to chat with the whole world (or to fling opinions like poo from a cage), to seek out those who agree with us, and to cancel those who don't. These are hard tools to lay down.

Would I hire a legion of orphans to put my books on the shelves of libraries like Gwendolyn did with her pictures? No, of course not. Orphans are *far* too expensive. Would I use an algorithm to write a story for me in the blink of an eye? No, I find writing far too enjoyable to outsource. But that doesn't mean someone else isn't out there, thinking: "Hey, I bet I could hit the best seller list if I could just get a million re-tweets…"

That's the world we live in. Not so different than Gwendolyn's, I fear.

Started: March 2018
Finished: July 2018

AFTERWORD: WE WILL BUILD A
HAUNTED HOUSE

Stories are shapeshifters, taking on multiple forms over the years of their creation. The first shape this story took began in 1993, when I stood before a nearly four-hundred-year-old door in Deerfield that still bore the hatchet-marks of a raid. Years later, that image merged with another story, a voice driven haunting that I hadn't quite gotten right. I thought of those two forlorn stories often, but something hadn't congealed.

Then the table moved.

For a writer who dabbles in the speculative and supernatural, my life is surprisingly free of events that I can claim to be paranormal. No family crypts where dead girls rise from the mist. No walls that bleed and scream and stretch out clawed hands. Yet one night, while watching TV with my wife, the dog asleep at our feet, something moved an old oaken table and the lamp a foot to the left. No passing trucks, no micro earthquakes, no swaying chandeliers. Just a sudden rumble and groan as four wooden feet slid across hardwood and settled before our wide eyes. It was as if some invisible kid had run smack into the table.

Of course, telling someone about moving furniture is about as thrilling as describing a dream; it's the ultimate You Had To Be There story. But that sudden *thump* got me thinking: What if the ghosts in this tale were on a different timeline? What if the haunt-ings stretched out not over weeks or a month but over decades, even centuries?

Point of view is a difficult in haunted house stories. As a reader, you're often one step ahead of the characters and the tension comes from the balancing act of when they'll catch up, catch on, and confront the menace. But what if the point of view *is* the menace and the land it sits upon? What if this perspective stretched over hundreds of years?

Thus, this story was born from the fusion of time and history and something curious that made an oak table go bump in the night.

Writing is lonely, sometimes to the point of psychological torture. Something I wondered while fleshing out the first draft: What would such loneliness do to a house? Would it crave company? And how could it ensure there were always a few friends around? What would the house look like after four hundred years?

I do most of my first drafts by longhand and my best writing at night. Like the many rooms built by the ghosts, I crafted this story page by page, often to the song of crickets and frogs and the rustle of nocturnal creatures among brambles. I kept my eyes on the old oaken table, waiting for it to move, daring it to. And some-times, when the words really flowed, when the night grew loud with frog song and crickets, when my eyes drifted back to the pages that almost wrote themselves, on those nights it felt like that old oaken table might just move once again.

Started: March 2019
Finished: January 2020

ABOUT THE AUTHOR

A child of the eighties, Andrew Van Wey was born in Palo Alto, California, came of age in New England, and lived as an expatriate abroad for nearly a decade. He currently resides in Northern California with his wife and their Old English Sheepdog, Daeny.

When he's not writing Andrew can probably be found mountain biking, hunting for rare fountain pens, or geeking out about D&D and new technology.

For special offers, new releases, and a free starter book, please visit andrewvanwey.com

instagram.com/heydrew

facebook.com/andrewvanwey

goodreads.com/andrewvanwey

bookbub.com/authors/andrew-van-wey

amazon.com/author/andrewvanwey

ALSO BY ANDREW VAN WEY

Novels

Forsaken: A Novel of Art, Evil, and Insanity

Head Like a Hole: A Novel of Horror

Head Like a Hole

By the Light of Dead Stars

Blind Site: The Clearwater Conspiracies (Book One)

Refraction: The Clearwater Conspiracies (Book Two)

Collections

Grim Horizons: Tales of Dark Fiction

9 780984 015771